The Betrayal

Linda Tweedie
Kate McGregor

Published by Fledgling Press 2015

www.fledglingpress.co.uk

ISBN 9781905916047
Printed and bound by:
Bell & Bain Limited, Glasgow

Acknowledgements

The Betrayal, the second book in the Coyle trilogy, was written by Linda Tweedie in partnership with Kate McGregor. Linda is the storyteller (a much better liar!) and Kate makes the book come alive.

Once again we have to acknowledge the help and assistance of Clare Cain for her input, patience and the provider of decent coffee. If we were overbearing and loud before, you can't imagine how much worse we are now after enjoying the success of *The Silence*. And yet she is never fazed by us

Again, Graeme, Fledgling Press's designer, has done the business – we love the cover! And thanks to Paul for actually getting the book out there.

Once more, thanks to my husband David who has eventually figured out what goes where (in the kitchen!) and gotten so good at it, I might consider keeping him.

Linda Tweedie

I Belong to Glasgow

"She's had the sprog. It's a boy," Bobby informed his house guest.

"Congratulations," the old man whispered. "Your dad would be pleased as punch. A boy. Well done."

"What do you mean, well done? I'm having bugger all to do with it. How do I know it's even mine?" the young man stormed. "I'm not getting caught out that way. She and her scumbag family can get on with it."

"Look, lad, it's understandable given the circumstances, but this is your son we're talking about and let's face it, if you really want revenge on the Coyles, then this child is the answer. I'm telling you, he's the key to Paddy Coyle's destruction. Think about it. Meanwhile, go and tell your mother she's a granny. That should cheer her up to no end," ex-canon O'Farrell chuckled.

Despite all the protests from Diane Mack, Frank O'Farrell had been recuperating in their pool house for the past few months, ever since Bobby had collected him from the monastery. Diane still hated the old bastard with a vengeance and held him equally responsible with Paddy Coyle for the death of her husband. No amount of persuasion would change her mind on that score. It was only due to the threat of Bobby also leaving, if she persisted in evicting O'Farrell, that he was still in residence.

How the old fiend had survived to tell the tale was nothing short of a miracle. He had spent days in the water, under the lethal Spanish sun, clinging desperately to a piece of flotsam, after Coyle had thrown him overboard. His would-be murderer had been unaware that in his youth, O'Farrell had swum off the coast of Galway daily, in the wild and treacherous Atlantic Ocean. The calm Mediterranean had given him a fighting chance and maybe it was true that God *did* look after his own. If not, then the devil surely did.

Somehow he'd made it ashore. Thanks to the dedicated care of the monks from a local monastery and despite a few brushes with death, O'Farrell had lived to tell the tale. He didn't get off scot-free however. Exposure to the sun's rays had damaged his skin to such a degree he was almost black and the effects of the salt water had dramatically affected his vocal chords to the extent that he now spoke in the merest of whispers. But, when all was said and done, he was, miraculously, still alive and for the moment, safe.

The ex-priest knew it was imperative that the new father establish a link with the Coyles immediately.

The longer Bobby refused to acknowledge his son, the more difficult it would be to connect with the mother. He had to convince the young man it was in his best interests to return to Scotland immediately.

To accomplish this, O'Farrell would need the help of his most bitter opponent: Diane, Bobby's mother. That was not going to be easy. Good God, if he could survive all those days in the Mediterranean, he could surely talk that pair round?

He had no remorse whatsoever for the vile deeds he had executed with his business partner, Bobby's father, and he had every intention of shaping the son to be his next cohort. But first things first: 'Operation Glasgow' had to get underway.

"If you want any kind of relationship with your grandson, Bobby has to go to her now. Trust me, I know the Coyles and the way these people think."

"Trust you? I'd rather take my chances with a rattlesnake. You're forgetting one thing, I *am* one of these people and I know *exactly* how they think," sneered Diane.

There was no way she could let the old sod think he had one over her, or that he was in any way in charge. But he was right. Bobby did have to lay claim to the child and to do that he would have to return to Glasgow, pronto. The main problem, however, was Bobby's hatred of the Coyles. He was still grieving for his father. Could she trust him to keep his cool if he came face to face with Paddy, or any of them, baby included?

Bobby paced angrily back and forth across the terrace while his mother and Frank argued the case for his return home. It seemed there was no convincing the new father that he should listen to them, and he refused point blank to acknowledge that he had any connection with the child. Eventually, however, Diane's argument won: should the child prove not to be his, then all the more reason for him to establish paternity. That would do more damage to their enemies in the long run.

"This is your Captain speaking, welcome aboard Flight BA355 to Glasgow. We are now cruising at 50,000 feet and the temperature outside is minus 40 degrees. Our estimated time of arrival is 11.05 a.m. and the weather in Glasgow is 10 degrees and raining."

"Shit, is it ever anything else?" moaned Bobby Mack.

The Prodigal

The room was full of balloons, floral arrangements, dozens and dozens of cards and well-wishers. No way was he making himself known to the crowd milling around her bed. Christ, it looked like the whole Coyle clan were in attendance. He'd probably get lynched! Watching the proceedings from the nurses' station, Bobby had forgotten just how hot Erin Coyle was and, just twenty-four hours after giving birth, she still looked amazing.

"Can I help you?" asked one of the nurses.

Pointing to Erin's room, Bobby replied, "No, it's okay, I'll come back when it's a bit quieter." He switched on his most devastating smile, the one which usually had women eating out of his hand. Not so this one. She just nodded and turned away. "Lesbian," he muttered.

He wandered round the private hospital for quite some time, drank enough coffee to keep him awake all night and finally made his way back to the maternity unit. Thankfully there was only a young nurse in attendance and it looked like Erin had fallen asleep. Standing over the crib, Bobby Mack knew at once there was no denying this was his son. He could see his father staring right back at him.

"Do you want to hold him?" the young nurse asked.

"Oh no, I'm not sure, I've never had much to do with babies," he blustered.

"Go on, he won't break, you know," and she lifted the swaddled infant and placed him in Bobby's arms.

Where was the amazing feeling you were supposed to experience, holding your child for the first time? Weren't you supposed to fall immediately in love with it? Well, that wasn't happening to him. In fact it was exactly the opposite sentiment; the critter started squalling and he wanted rid of it.

"Bobby? Is that you?" a very sleepy voice asked. "What are you doing? Put him down!" the voice was accusing.

"She gave me it," he replied.

"I thought you were the father," the young nurse stammered.

"He is."

"I am."

"Look, I'm sorry, Erin. I should have waited till you were awake, but, well, he is my son."

"Are you sure? I heard it on good authority that you wanted nothing to do with us, and that no way were you getting lumbered with a baby."

At that moment it dawned on Bobby. Erin was speaking. "Hey, you can talk."

"Yes, I can. It's amazing how seeing my father about to be shot by yours can traumatise a person into finding their voice again." She noticed the dark shadow pass over his face.

"Look, I had nothing to do with that carry-on and when all's said and done, yours is still alive."

"I'm not sure if you'll be, if he catches you here," the new mother challenged him.

This was an entirely different person to the girl he had had a holiday fling with. She was very much in control, not the silly naive chick he'd played fast and loose with. He was going to have to rethink his strategy. This one certainly wasn't going to just fall into his arms. Fuck, his mother and that other old coyote had made it sound so easy.

"Well, well, what have we here?" A contemptuous voice interrupted his thoughts.

Shit, this could only mean trouble. Bobby steeled himself to face Paddy Coyle. No coward, he turned to face Erin's father. But before he could defend himself a crashing punch knocked him clean out.

Picking up the inert new daddy, Paddy threw him bodily out into the car park. By now, most of the hospital, patients and staff were agog at the proceedings.

"What the devil is going on here?" The stern lesbian nurse (who was happily married with two kids) roared at the father and grandfather who were squaring up once again.

"You, Mr Coyle, no matter how generous a patron you are of this hospital, you will be barred from entering the grounds if I have any more of this ridiculous behaviour. And the same goes for you, young man."

Shamefaced, Paddy made his way back to his daughter's bedside, followed by a somewhat battered Bobby.

"For God's sake, Dad, have you always got to make a show of us?" Erin was furious with her father. "Take him and get him sorted, it looks like his jaw is broken."

"I'll sort him alright," the Big Man snarled and again the two squared up to each other.

"Will you two stop it?" Erin shouted. "Imagine fighting over the baby. Get out now!" She frantically rang the nurses' bell to summon help.

Seeing the fierce Sister on her way, the two men backed out of the room, leaving Erin to the ministrations of the nursing staff.

"Keep away from my daughter, do you understand me? If I catch you near either of them, you really will need a fucking hospital."

"Fuck off, old man, that's *my* son in there and unless Erin tells me otherwise, I'll be sticking around."

Narrowly avoiding another right-hander, Bobby headed off to A & E.

Homecoming

Erin was discharged from hospital the following morning and was dreading the next few days. God only knew how she was going to manage, with Bobby demanding to see his son and Paddy threatening to beat the crap out of him, refusing him entry to his home and having a dig every time their paths crossed. It didn't look like it was going to be the tranquil homecoming she'd envisaged.

"God, Carol, I'm exhausted, and those idiots are certainly not helping," she said as she put the baby back in his crib, having eventually settled him down to sleep.

"I have to say, it's a brave man who would front your father up. Bobby Mack has certainly gone up in my estimation," her friend chuckled.

"It's not funny, and what about those goons outside in the Porsche?"

"Who the hell are they? And would you listen to that music?" sneered Carol.

The cacophony of noise emanating from the flash black car was unbelievable.

"They're some relation or another of Bobby's, cousins I think. His backup, apparently."

"Backup? Do they know who you are and who they're taking on?" Carol was amazed. "Jesus, Erin, if they don't move by the time your dad gets home, there really will be murder."

"You think I don't know that?"

"They certainly don't look as if they could afford a car like that."

"Oh, I'm sure they can't," Erin laughed. "It was a Mercedes yesterday, so I think they just 'borrow' them."

"Shh! Here he comes. Hi, you okay?" Erin asked the father of her child as he presented her with an enormous bouquet and an even bigger teddy bear.

"These are for you."

"Thanks. Carol, could you take the flowers out to the kitchen and see if you can find anything to put them in?"

"A dustbin perhaps?" Carol muttered as she left the couple alone.

"How's my son this morning?" asked Bobby, standing over the crib and poking the sleeping baby.

"For heaven's sake, Bobby, I've just spent the last half hour trying to settle him," she snapped as the child began crying again. "Pass him over to me."

"No way, I don't do babies." Bobby backed right off.

"He's not 'babies', Bobby, he's your son and you have to get used to handling him."

Not a chance, thought Bobby. That's her job, not mine. "He's too little for me, maybe later when he's bigger. I thought we could go and register him today?"

"Plenty of time for that, and are you sure you want to make this legal, especially after all your doubts?" Erin faced him. "I mean, you were mouthing off last night about his parentage and your virility."

"How the devil do you know that? I only had a couple of beers with my cousins! I wasn't out on the lash or anything, we were only having a laugh." Bobby was more than a little perturbed that she knew anything about his movements, never mind a conversation between him and his family.

"Glasgow may be a big city, but when it comes to the Coyles, we know everything. Nothing is secret and especially not somebody dissing Paddy Coyle's daughter and grandson."

Christ, this was unbelievable. He'd met up with his two cousins immediately after leaving the hospital. A phone call had brought the two lads, John and James, immediately. Even though Bobby hadn't seen, or kept in touch with his mother's side of the family for years, that didn't matter, they were more than happy to give Spanish Bobby, as they called him, a bit of backup.

Especially when the guy obviously had a few bob and was the co-owner of the biggest nightclub in Spain. If they played their cards right, that would be the holidays sorted for the next few years.

Sitting outside the house with music blaring, the cousins shared a spliff and were fantasizing what they would do to the Big Man if he turned up.

"I'd fucking knock him out," John caressed his trusty baseball bat. "A couple of taps should do it," he smiled at the thought.

"Naw, I'd just fuckin' shoot him," said James, checking out his weapon.

"Is that a fact, big boy?"

James was hauled from the passenger seat by his hair and unceremoniously kicked about the gravel path.

John was out of the car and halfway down the drive in a flash to avoid receiving the same treatment, but he was still shouting insults and obscenities from a very safe distance.

"Fucking morons. What the fuck are those two idiots doing on my property?" Paddy roared at no-one in particular.

The racket had Erin, Bobby and Carol all at the window. Bobby, seeing his cousin lying injured on the path, ran outside.

"You have to be kidding, boy. You don't really think you can take me on, do you? Erin, dial 999. This stupid fucker's going to need an ambulance." Paddy sneered at the young guy.

Bridget's car screeched to a halt as she pulled up to the house. Jesus, she'd only been gone half an hour. Seeing one body lying on the path, another young guy swaggering back up the drive, and her husband and grandson's father squaring up to one another, she was thankful there hadn't been a long queue at the chemist.

Fingers in the Till

"Just how long are you going to cover up for him?" Marie demanded. "It's bloody ridiculous. If it was anyone else, they'd be well sorted by now."

"I know, Marie. Trust me, I'm well aware of what's going on and I'll have a word, I promise," Michael Coyle answered his younger sister. This was the third occasion recently when Sean's behaviour had caused her to come to him.

"Have a word? Are you having a laugh? He needs sorting, Michael, before things get really out of hand. I don't want him back in the club, and I've put the word out, he's barred. So you better get someone else to do the collections, 'cos I'm not having him near any of the girls."

"Look, Marie, I've said I'll sort it and I will. I'll keep him away for a bit till things quieten down."

"Michael, you're not listening to me. Enough is enough. He comes in with those stupid idiots he hangs about with, acts like the big shot and helps himself to the takings. You know I sacked a good hostess, thinking she was skimming? And all the time it was my own damn brother. One girl has taken off because she was so afraid of him when he lost his temper. And to top it all off, last night he battered a punter so badly the poor guy was hospitalized. Just because he asked for a clean glass. A fucking clean glass! No! He's a liability and he's out, as far as I'm concerned."

"For fuck's sake, Marie, *you're* supposed to be running the club. If you can't deal with the girls or the punters, then maybe it's time you considered a change of career."

"Don't you dare suggest I can't run my club. I deal with heavier situations every night, but I certainly don't expect this kind of hag from my fucking *brother*. You know he's the talk of the town? No? Maybe you and the Big Man should climb down from your ivory tower and find out what's going on in the real world."

"What are you on about? Why is he the talk of the town?"

"He owes, Michael. He owes everybody and there are a few who are not willing to wait. Being a Coyle is not all it's cracked up to be nowadays, and something needs doing, and fast."

"Fuck! How did all this come about? What the hell is the matter with him?"

"He's always been like this, you just couldn't see it. I can understand that, you being his twin. But your big brother hasn't got that excuse. It suited him to ignore

Sean's behaviour. He knows what a conniving bastard he is. He'd sell his granny if the price was right."

"Look, let me sort this. I'll send him away for a bit if I have to, but please keep this to yourself, just for now."

"A week, Michael, then I'm going to Paddy, so you better do something quick."

The crunch of tyres on gravel signalled the arrival of the Big Man. Paddy Coyle was pleasantly surprised to see his younger sister's car parked outside the portacabin. It was unusual for her to come to the yard; she preferred the comfort of her plush office at the back of their flagship club, Fantasy.

He hoped there was nothing amiss, their mother seemed fine and the businesses were all doing well so maybe it was just a social call?

"Hi, titch, what brings you here? Didn't think this was posh enough for you," Paddy teased his younger sister.

"It's a secret, I promised not to let you know we're planning a party for you. Oops, I've gone and done it now," she laughed.

"No party for me, thanks," said Paddy.

"I was just passing and took a chance that one of you would be about to buy me lunch. It seems Michael here is too busy. What about you?"

"Sorry, but Bridget's got me on a leash, no can do."

Marie gave Michael a very knowing look which Paddy didn't miss and waved them goodbye.

"Okay, what was that all about?" he questioned Michael.

"What was what about?"

"There was no way she was just passing. What's the problem? Is she having trouble at the club?"

"If you must know, she's thinking about moving in with this guy she's been seeing and she wanted my opinion."

Never in her life had Marie asked for anyone's opinion, and certainly not from her brothers. Either this was a pile of bullshit, or at long last his little sister was growing up. Paddy knew which option his money was on.

Problems

The news of Canon O'Farrell's disappearance had just reached the ears of his parishioners. Most, quite frankly, couldn't give a damn. He was a surly, miserable old sod most of the time, but it had hit one in particular, hard. Not for his clerical devotions, or his ministrations to his parish, but his input to Sean Coyle's income.

How could that stupid old fool go missing? What the fuck had he been up to, going swimming at his age? He must have been well into his seventies, maybe even eighty-odd and he, Sean, was supposed to be taken in by some tale about the old bastard being swept out to sea. Rubbish.

Sean didn't believe for one minute that the illustrious Canon Francis O'Farrell was dead. He knew deep down that O'Farrell was out there somewhere, avoiding him, on the missing list just to cause him problems. Why he would be avoiding Sean was neither here nor there. Like most addicts, not only was Sean paranoid, but everything, absolutely everything, was centred on him and his needs.

Whatever had happened to the canon, it was making life extremely difficult for Sean Coyle. Not only had O'Farrell's disappearance cut off his supply, it had ended a nice little earner which proved impossible to replace without giving the game away. Nobody, especially his brothers, would ever believe he had been in cahoots with the canon for the past few years. Their partnership had worked like a dream.

Like most successful enterprises, it was simplicity itself. Sean acquired a shipment of drugs and the 'Micks' boarding at St. Jude's would sell them on. There was a cut to the Irishmen, a decent cut to the canon and an even better cut to Sean. That, and any amount of the white stuff he could handle, had created a very expensive habit which he could now not afford.

With the disappearance of the canon, St. Jude's had no 'student' residents, depriving Sean of his chain of pushers, but worse still, almost every dealer in the city was out looking for him. He owed, big time, and frankly, he couldn't see any way out. It was the name Coyle that had saved him up until now. There were few brave hearts who would tackle a Coyle brother about a debt, but it was becoming obvious that Sean was just taking the piss and, Coyle or no Coyle, a few aimed to have their money, or a piece of him.

"Are you ready?" Sean called to his mate, Johnno. "I

thought we'd go out of town tonight, maybe Paisley. See what's happening. Eh? What do you think?"

Johnno knew exactly why the posse would be heading out of town: it would be safer for Sean. But the boys were Weegies and not welcome outside their own territory. So whether they ventured out of town or stayed on home turf, it looked like there was going to be a scrum and Johnno, like most of his mates, was getting a bit hacked off with Sean and his problems. He was always on the tap, never had any dosh, and expected them to carry him. The fact that he had been the banker for years was only to be expected, he was a Coyle and everybody knew they were loaded.

"Sorry, Sean, no can do. I've got to meet Susie. I promised her I'd take her out for a meal and a few drinks. Sorry, pal, you know what she's like if she doesn't get her own way."

Sean could be heard muttering to himself on the way out, "Fuckin' birds. Imagine picking a bird over the boys."

The truth was Johnno had had enough.

Sean called round for Malky, only to find an empty flat and his calls going to voicemail. Sean was becoming more and more aggravated; he knew that the brothers, Scott and wee Peem, were both out of action today. They were on their way back from Ireland after attending their granny's, or auntie's, funeral, so it looked like he was on his own.

Money. If he was on a loner, he needed some dosh. Looking at his watch, he reckoned it would be unlikely Marie would be on duty yet, so, making for the Fantasy, he planned how to finance his evening's pleasure. He'd already had a run in with his little sister the last time he'd helped himself, but she could go fuck herself. He was a partner, unlike her, and it was his due, he told himself.

The club was, as he suspected, pretty quiet at this time of the day. Waving to Stella, the head girl, he made his way to the bar.

"Jackie D and coke, luv," he smiled to the barmaid. "Bring it into the office for me."

"The office is locked, Sean. Marie took the keys with her, sorry."

"I need to get in. I've to collect some paperwork for Paddy and there will be fucking murder if I don't get it. When is she due back?" he asked the nervous girl.

The staff had been instructed that under no circumstances was this brother to be allowed into the office or behind the bar.

"I don't know, probably about eight. I could ring her."

"Yes, you do that." Sean faced up to the girl, knowing full well that Marie was more than likely to have her phone turned off so that she could have some time with their ma and Errol. If she did happen to answer, he'd bluff it, but he was right.

"Sorry it's just going to voicemail, Sean." The girl was visibly shaking. He looked like he was ready to kick off.

"Are you telling me there is only one key to this office? No way. I'll kick the fucking thing open if I have to."

Seeing that trouble was brewing, Stella walked over to the bar. "Sean, what's up? Why are you having a go at Pattie? She's only the bartender. Speak to your sister, she's the one giving out the orders."

The expression on Sean's face changed "Orders, what orders?"

"Look, there is only one key on the premises and Marie takes it with her when she leaves. We don't have access to the office. She should have told you herself. We're not allowed to let you behind the bar or into the office. That's why she takes the key."

Stella had worked clubs and bars for years and could spot a move before it happened, but she wasn't quite quick enough for Sean. In a fury which surprised even himself, he grabbed both women by the hair and smashed their heads, face down, on the granite bar top. There was blood everywhere.

He emptied the till and left the club with only one thought in his head – where to score – without a vestige of regret or guilt for the mess he'd just left behind. It was Marie's club and if she was going to treat him like a cunt then she could clear up the mess. It was fuck all to do with him.

Stand Off

God almighty, she had been away precisely thirty minutes. After a quick trip to the chemist for a colic preparation for the baby, she came back to this? Having waited until Paddy had gone off to meet Michael, and Carol had arrived to sit with Erin, Bridget hadn't foreseen any problems. She certainly hadn't expected to find Paddy and Bobby squaring up to each other on the driveway.

And whose was the black sports car? Doors wide open and blaring music so loud she couldn't hear herself think. There was one comatose youth and another who was likely to end up the same if he didn't shut that blasted music off. Her home was turning into a bloody three ring circus and she'd just about had enough.

"For the love of God, what's going on?" She barged between Bobby and Paddy. "You," she pointed to Bobby, "I can understand. You're only a bloody kid, but you," she turned to her husband. "You're behaving like a damned five-year-old, and I'm telling you, Paddy, I've truly come to the end of my tether."

"It wasn't me who started this," Paddy sulked.

"Well, it certainly wasn't me. I was with Erin when this madman –" Bobby stood his ground.

"I don't care who the hell started anything, enough is enough." Turning to Bobby she spat, "Get that pair of neds out of here and shift this stolen car off our property. You can come and visit with Erin this afternoon on your own. You will not, I repeat, not, discuss our business or make any remarks concerning my family with anyone. If you do, you will have me to deal with. Now get moving, and take these idiots with you."

A sheepish Bobby collected his backup and screeched off in the hot car, music once again blaring.

Paddy was pacing back and forth in the hallway, ready to kick off. "How could you embarrass me like that in front of those fucking arseholes?"

"Me embarrass you? You managed that all by yourself, you stupid fool. And I'll tell you something now, Mr Big-Shot-Paddy-Coyle, I'll do more than embarrass you. If I have to put up with any more of your moronic behaviour, you'll be out on your ear, do you understand me? I've had enough. For the past six months I've put up with the way you've treated my daughter like she was some kind of tramp you employ in one of your clubs. You've snubbed her, had nothing to do with her and made her feel cheap and worthless. But now you're playing the fucking doting grandfather?

"The whole of Glasgow thinks you're some kind of hero, delivering the baby single-handed. What the whole of Glasgow doesn't know, Mr Big-Shot, is that you had your daughter in such a state that she almost lost him. So think on, Paddy, just think what you might be about to lose. And while I'm at it, for however long that lad is in Glasgow, he'll be welcome in my house to visit with his son."

Paddy and Erin stood open-mouthed watching Bridget march through the house to check on her grandson.

Only once before had her husband witnessed the full force of her wrath, and that had been on the night of her father's murder, almost twenty years ago. Fortunately, then it had not been directed at him, but this, well, he was damned if he was putting up with her bloody menopausal tantrums. He would show her what she was about to lose. So, for the second time that morning the building shook to the foundations as Paddy Coyle left his home.

The Family

"Hello, Michael, it's me. You need to get over here, pronto. Your beloved twin brother has caused fucking mayhem yet again," Marie snarled down the phone line.

"For fuck's sake, Marie, what's he supposed to have done this time?"

"Supposed to have done? What do you mean supposed to have done? You better get on over here and see for yourself before I do something we'll all regret."

"C'mon, Marie, taking a few pennies out the sweetie jar or having a bit of a dust up with some leery punter doesn't exactly make him public enemy number one."

"You don't think so? Well, he's gone one better this time. He's only put two of my best girls in hospital because they wouldn't give him the key to the office."

"Why wouldn't they give him the key?"

"Because they didn't have it, I had it with me. The bastard is thieving from us, and I wasn't having it."

"I told you to cut him a bit of slack till I got it sorted."

"Piss off, Michael. I warned you just three days ago I didn't want him anywhere near. He was to stay away, him and his mates, and you promised me you would sort it. Have you even spoken to him?" Marie quizzed her older brother.

"I haven't been able to catch up with him, and bad though it is, Marie, if he didn't know you'd barred him, he would think that the girls were taking the piss. I would do the same if some tart told me I couldn't go behind the bar or get something out of the office."

"Don't talk bollocks, Michael. You'd understand immediately if one of the staff even intimated something like that. You'd go howling for my blood, not the wee lassie pouring you a sherry. So don't talk shit, and don't insult me by thinking I'll swallow it."

"So what exactly has he done to upset you?"

"Upset me? He's done more than upset me. He's put Stella and one of the bartenders in hospital. He smashed their faces beyond recognition and walked out with almost a grand from the till. But tell you what, it seems you're too busy to deal with my little problem, so sorry to disturb you. I'll just see what Paddy has to say about it," and with that Marie hung up.

"Fuck," Michael swore to himself. He'd had a shit day already because of Sean, but his antics at the club were just the tip of the iceberg. Joe Malloy, an old associate of the Coyles, had paid a call on Michael earlier that day.

"Look, Michael, I'm vexed that it's me having to do this. We go back a long way, so you know I wouldn't dig you up unless it was serious. But the pressure's on me to sort Sean out."

"Old mate or not, Joe, you better have a damned good reason for dissing my brother."

"He owes money right, left and centre, Michael. And a few of the boys are wondering if the Coyles have cash flow problems. You know if one of the brothers can't or won't pay their debts, rumours get about."

"You are having a laugh. A cash flow problem? Fuck off, Joe."

"That's the word out on the street, Michael."

"How much are we talking?"

"About ten thousand."

"How much?" spluttered Michael.

"It's been building up over the past few months. No-one really bothered at first. C'mon, he's Paddy Coyle's brother, and he's surely going to be good for the dosh. But he's taking the piss big time, and now he's down to beating up the odd street peddler to score. He's got a serious and expensive habit, Michael, and my advice is he needs sorting."

Michael had opened the office safe and handed

a bundle to the man. "Count it. And thanks, but the Coyles don't take advice from anyone."

"Sorry, Michael. Sorry I didn't let on sooner, but you know how it is."

Michael spent most of the day trying to trace his brother. He left messages at all his known haunts and watering holes. He left God knew how many voicemails, to no avail. Sean had gone underground and would resurface when he was good and ready, or when the heat was off.

His problem was how to cover the bundle he had handed over to Joe Malloy. It wasn't exactly petty cash and now he had Marie on his back, screaming for blood. So much for a pleasant night in with Margee. He'd fucking swing for him when he eventually caught up with him.

Sean was well aware his twin brother was on the hunt for him, and he was pretty sure he knew why. Over the past couple of weeks he'd lost count of the number of threatening messages he'd had from dealers around the city. Who the fuck did they think they were, threatening him? Sean Coyle wasn't some no-mark junkie that they could put the frighteners on. He'd pay them, they'd get their money when it suited him, but it did look like a few were getting impatient and it was becoming harder to score these days.

What about that cunt of a sister of his? Telling a couple of brasses that he was barred from the club? Him barred? What a fucking liberty. Well, he'd soon put them right and as for the cash, she could consider it as being an advance on his wages. He, Sean Coyle, answered to no-one. And sister or no, Marie was due a proper right-hander. Who the fuck did she think she was?

No doubt she'd go running to Paddy, Mr Big Man himself. Let him say anything and he'd soon find out who the hard man was. It was about time his brothers gave him a bit of respect. He was sick of the way they treated him like he was some kind of errand boy. He was nothing more than a gofer. Well, not for long. They might be in for a bit of a shock. But first he had to score.

Paddy

Threatening to throw him out on his ear? Who the fuck did she think she was? Telling him what to do, or what to say, mugging him off? Well, he'd show her. In fact, he'd show them all who was boss. To think she actually took that little fucker's part against him. Bobby fucking McClelland. And in his own home? Well, he was the boss and it was about time a few people remembered that. Paddy fumed as he raced towards town.

Oh, for fuck's sake. He couldn't believe it when he saw the blue light flashing in his mirror; the boys in fucking blue. He wasn't in the mood to deal with this, but he pulled over anyway.

"Can you get out of the vehicle, sir?" asked the rookie copper. They say you're getting older when the police start looking younger. Well, this one didn't look like he was long out of short trousers. As for his partner, if ever there was a dyke, there was one standing before him.

"Do you know what speed you were doing sir?" Supercop asked.

PC Wright was just out of Tulliallan Training College. In fact, this was his first day on the job. He couldn't believe his luck. Some rich sod driving a brand new Range Rover at the speed of light was going to be his first collar.

"No, but I'm sure you are going to enlighten me, officer." Paddy really wasn't in the mood for this shit and was barely containing his infamous temper.

"Is this your vehicle, sir?"

"Yes, officer, this is my vehicle."

"Can you tell me the registration number of the vehicle, sir?"

"Yes officer, it is PAD 1 and it's registered to me, Mr Patrick Coyle, The Grange, Kilmacolm."

This meant absolutely nothing to the rookie, but his sergeant, Grace Thomas, almost jumped out of her skin at the mention of the driver's registration number and even more so at the name and address.

"Okay, Mr Coyle, so sorry for the intrusion, my colleague mistook you for someone else. Please don't let us detain you and we hope we've not inconvenienced you," she spluttered.

Paddy took off like a bat out of hell.

"Fuck, look at him, Sarge, what was all that about?" The rookie was baffled. Why on earth was the sergeant letting this big ponce off with a caution? This should have been his capture, not hers.

"Have you any idea who you just stopped?" the sergeant quizzed him. "No. Well let me tell you, sunshine, if you had persisted in booking that big bastard, it may well have been the last thing you ever did. That was the infamous Paddy Coyle, and believe me, we wouldn't have walked away intact."

PC Wright was known until the day he retired as the mug who tried to arrest Paddy Coyle.

Pulling into the yard, the Big Man was annoyed to see neither Sean nor Michael's cars were in evidence.

"Lazy bastards," he muttered to himself as he entered the portacabin. He knew fine well that wasn't the case, and that both brothers would have been out until the early hours of the morning. The yard was busy and the three guys who worked there waved cheerily, but continued with the day's tasks. It wasn't unusual for any of the brothers to appear throughout the day and even, occasionally, at night. These boys all knew the drill. If Paddy wanted something he would call.

Paddy pulled out the bottom drawer of the old, battered filing cabinet, produced an almost full bottle of Black Label whisky and poured a healthy dram. None of the brothers were drinkers, thanks to years of watching their father, but there were times, and this was one, when a bender was the only cure.

He was cut to the quick over Bridget's outburst. Telling him she was sick of him and wanted rid. He had worked his bollocks off since the day he'd met her. She had wanted for nothing. He had more than provided for her and her daughter. He didn't smoke, drink, do drugs or gamble, and as far as other women were concerned, well, they were strictly business. Oh, he'd taken a couple of flyers over the years, but they were few and far between and usually when Bridget was off somewhere and he was on his own. Mr Big, Paddy Coyle, hated being on his own, but really, there wasn't another woman alive that could take his Bridget's place. Up until now that was.

He finished the bottle in jig-time and, despite not being a frequent drinker, he could hold his liquor along with the best. He wasn't however, like many Scotsmen, a happy drunk. The more Paddy consumed, the more morose he became, and he was on that slippery path.

His next port of call was into town to the Horseshoe Bar. There were bound to be a few friendly faces in there. Paddy was seldom in town and even more seldom on his own. But he was right, there were several well-known characters in the bar, even at this early hour of the day and surprise, surprise, they all knew the Big Man and were happy to take a drink with him. He went from pub to pub, and by mid-afternoon Paddy Coyle had reverted to type. He was a 'fighting Mick'. A cheerful 'hello' was taken as a grave insult and from St Enoch's Square to the Fantasy he left a trail of broken heads and bloody noses.

"Where the hell have you been?" demanded Marie. "I've been trying to reach you since this morning."

Here we go again, he thought to himself. Another woman who thought she could tell him what to do, another harpy on his case. Well, she could fuck right off. Let's face it, she was only here because of him and if she didn't like it, too fucking bad.

"And since when have I had to report to you? What fucking business is it of yours where I go or what I do?" The Big Man was lurching all over the place. "I'm the boss and I say what's what." He turned to the barmaid, "A large scotch. Now."

"I don't think so, you've had enough for today, boy," his sister endeavoured to get him away from the bar.

"Fuck off, Marie. And you," He pointed at the bartender. "Get me that scotch, if you want to keep your job."

"Jesus, Paddy you're drunk. Get through the back before the customers see you. Now move!"

"Fuck off, Marie, before I get really pissed off."

The altercation was attracting attention from both customers and staff and although Marie wanted him out, she knew it was time to back off.

What the hell was wrong with her brothers? This certainly wasn't the time to tell Paddy about Sean's activities and she was devastated seeing him like this. The whole family prided themselves on their name, but Christ, it was taking a battering today.

Paddy had wandered off to the end of the bar where the hostesses sat waiting for clients. "Give the girls a drink, and same again for me," he called.

They were all a bit wary after Sean's performance earlier in the day, and now, seeing Paddy drunk, a few were dubious, but not enough to refuse a drink.

It was well known that Paddy seldom, if ever, played away from home and if he did, it was well, well away from his own doorstep. That didn't stop a few of the dancers from trying.

One in particular – Chantelle, a tall leggy blonde, one of the most popular girls and one who had worked for the Coyles for years – had always had a thing for Paddy but had never struck lucky. It looked like he was game tonight and she was going to give it her best shot. First things first. She had to dodge Marie and get out without being noticed. She needed to create some kind of diversion.

Within minutes she had two of the girls scrapping over a customer, a ploy she'd used for years. Now to get her prey, she thought.

Grabbing him by the hand, she led Paddy out of the club and into a cab without being spotted, and he was more than a willing participant.

"Your place or mine?" he grinned at her. "Oh, sorry, can't be mine, the wife might object."

By now Paddy was as drunk as he'd ever been, but after a couple of lines he was ready to party. Fuck sitting at home with his pipe and slippers. He was

in his forties, not his fucking dotage and if his wife
didn't want him, there were plenty of other tricky little
pieces who did, and he had them on tap. He felt not the
slightest bit guilty.

In The Morning

Sean was a major problem, but Marie was becoming just as bad, thought Michael. Why the hell was Paddy keeping her in a job? She obviously couldn't hack it. She was never off the bloody phone, screaming the odds about their brothers. First it was Sean. Okay, he was a bit out of order, but the guy was having a bad time just now and she should cut him some slack. Then she calls to get him over to the club to sort Paddy out. Paddy, for God's sake! Their oldest brother, she alleged, was out of his skull, creating all sorts of hag and she couldn't handle him. What a load of shit.

Michael had only seen Paddy pissed a couple of times, the last time being when McClelland and the canon had been dumped in the Med. As for drugs, on an even rarer occasion he'd maybe dabbled, did an occasional line of coke perhaps. Now, here she was on the blower, screaming blue murder for him to drop everything and come and sort things out. The truth was, it was only she, old rent-a-gob herself, who had the nerve to face Paddy up when he was out of order. To top it off, when he did arrive at the club, Paddy had already buggered off home. No apology from his sister, just a litany of all that was going wrong. Well, he too had had enough.

"What a fucking day," Michael moaned to himself, "one bloody thing after another," he muttered as he climbed over the sleeping Margee.

God, he was knackered. He would get to grips with things in the morning, but for now he had to get some sleep. As he was just about to drift off, the shrill noise of the phone startled him awake.

"Bugger," he said as he lifted the receiver.

"Hello, Michael, you weren't sleeping, were you?" asked Bridget.

"Naw, I had to get up to answer the phone," he replied sarcastically. "What is it?"

"Paddy's not home."

"Well, he's not in fucking bed with me," her brother-in-law barked back. "What time is it?"

"Half past two."

"Fuck, he's probably still at the club. He'd tied a few on earlier, according to Marie. What you worrying about?"

"We had a massive fight and he walked out."

"For God's sake, Bridget, he's a big boy, he'll turn up. Go to bed and stop worrying, and more to the point, let me go back to bed, I'm shattered."

There was no way he was letting on that Paddy was

on a bender. He could make his own excuses in the morning. Michael was sound asleep almost before she'd put the phone down.

For probably the twentieth time that day Bridget rang Paddy's mobile, but again it went straight to voicemail. She knew she was being ridiculous, but Paddy, for all the villain that he was, and all the nefarious deeds he was involved in, seldom stayed away from home and never without telling her.

If he had, as he put it 'a bit of business to attend to', he told her. If he was going to be late, he phoned. This absence was so out of character. Maybe she *had* been a bit over the top this morning, but between him and the McClelland boy, she'd had enough. Maybe she could have dealt with the situation differently, but there was only so much a body could take and she had definitely come to the end of her patience. She'd sort it in the morning, one way or another. Oh my God, did that child never sleep? She might as well see to him and let Erin sleep on. Let's face it, there was no way she, Bridget, would get any sleep tonight. Not until her errant husband turned up.

It said much about their marriage that not for one minute did Bridget think Paddy was out on the prowl. She was quite sure he could get himself into trouble, but trouble of a different ilk. He was far more likely to be locked up for fighting than shacked up in some tart's bed. If only that were so. Unknown to Bridget the tide had turned. Tomorrow would take care of itself, or so she hoped.

Early Bird

Languishing in her warm, comfortable bed, Erin Coyle forgot she was a new mum for a split second, forgot the nightly feeds and forgot the tiredness. Jesus, she'd slept right through, she hadn't wakened to feed or change the wee soul. Panic set in. But there, nursing her son, rocking to and fro, was her mum.

"Have you been there all night?" Erin asked, relieved.

"Yes, don't fret. I couldn't sleep and this little man was grouchy so I left you sleeping. There was no point in the two of us being up all night. You'll feel better today and more up to coping with him."

"Thanks, Mum, but you shouldn't have. I take it the Big Man's not home?" Her daughter nodded towards the door.

"No, he's obviously out to make a point, but if the stupid fool thinks this is the way to sort things, he's dafter than I thought."

"Och, he'll be back soon, tail between his legs and hollering for his breakfast."

"Hmph." Bridget handed the little bundle over to his mum and left the room.

Around the same time, the man in question was just coming to. Where was he? Wherever it was, it sure as hell wasn't home. The usual morning scents of breakfast and freshly brewed coffee were absent. The bed wasn't his and the room had a peculiar, unfamiliar odour. But more to the point, the underwear strewn about the room definitely did not belong to Bridget.

"You've joined the land of the living then?" a female voice from behind a screen addressed Paddy. "Do you want some coffee? It'll have to be black as I've no milk, unless you want to nip downstairs to the shop?"

Vague memories of the night before were circulating in his brain.

"Feeling bad, big boy? Do you want a pick-me-up?" questioned the voice as its owner appeared from behind the screen.

"Chantelle, what the fuck am I doing here?"

"Well, you weren't kidnapped if that's what you think. You came quite willingly, in fact you came quite a few times," the hostess laughed.

It all came rushing back, the fight with McClelland, the argument with Bridget, the storming off, and the tour of most of the East End pubs. He vaguely remembered arguing with Marie, but how he had ended up here, God alone knew. Shit, he was in big trouble. If Bridget ever found out she'd skin him alive, if he was lucky, but it would more likely be the finish of them.

Checking his phone confirmed this. There were twenty-three missed calls, nineteen from home. The voicemails from his wife went from pleading to vitriolic throughout the night. Maybe going straight home was not the best idea. Maybe he should let her calm down a little before making an appearance.

Dear God, he was feeling rough. He must have shifted some amount of booze over the course of the day and his head was exploding. He desperately needed a hair of the dog, or something, to straighten him out.

"You got any gear, girlie? I'm decidedly fucked."

Setting up a modest line of coke, within minutes Paddy was raring to go. Well, he thought, might as well get hung for a sheep as a lamb. "C'mon, girl. Let's go eat, I'm starving."

Half an hour later they were ensconced in the brasserie at the Hilton, drinking champagne and devouring that establishment's famous Scottish breakfast.

Paddy Coyle was buzzing from the combination of coke, champagne and the residue of the previous day's alcohol. This is the life, he congratulated himself, and signalled for another bottle of Cristal. Fuck the licensing laws, they didn't apply to folks like him. In fact, fuck the lot of them; he was having another day's holiday. 'Them' being Bridget and the twins, he never really counted Marie. She could bloody well get on with things, earn her crust for once. There, it was sorted.

Michael tried Paddy's phone, but as he expected, no answer. The stupid bastard would be dossed down somewhere, nursing a monumental hangover. He'd likely appear as rough as a badger's arse around lunchtime, barking out orders in a filthy temper. Well, Michael, for one, wasn't putting up with it today. As soon as either of his brothers appeared, he was off.

He didn't hold out much hope for Sean appearing, he'd tried his mobile half a dozen times this morning already, with no luck. One of them would surely appear at some time. He dived to retrieve his own shrilling mobile, convinced it would be one of the prodigals, only to receive an ear bashing from his sister.

Big Score

"Hi, Mum, how are things in Spain? Everything okay?"

"Everything's fine, sweetheart. How does it feel being a new daddy? Have you seen your son yet?"

"I saw him yesterday, just after I arrived, and then spent most of today with him."

"Is he okay? Who does he look like? What is she calling him?"

"Hey, one question at a time," Bobby laughed. "He's good, and honest to God, he's Dad's spitting image. It's incredible, it's like a mini-Pete staring back at you."

"Really? Has she decided on a name yet?"

"It's not official, but Ryan seems to be the favourite."

"Yeah, that's okay. How are the Coyles treating you? You've not had any stick from Big Paddy, have you?"

"Nothing I can't handle, but fortunately he seems to have gone AWOL. Nobody has seen him since yesterday and you could cut the atmosphere with a knife. The mother stuck up for me and he took it really bad."

"Shame!"

"I'm going to try and get Erin to register the baby tomorrow. Once my name is on the birth certificate, we're home and dry. After that I'm out of here."

"Look, son, you need to stay just a bit longer. Make sure everybody that needs to know knows you're the boy's father. Go to mass, go and see Father Jack. Get in with old Lizzie, she'll be in your corner. Just get as many people on your side as you can."

"I never signed up for all this shit. You and the old man made out I just had to come over here, smile, get my picture taken and leave. None of this bonding shit or meeting the family. I don't feel anything for this kid. I'm only interested in using it to destroy the Coyles."

"I know you don't want to do this, but if you want revenge you have no choice. At the end of the day he is your son, and you have to step up to the plate."

"Cut it out. Remember, I'm here on a mission and the quicker it's over the better."

"Bobby, Bobby . . ."

But Bobby had heard enough. It was time for him to meet up with those two idiots, his cousins. The trip was worth it just to spend time with them. Bobby Mack had never come across two more delinquent half-wits in his life. They were unbelievable, thick as two short planks and a total fashion abomination. They dressed exactly the same, like some kind of freakish child-twins, and always in Burberry. No-one had told them they were at least two years out of date and that knock-offs didn't really hack it anymore.

They swanked around town, in whatever top of the range car they had nicked that morning and were convinced they were the real thing.

Both young lads desperately wanted to join a crew; it was their life's ambition. In fact, if it hadn't been for this family feud, they would willingly each have given a testicle to join up with the Coyles. That didn't look like it was going to happen. But having had his jaw broken by the Big Man was kudos enough for John.

The story had now reached epic proportions, with the two lads now having taken on all three brothers in their cousin's defence and of course no-one could expect to walk away from a scrum without a few battle scars.

Bobby could hear the music from a couple of streets away. Several pedestrians were aware of the racket and were looking for the source. One couple, at the top of the steps of the Hilton Hotel, were particularly noticeable. They looked a bit worse for wear this early in the day and were certainly very striking. She was a tall, supermodel blonde and he was tall, dark and handsome. He was also his child's grandfather.

Well, well, that was a turn up for the books.

Sean's Song

For once in his miserable young life Billy Riley actually had something to smile about. He couldn't believe his luck. This was probably going to be one of the best days of his life. He had the chance to make some real money and he sure as fuck wasn't going to screw it up.

Situated on the corner of Glebe Street and Church Street, definitely one of the best pitches on the turf, Billy had a clear view of his empire from the top to the bottom of both thoroughfares. The lad could spot potential customers from afar, but more to the point, he could spot the polis from the same distance. The beat cops seldom walked these streets, knowing full well there was a distinct possibility they might not get out of the estate alive. And undercover CID stuck out like two sore thumbs. They were a joke, with their highly polished shoes and neat, well-trimmed hair. But if by chance they did happen to appear, Billy's pride and joy, his black and silver Chopper, was his trusty getaway vehicle.

Yes, this was a fantastic spot and he was going to make some decent mullah, thanks to his elder brother, Tommy. Well, actually, it was really thanks to their mother and her abominable kitchen skills that he was strutting his stuff and lording it over his two best mates.

Tommy Riley was well known in the area and had built up an extensive and regular customer base from all walks of life. He had respectable businessmen, single mums, who, finding life difficult, were not bright enough to realise it had just got a whole load harder. And of course, his hard-core junkies who needed a fix, twenty-four-seven.

He had worked his pitch for over a year and had miraculously survived numerous takeover bids. Despite having been stabbed, shot at and beaten up, Tommy had clung on with great tenacity. Ridiculously, he'd been trumped by a plate of his mother's mince and tatties, the ubiquitous staple diet of every Glaswegian.

Mary Riley, mother of Tommy and Billy had, the previous day, been struck with an attack of conscience after the consumption of a two litre bottle of electric soup. Somehow, and she had no recollection whatsoever of how, she had acquired a quantity of minced beef and potatoes. Her cooking skills left much to be desired, but it had been some time since the boys had had what they termed a 'proper meal'. Billy ate his straight from the pot and came to no harm.

Tommy on the other hand, hadn't returned home till the wee small hours, and the 'proper meal' had been subject to various temperature changes and contamination by numerous flies crawling all over the food. He devoured the lot. Eight hours to the minute, botulism had reared its ugly head and Tommy was due to spend the next few days on the lav.

The brothers knew that if Tommy failed to secure his pitch for even one day, it would be gone and there was no way he'd get it back, even with Paddy Coyle's protection. So it was down to the youngest Riley to take over.

Billy's first transaction of the day was to an old brass. Twigging how green young Billy was, she turned on the charm and got the wrap in her hands before parting with the money. For an old bugger she could surely move. Big mistake, he wouldn't do that again. Apart from a few arguments with customers chancing their luck, the rest of the morning was good, business was brisk and he was having the time of his life.

He was just finalising a deal when a black Range Rover pulled alongside the young entrepreneur and the imposing figure of Sean Coyle emerged. Panicking that he'd be chased off the pitch, Billy didn't know how to play this situation.

"Who the fuck are you?" snarled Sean Coyle.

"I'm Billy Riley, Mr Coyle. Tommy's brother."

"Where's Tommy?"

"He's sick, sir. I'm just covering for him."

Immediately Sean saw an opening. Okay, he had enough cash to pay for what he wanted, but so what?

"A couple of your punters have been complaining you're dealing shit. What have you got to say to that?"

"It's good stuff, Mr Coyle. Here, try it for yourself."

"Try it for myself, you cheeky wee cunt. Are you trying to make out I'm some kind of smackhead?" Sean roared at the young boy.

"No, sir! Honestly, it's what Tommy always sells."

"Well, it will be fucking shit, then. How much is left, boy? Hand it over."

Billy didn't know what to do. If he didn't do what Sean Coyle said, Tommy might lose his pitch. If he did hand over the gear, his brother would surely kill him.

"I've only got a couple of wraps left. Here, look." He produced a few small paper wraps from his jeans pocket, hoping Sean Coyle would believe him. But he knew that anyone in the game would know a dealer never kept his stash on him, but close by.

Sean grabbed the boy by his ear. "Are you making a cunt out of me, sonny? Get the rest of the gear now," Sean hissed in the lad's face. He delivered a hefty blow to the side of Billy's head and the kid went down like a ton of bricks. Sean, busy picking up the few wraps that had fallen, gave Billy a lethal kick to get him moving, but the young dealer was deathly still.

"For fuck's sake, what a fucking day. Is everybody out to get me?" he muttered to himself. "That's all I need, another fucker messing with my day. If this little bastard's playing possum he'll wish he was dead when I've finished with him." Slinging the inert body of Billy Riley into the boot of Michael's four by four, Sean Coyle drove off with only one thing on his mind and it wasn't Billy Riley.

Culprit

Bobby jumped into the cousins' latest acquisition, a bright red Audi, and told them to go round the square again. He wanted to double check; it couldn't be him, could it? But yes, there he was, no mistaking him. In glorious technicolour, Mr Happy Families himself, Paddy Coyle. And by the way he was clinging onto Miss Supermodel, they were definitely good friends. He blasted the horn to attract their attention and Paddy Coyle looked decidedly pissed off when he realised who was making all the commotion.

"Need a lift anywhere, Mr Coyle?" Bobby shouted at the top of his voice for the entire world to hear. "We're definitely going your way."

The three guys who were blasting the horn and turning the music up even louder were certainly drawing attention to the guilty couple.

"Naw, you're alright, sonny, but you could maybe do me a favour," answered Coyle.

Expecting a plea for his silence, Bobby was somewhat taken aback by Paddy's request.

"Aye, son. You could tell my wife and daughter I won't be home for dinner tonight. In fact, not for the foreseeable future," sneered the Big Man.

There was no way that trio of morons were getting one over on Paddy Coyle, and taking his companion by the arm, they walked away from the parked car.

"Yes!" laughed Bobby, punching the air. "Head for home, boys, and don't spare the horses."

They arrived at Chez Coyle in record time.

"Wait outside the gates, lads. She doesn't know it yet, but I'm taking Erin to register the chav, so I shouldn't be long." Bobby told his chauffeurs. "And not a word about that old wanker not coming home soon, I'm not sure how I'll break that news to her."

"No problem, we'll keep schtum. And take your time, cuz, no hurry, we're free all day. This little beauty won't be missed till late on this afternoon," John, the oldest cousin, assured him.

Erin opened the door as Bobby was walking up the drive.

"Obviously been looking out for me," Bobby smirked at her. And boy, for someone who had just given birth a few days ago, she certainly looked a knockout.

"Morning, you're looking good," he complimented her. "Ready for a trip into town, make the little man legal? Surely your mum will look after him for a couple of hours?"

"I'm not sure, my dad's been on the missing list since yesterday's fiasco and she's a bit upset."

"He's okay. We just met him and he sent a message home too."

"You met him and you're still standing?" the girl was dumbfounded.

"Oh, we were in the car. Anyway, he says he's not coming home for dinner."

"What do you mean he's not coming home for dinner?" Erin was beginning to panic. "What kind of message is that?"

"I don't know, he just said 'Tell my wife and daughter I won't be home for dinner tonight.' Maybe he's got a job on or something?"

"Where did you meet him?"

"He was coming out of the Hilton with his secretary." Christ, she was so gullible, thought Bobby.

"He hasn't got a secretary," snapped Erin.

"Whoa, don't shoot the messenger. I just bumped into him and offered him a lift," Bobby shot back at her.

"What did this woman look like, was she young, old, what?"

"Erin, it was a bird. I didn't pay much attention. She was tall, blonde, maybe mid-twenties, but as I said, I didn't pay that much attention." Bobby knew exactly how to pull her strings, and she was visibly distressed.

"Look, why don't we go into town, sort out our business and then see if we can find him?" Bobby suggested.

Erin disappeared into the house and returned a few minutes later with a face like thunder.

Erin

"For God's sake, slow down," Erin yelled from the back seat of the car. "You'll get us all killed!" But none of the others, especially the driver, paid the slightest bit of attention to her.

Christ, it wouldn't be her son's birth being registered, but four death certificates if they didn't stop their stupid joy-riding. She was terrified. So, when they pulled up to the traffic lights, she was amazed they hadn't run them but had actually stopped, and she opened the passenger door and fled across the road.

"Don't be stupid, get back in," Bobby shouted to her. "Get in, he'll drive slower, we were only having a bit of a laugh. Honest, he'll behave. I promise."

Shaking like a leaf, Erin crossed the road and flagged down a passing taxi. "No chance. I'm not getting back in there with those fucking idiots. If you want to register your son, come with me, otherwise forget it."

"Okay, hold on. Wait a minute. Sorry, boys, catch you later, I've got to keep her sweet."

"That's okay," said John, "we'll meet you at the registry office."

"No, listen, you could do me a big favour and have a quick look around and see if you can spot Coyle. He had the look of a man on a mission, and I'll bet anything he and the tart hit the first pub they came to and might well still be there."

"Will do, but we might need to dump this beauty if we're hanging about the town, keep you posted." The car vanished into the distance.

"Why in God's name, Bobby, are you hanging about with those two imbeciles?"

"They're family, Erin. They're okay, just a bit exuberant, and don't you forget I came over here, right into the lion's den with no backup, nothing. So give it a rest, or I'll be back on the next flight out of here."

"Please yourself, I'm sure as hell not holding you back. Let's face it, there's been nothing but aggravation since you arrived. So if you want to go back to Marbella, be my guest. I'll tell you something, though, you can forget seeing your son and I'll be damned if he'll have the McClelland name."

Wow, the worm had certainly turned. Erin had even surprised herself. She was no mug, and despite her mother's endeavours to keep her well away from the family business, Erin had seen and heard far too much over the years for some of it not to have rubbed off on her.

So, much as she wanted him back in her life, there was no way she was being dictated to by anyone, much less Bobby Mack.

As the taxi pulled up outside the registry office, Erin was having second thoughts. What was the rush? They had plenty of time to do this. The baby was less than a week old and the fact that neither her mum nor dad were with her just didn't seem right. Her dad had never been away from home like this before, and she had never known her mother to fret over him like she was doing now. But more to the point, why was she giving in to pressure from Bobby? No. Stuff it, she wasn't ready to do this and she certainly wasn't going to play along just to keep the peace.

Standing outside the grey, sombre building on a wet dismal day, Erin Coyle told the love of her life to do one. "Sorry, Bobby, but we'll have to do this another time. I want my mum and dad here with me, so we'll just have to come back when they're both here."

"Don't hold your breath, darlin', you could have a long wait."

"What do you mean?"

"Just what I said, you'll have a long wait."

"Shut up! What do you know about us?"

"I know your dad's shacked up with some brass and he has no intention of coming back in the near future."

"Don't talk rubbish. My mum and dad have never been apart for more than a few days at most, and the last person on earth he would send a message home with is you."

"Believe what you want, I don't give a fuck. Your father categorically informed me, and half the population of this city, that he had no intention of returning home in the foreseeable future. So, if you don't mind, let's not waste any more time and get this over with."

Bobby marched into the registry office leaving her standing alone on the pavement, tears streaming down her cheeks.

Marie

What in God's name was happening to her family? Two of her three brothers had gone absolutely fucking doolally, to say the least. Completely lost their marbles, and behaving like fucking teenagers. Gone off the rails was putting it mildly, and the third had his head so far up his arse he could probably see daylight.

Sean was careering round town beating people up for little or no reason, running up enormous debts, stealing from his own family, and for most of the time he was completely off his head on a cocktail of booze and drugs. He was way out of control and if something wasn't done to curb his behaviour soon, it could be too late. He'd pissed off some serious people, people who wouldn't back down simply because he was a Coyle. And the most worrying thing was that she seemed to be the only one who recognised the situation.

To make matters worse, if they could be any worse, the other brother had apparently dumped his wife, gone on the trot and was shacking up with some two bit whore. The gossip about him was just as bad: booze, drugs and sex, and God help anyone who crossed Paddy. Like Sean, he had left a trail of broken bones over the past week.

Neither had checked in with her or Michael for days. Anything could be happening in their business and they would be oblivious. Word was out on the street that the Coyles had problems. As far as Marie was concerned, the word on the street was right, the Coyles did have problems and they were all of their own making.

She had tried to enlist Michael's help with Sean. She'd been to him on three separate occasions, only to be told that she was somehow at fault. He'd implied she couldn't do her job and when he got round to it, he'd have a word. Have a word? If they didn't act soon they'd be doing it through fucking Psychic Sally. The vultures were beginning to circle.

"Michael, it's me. Any word?" He could hear the concern in her voice, but that only aggravated and irritated him even more. He was definitely going to have a serious word with Paddy about their sister when he eventually deigned to put in an appearance.

"No, nothing, and if you're phoning to tell me how hard done by you are, you can piss off. I'm up to my neck in work, so you'll have to sort out your own shit. I've got more than enough to deal with myself."

"Listen, for Christ's sake! We have to get them back

on track, Michael. Things are beginning to fall apart."

"Don't talk fucking nonsense, girl. Are you trying to tell me that if Paddy went off on his jollies to Benidorm for a week the businesses would fall apart?"

"Of course not, but the fact is that Paddy has been seen about town, pissed out of his box, hanging out with a young brass, and obviously *not* taking care of business. And the other brother is on some kind of wrecking spree, way out of control. Sean's been upsetting more than a few major players in town and tongues are beginning to wag. So yes, we're ripe for the picking and there are certainly plenty who would chance their luck, don't you think?"

This was the second time their viability had been called into question. Joe Malloy had hinted as much and now his bloody sister was saying the same. A strange feeling in his gut made Michael sit up. For fuck's sake, what was wrong with everyone? He knew he had to do something, but what?

Michael was the numbers man. He could handle himself well enough in a scrum and he wasn't shy of wading in where necessary, but he wasn't, and never would be, a 'heavy' like his twin or his older brother. Paddy and Sean would both use any means to get a result and in a situation like the one he was facing, there would be no argument. Paddy would gather the troops and go out and smack a few arses, but that wasn't Michael's style and he was out of his depth.

"Okay, what do you suggest? If you think the situation is that serious, and we can't capture either of them, what do you propose?"

"We'll need to show some force. I've had a few strange faces in the club this week and I know at least two were sussing the place out."

"So we double up security and at the first sign of any trouble we give out a few serious leatherings. Show that we're not mugs and that certainly the Coyles are not to be messed with."

"Yeah, that's okay for starters, but it doesn't really say anything other than we've got a huge workforce. Seriously, Michael, I'm not sure what to do. We could start a turf war here and everybody becomes a loser. I hate to admit this, but we have to get Paddy back in."

"What do you want me to do? Put a fucking ad in the lost and found column? I've had bodies out day and night looking for the fucker, with no joy."

"What's this all about anyway, Michael? I would have staked money that he and Bridget were rock solid. I know they've had their ups and downs like any couple, but I honestly never saw this coming," Marie was upset. She loved her brother, and Bridget truly was the sister she'd never had. This had to be sorted, for the whole family's sake.

"I reckon he'll stay away till the McClelland kid leaves. There's no way Paddy would entertain that little shit swanning around his home, and from what I can gather, Bridget and Erin have sided with him."

"For Christ's sake, Michael, I thought it was something serious. Just because he lost face, he's gone on the trot?"

"It's serious to Paddy. You know what he's like. It's all about respect, that's how we got where we are and if we're not careful it's what will bring us down." Michael was worried now, seriously worried. He would never want to let Paddy down and he'd spent most of his life covering for Sean. He had to find them, and soon.

Having Fun

Christ, he was bored, he thought as he wandered around the small apartment. What a dump. Days filled with booze, coke and sex had blown him away at first, but honestly, the attraction was wearing thin and he was fucking knackered.

Freedom and lack of responsibility were all very well, but the novelty of sticking two fingers up to everyone had soon worn off. Paddy was used to work, discipline and order. For God's sake, he had hardly had a day off since he was fifteen and he needed to get back to work. Not only that, he wryly admitted to himself, he missed his home comforts. It seemed the excitement of dirty sex on tap couldn't make up for a clean shirt and a full English.

He caught sight of himself in the grubby mirror. Jesus, he looked rough. For a man who prided himself on his appearance, he was in some fucking state. It was time to go back to the real world, well, his real world.

He was pretty sure that no-one knew exactly where

he'd been shacked up or with whom, and he intended to keep it that way. Chantelle was a brahma and if things were different, well? Who knows! But they were what they were, and if she played ball she'd be well taken care of. As long as he could make her understand there was no going back, her days at the club were over. Hopefully she would take this on the chin, but he couldn't have a constant reminder of his indiscretion, or take the chance she would let something slip.

"Breakfast," called Chantelle as she opened the door and placed two McDonald's bags on the cluttered table.

"Not for me darlin', I can't stomach that shit under normal circumstances, but with a hangover like this . . . Fuck, no."

"Drink the coffee and I'll sort you a pick-me-up," laughed his companion, all the while taking in the fact that he was dressed and his possessions had gone from the table, his keys and wallet.

"No pick-me-up, I've got to straighten out," Paddy shuddered at the thought.

"Are you off somewhere?" she asked, frowning at the man in front of her.

"I've got to get back to work, sweetheart. I've stayed away too long. Not that being here hasn't been off the scale, babes, but I have to go. Got things to do, people to see."

"Yeah, of course. We both knew it wasn't for real, just a holiday romance," she laughed.

"Chantelle, come and see me at the club tomorrow

morning and I'll see you alright. I'll sort you out, make things good."

"Look, Paddy, you don't have to do anything, and I know I can't go back to work there. Some arsehole would put two and two together and make ten and then we'd all be in the shit. Don't worry about me, I'm a big girl and I can get work anywhere."

"Come in at ten and I'll you fix up."

As the door banged closed, she fell apart. Chantelle would never go cap in hand to anyone, especially not to Paddy Coyle.

Running downstairs and out into the bright sunshine, Paddy could hardly believe his eyes. The area was like a bomb site. What the fuck was he thinking of? And where the hell was his car? He dreaded to think what state it would be in, as he surveyed the number of burnt-out vehicles strewn about the green.

Fortunately, across the other side of the road, standing like a beacon and intact, stood his brand new Range Rover, surrounded by a small group of neighbourhood kids.

"We watched out for your car, Mr Coyle," spoke a lad of about twelve.

"We took good care of it, sir," piped up another gallus young chap.

"Yeah, we made sure no-one nicked it or keyed it. We done it in shifts."

"Thanks, boys, and if I'm ever back down this way I'll be sure to leave it in your safe-keeping."

Taking two twenty pound notes from his wallet, he handed them to the oldest lad. "Go get yourselves a McDonald's or something."

He jumped into the car, gunned it and sped off. There was no chance he'd have to fork out for his car again because he'd never be anywhere near this place again. Ever.

"Jesus Christ, Paddy! Where the fuck have you been? And look at the fucking state of you." Michael was disgusted at the condition of his older brother; older being the operative word. Paddy looked like he'd aged ten years since he last saw him.

"Never you mind where I've been, I'm back now and that's all anyone needs to know."

"We all know who you've been with, but why? Bridget's going fucking ape-shit, threatening all sorts." His brother was furious at his disappearance but relieved to have him back.

"Don't you worry about Bridget. She'll be fine. And if she ain't, fuck it, I'll be off again."

"Don't say that, Paddy, it's been blue murder. Fuckers chancing their luck, and Sean's been on the trot almost as long as you have. I need you here."

"Okay, okay, calm down. I'm off home to get changed and I'll be back in a couple of hours, you can fill me in then. What about the McClelland pup? Is he still on the scene?"

"Yes, as far as I know."

"Well, he's first to get his arse kicked."
Paddy made for home to face the music.

The Worm Turns

Erin was distraught, standing alone on the pavement outside the registry office. She couldn't believe what Bobby had just thrown at her. Her father was not coming home? No way would he abandon them; they were family.

But what if it was true? Paddy was all for loyalty and she knew that, deep down, he felt she had betrayed him, even though it had been unintentional. Erin had not known that Bobby was the son of Paddy's sworn enemy, and, much as he loved his new grandchild, he detested the McClellands more. Add that to the fact that her mother had taken a stance against him and it would be more than Paddy could tolerate.

Could it be true?

Whatever, she was certainly not being held to ransom by Bobby and if he thought that the news he had just imparted would sway her, he had another think coming. The bloody nerve of him, thinking he could dictate to her. Erin waved down a taxi, jumped in the back and gave the driver instructions.

"What are you doing here? I thought you were all loved up with Señor Bobby," laughed Carol.

"Don't talk to me about that prat," stormed Erin. "You'll never believe what he just told me."

"Well, I'm not into guessing games, so spill. What did Mr Wonderful say that's got you this upset?"

"He's only after telling me that Paddy's left my mum and won't be back. The bloody cheek of him. As if my dad would tell *him* anything."

"Whoa, where did this come from? And why did Paddy tell him, of all people?"

"He says he met him in town and Dad told him he wasn't coming home for dinner, or ever again."

"Don't believe a word of it," said Carol.

"Well, he hasn't been home and my mother is beside herself with worry."

"That doesn't explain why you're here in the middle of the day. What else has happened?"

"I've just left Bobby at the registry office. He wanted to register Ryan's birth and I refused. I want the family to be there, to make it an occasion, and that's when he told me not to hold my breath, my dad wasn't coming home."

"Paddy and Bridget are solid and it's up to you to decide when and where you register Ryan. He's your son. Listen, Erin, you're not going to like this, but I'm going to say it anyway. He's a player, is Bobby. I know I don't know him very well, but he really is a chancer. I've a feeling that when he gets his name on the birth certificate he'll be off like a shot. It's worrying that he may have some kind of agenda about the baby. I hope I'm wrong, but be careful."

"When he's with us, Carol, he's brilliant, but when there's an audience he's a completely different person. And he and my dad really hate each other. I don't know how I'm ever going to solve that. Did I tell you he wants us to go and live in Spain?"

"What!"

"Yes, he's been going on about it since he got here. He knows my family will never accept him, but he insists he wants to be in Ryan's life. I don't know what to do."

"Nothing. You do absolutely nothing until you have no doubt that what you're doing is the right thing, and from what you're saying that's certainly not what's happening at the moment."

"You're right. I'll sort things out in my own good time. If my dad's not home next week, then I might register the baby, but that doesn't mean to say I'll put Bobby's name on it. We'll see."

The Prodigal Returns

"Gran, Gran, Uncle Michael's here," young Errol squealed, jumping up and down excitedly at the window.

"Michael? Your Uncle Michael? At this time of the morning? Holy Mother of God, there must be something up," and without a moment's hesitation Lizzie ran out to the car. The windows on the monster were blacked out and the fact that they were also steamed up made it doubly impossible to see into the vehicle.

"Michael, Michael, open the door," Lizzie was knocking on the passenger window and calling to her son.

The occupant, drifting in and out of a drug-induced sleep, could hear his mother calling and for one split second he thought he had died. He appeared to be in some black tomb. It was that grim thought which shot him back to consciousness.

Fuck, what was he doing here? Passed out in his brother's car, outside his mother's house? This was the last place on earth Sean wanted to be. He rolled down the window and faced his concerned mother.

"Lord above, Sean, you frightened the life out of me. What the devil are you doing sleeping out here? What'll the neighbours think?"

"As if you'd give a toss what anyone round here thought," Sean snapped back at her.

"Maybe so, but what a state to be in. Get yourself inside and I'll fix you some breakfast while you get cleaned up."

"It's okay, Ma. I just rolled up late and didn't want to wake you. I'll shoot off, I'd better get Michael's car back to him."

"Get yourself indoors and not another word, I'm not standing here arguing with you," Lizzie turned and made her way back inside.

Sean had no alternative but to follow her. Even to this day the boys seldom, if ever, argued back with their mother.

There was something niggling at the back of his head, something that he had to do. Whatever it was, it escaped him for the moment. He was soon tucking into his mother's famous 'full Monty' breakfast. It was probably the first food he'd eaten in days, he couldn't remember. He'd existed on a diet of whatever drugs were available, washed down with copious amounts of alcohol and, boy, was he paying for it.

"Uncle Sean, can I go sit in the car 'til you get ready? Please, I won't touch anything, I promise. Please?"

The young lad was besotted with cars, his head was to be found under a bonnet whenever possible. He pestered the life out of his uncles to go driving with them or if they were visiting his gran, he'd clean and polish the vehicles. There was no doubt when he was older what line of work he'd end up in.

Sean threw the keys over to the lad, "Go on, but no starting the engine, mind. And no mucking about."

Sean still had a niggling feeling that he had to sort something to do with the car, but it eluded his coke-befuddled brain.

Errol was off like a bullet. He let himself into the driver's side and was lost in the gadgetry of his uncle's top of the range vehicle. Climbing over onto the back seat, the young lad fiddled about with the in-car videos and soundtrack. He'd have to get into the boot to change his uncle's crap music. Just as he was about to disappear between the seats, his uncle Sean appeared.

"Go get ready and I'll give you a lift to school," Sean offered. Anything to get away from his mother and the fear of being confronted by Marie, who, thankfully, was still asleep.

"I'll put my bike in the boot, Uncle Sean, I need it to ride home."

"Okay, son." Just as Errol pressed the button to open the huge, cavernous trunk, a vivid flashback hit Sean. The boy! Fucking hell. He remembered with great clarity what it was he had to 'sort out'.

He jumped out of the driver's seat and bolted to the back of the car. Thankfully, Errol was still struggling with his bike. Slamming the boot shut, Sean grabbed the youngster's bike and threw it on the back seat.

"Oh, no, Uncle Sean! Uncle Michael will go mad. I'm not allowed to put my bike there. Honest, he'll go off his head."

"Don't you worry about Uncle Michael, I'll fix him. Now let's get you off to school, young man."

"Are you okay, Uncle Sean? You look a bit funny." the young lad looked quizzically at his uncle.

Feel a bit funny? Sean thought he was going to have a fucking heart attack. Christ, that was a near one. He'd forgotten all about that poncey little drug dealer. He'd see about getting rid of him as soon as he got shot of his nephew. What a fucking carry-on. Could he not get a break? he moaned to himself.

Errol chattered all the way to school and Sean was now regretting having offered the lad a lift. He wasn't used to kids, and certainly not first thing in the morning when he felt as rough as a badger's arse.

"They found his bike and Billy would never leave his bike. He loved it and he'd spent a fortune on it, but he's been missing for three days now. So what do you think, Uncle Sean?"

"Think about what?" Sean had obviously not listened to a word Errol had said.

"What do you think about my mate going missing?"

"What mate? And going missing where?" said Sean, exasperated.

"My mate Billy, he hasn't been seen for three days. He was punting some gear near Gran's and he's gone, vanished. Nobody's seen or heard from him."

"You better not have anything to do with punting gear, my lad, or I'll personally tan your arse," Sean warned the boy.

"No way, I'm just telling you what happened."

"Okay, but remember, I'm not joking. So, tell me about this missing pal then."

"Well, as I said, he's not been seen for three days, but his bike was still there. Billy would never leave his bike, he wouldn't let anyone even have a ride on it. The cops are all over the place. Somebody said he was taken away in a big black car, but I don't know if that's true. Are you sure you're okay, Uncle Sean? You really look funny."

Sean dropped his nephew off at the school gates and headed back to his flat in town. He needed to have a snort and work out what the fuck he was going to do. Sean had a strict rule about his home. He never, ever brought anyone back and he never kept anything incriminating indoors. Many's the fool who'd been nicked, not by stashing their cash or goods in safety deposit boxes, but by keeping a little in reserve under the floor boards, or even more unbelievable, under the bed in case of emergencies! It was a rule Sean never broke, no matter how off his head, or out of control he might get, his flat was as clean as a whistle. In the unlikely event that his place was raided, the filth would find nothing. It also allowed him to employ the services of a respectable widow woman as his cleaner without fear of the old biddy innocently finding something. But this was an emergency, so he cut a couple of lines.

The disposal of the car and the body through the crusher was an easy enough task. It would certainly not be the first Range Rover to finish up as a metal ashtray. However, Sean reasoned, some nosey fucker might question the destruction of such a new and expensive vehicle. Therefore he decided it would be best done later that night. It was imperative that the vehicle remained hidden until then.

Sean arrived at the scrapyard and parked the car round the back, out of sight. It was most unlikely anyone would think it strange or poke around, but he had no inclination to bump into either Michael or Paddy until the deed was done.

He had arranged for a taxi to pick him up a couple of streets from the yard and take him into town. A few drinks were in order, then home to get his head down for some much needed kip.

Standing at the bar, minding his own business, Sean reflected on the morning's incidents. Christ, he'd had a couple of near misses, but the job was almost done, he smirked to himself. All he had to do now was wait a couple of hours, get back to the yard and do the deed.

"What you smirking at?" the words broke into Sean's thoughts.

"You talking to me, ya bampot?" answered Sean. Then blackness descended.

"For fuck's sake, somebody call an ambulance," screamed one of the more sober customers.

"Get him out of here first. If he's done for, it's fuck all to do with us," replied the barman as he and a couple of customers dragged an unconscious Sean outside to the alleyway next to the pub.

For the second time that day he heard his mother's voice, off in the distance.

Bobby

"Where the bloody hell is she?" said Bobby, striding up and down George Square. There was no sign of her. She wouldn't have gone off and left him, no way. No-one dumped Bobby Mack, well not usually. He was fed up with the whole bloody fiasco.

His intention had been to come to Glasgow, despite the fact that he hadn't been in the city since he was a nipper, meet up with the Coyles, charm Erin, sort out the birth certificate and piss off back to Spain, all in the shortest possible time.

Well, that plan sure as hell wasn't working. So far, he'd acquired a broken jaw (which was giving him gyp by the way), collected two idiotic relatives who were sure to land him in jail and the mother of his baby had buggered off and left him stranded. Now he was freezing his nuts off in the pouring rain, in what passed for summer in Scotland. No wonder his parents had left.

Bobby was positive that Erin would have headed

for home and if he wanted to sort this mess out once and for all and get back to his home, he'd better get there, pronto. The last thing he wanted was her having a long heart-to-heart with her mother, who would definitely talk her out of returning to Spain with him. To be fair, he knew there was little or no chance of that happening, but he had to convince Erin that that was what he wanted and if not now, then in the very near future.

He was surprised to find no-one at home when he arrived at the house. Testament to Paddy's reputation, the house was unlocked.

"Is there anyone home?" Bobby called, entering the silent hallway. What should he do? Well, a cup of coffee wouldn't go amiss and with Paddy out of the way, he was sure neither woman would object to his waiting inside.

Through in the lounge, he settled down to watch the sports channel and wait for Erin. Within five minutes he was dozing comfortably, oblivious to the world.

Bobby shot off the sofa, "What the fuck?" For a few seconds he had no idea where he was or who had grabbed him.

"Precisely. What the fuck?" snarled Paddy Coyle. "What the fuck are you doing in my home on your own?" he glowered at the intruder.

"I lost Erin in town and came back to wait for her, but there was no-one home."

"So you took it upon yourself to break in?"

"The door was open," Bobby was beginning to realise just how much danger he might be in. This was probably the most vicious man he'd ever meet. The man who had cold-bloodedly murdered his father. And who would think nothing of snuffing out *his* life in a puff. And there would be no witnesses. He could have been a burglar caught in the act.

A similar thought was passing through Paddy's head. It would solve everything. But no, this was his home and no matter how bad things were between him and the family, he wouldn't contaminate it. Marching out of the lounge and taking the stairs two at a time, Paddy left a gobsmacked Bobby slumped on the sofa, thankful he was still breathing.

Should he make a quick getaway or chance his luck and wait for someone to return? His dilemma was solved immediately, as Bridget, carrying baby Ryan, stormed into the house. Having seen Paddy's car in the drive, she was ready for battle. She was extremely surprised to find Bobby in her sitting room and not Paddy.

"What are you doing in here?" she snapped at him.

"Look, I've already been through this with your old man. He's upstairs, by the way, and not in the best of moods."

Bridget practically threw the baby into Bobby's arms and she too ran up the stairs.

"What the . . .?" He had no idea what to do with

the child, but judging by the noise emanating from the upper floor, he certainly wasn't going to interrupt the antagonists to ask what he should do.

Saved again. A taxi cab pulled into the drive and the errant mother alighted.

"Thank God," Bobby shoved the baby into Erin's outstretched arms. "I'm off," and the young guy bolted out of the house and into the taxi. "Fuck, that was good timing. Head for town," he instructed the driver, but not quickly enough.

Erin appeared from the house waving frantically. "Hold on, Bobby. Wait, we need to talk!"

"Ignore her," Bobby told the driver, but knowing full well who the house belonged to, the driver reversed back up to the front door.

"Get out, mate."

"Just hang on until I see what she wants," he ordered as he got out of the cab. The driver, without hesitation, drove away, leaving Bobby stranded.

"Talk? We've done nothing but talk and got nowhere. Erin, your dad's a bloody maniac, listen to him. He and your mum are going at it hammer and tongs and believe me, I was lucky to get away without serious injury earlier. I'm so out of here."

"He won't bother you anymore, I promise. And I'm sorry about the registry office. I just got cold feet. It felt wrong without my folks being there."

"Even ones battling like those two? Real happy families."

"I'm telling you again, you don't know anything about my family so don't go making judgements."

"I couldn't give a fuck if he's with a different woman every night, or if he worships the ground your mother walks on. I'm here for you and my son and nobody else, but this is going nowhere."

"What did you expect? Did you think I was going to swoon at your feet because you took a cheap flight from Spain and bought me some flowers? Dream on, Bobby, step into the real world." Erin turned on her heel and walked back into the house to answer the phone.

"Hi, Gran. What's up? Oh, my, God. Calm down, wait and I'll get my dad."

Erin battered on the door of her parents' room and eventually made herself heard. No matter how angry Bridget and Paddy were with each other, this was urgent, her gran was in a terrible state and Erin had been hard pushed to understand her.

"Dad, listen, I've got Granny on the phone and she's saying something about Uncle Sean. I can't make out what's wrong."

Taking the receiver from his daughter Paddy listened stony-faced.

"Okay, I'll leave now and pick you up in twenty minutes." He replaced the receiver.

"Sean's been attacked. He's in ICU at the Royal and it's not looking too good. We have to go."

Immediately Bridget put their feud aside and got

ready to go with Paddy. It was family and Lizzie needed them.

Bobby saw his chance to escape and called the cousins to come and collect him. This was no concern of his. Maybe the uncle would die and that would mean one less Coyle to deal with.

The family made the journey to Lizzie's in silence. Bridget was still reeling from the row with Paddy.

Who did he think he was, laying down rules like she was some kind of muppet and not his wife of almost twenty years? He'd still be a bloody gas meter bandit if it wasn't for her. Playing the big man at home and telling her to mind her own business. Well, he'd keep. There were more important fish to fry at the moment, but he certainly hadn't heard the end of this. Not by a long chalk.

The Blackness

Police are investigating what they think was a vicious gangland attack in the East side of the city yesterday. An attack which left Sean Coyle, younger brother of Patrick Coyle, the well-known head of the Coyle family, fighting for his life in a Glasgow hospital. The victim is in a stable but critical condition. The attack took place in the late afternoon outside the Square Rigg in the Provanhall district. Police are appealing for witnesses. Anyone with information should contact the incident room . . . The newsreader continued.

There was nothing of further of interest to Gerald Fairnie so he turned the television to mute and with a grin mouthed 'Cheers' to the battered old set in the corner. He was still elated over the previous day's events. It was the first piece of good luck he'd had in God knows when.

It was fate, that's what it was, or karma (as they called it now) that had taken him into that particular boozer yesterday. Having been out of circulation for eight years, it was one of the few places he recognised. Inside it was as though time had stood still; the same barman slouched behind the same bar reading the paper, the same décor and definitely the same losers nursing the previous night's hangovers. Nothing unusual in that, until the door opened and in *he* walked. Gerry almost choked on his pint. The cliché 'Of all the gin joints in all the towns' sprung immediately to mind. Fuck, this was unbelievable. He'd probably never get a chance like this again.

Having vowed for years that he would 'do' Sean Coyle if he ever saw him again, Gerry had spent countless sleepless nights picturing Sean's demise. How he'd make him pay and pay in full for what the bastard had taken from him. It was that vow that had got him through the darkness that had become his life.

Gerald John Paul Fairnie was a small-time crook, stealing from his own, which was the most despicable crime in any community. He took from those who had little or nothing to begin with. He only just managed to scrape a living for his beloved wife and kids.

Gerry had somehow, and he never understood how, managed to capture the best-looking bird for miles around. Moira Grey was a local lass with the face and nature of an angel. She was a real stunner and Gerry knew he was punching way above his weight. Okay, she wasn't the sharpest knife in the drawer, and so gullible it was a crime, but she loved 'her Gerry' and their two kids with a passion and would hear nothing untoward said about her husband. She knew he was doing the best he could and she believed, like him, he would one day get a break and life would be better.

Well, the break came in the way of Paddy Coyle, a different type of fish altogether to his scumbag brother. During the 'Ice Cream Wars' era, vacancies for roundsmen came up frequently and as luck would have it, Gerry was in the right place at the right time. Or, maybe the wrong place at the wrong time. Whatever. On his first week on the job he was raided by the Serious Crime Squad and despite every effort made by Paddy, his lawyers and the vast amounts paid to ensure that his drivers never got a pull, Gerry went down for a ten stretch. The authorities were making a stand and poor Gerald Fairnie got much more than they all had bargained for.

He was promised that his wife and kids would be taken care of if he kept his mouth shut and did his bird with no fuss. They were, but not in the way Gerry had envisaged. Had he known what was ahead, he would have sung like a canary and fuck the consequences. Things certainly couldn't have got any worse.

At the beginning of Gerry's sentence, his wife received regular sums of cash and the money made the difference between the family existing or not. Moira was so grateful, and when Sean enlisted her help with a couple of deliveries she saw no harm in it – the extra money certainly came in useful.

Over the months the poke got less and less which meant Moira, out of necessity, became a regular courier. The young mum with two children, one of whom was in a buggy, traversed the city with her packages unnoticed, or so it seemed. She'd had a bad feeling that fateful morning and against her gut instinct made her way to the address and the pick-up went ahead as planned.

With the consignment stashed in the buggy under her son's blankets, she set off for home. It was a miserable rainy Glasgow day and in her hurry to get home, Moira bumped down off the pavement into a particularly deep puddle and the wheel came off the pushchair. Child, blankets and package scattered. In the confusion she became aware of two police officers who had appeared on the scene. Despite Moira's efforts to recover the situation, she knew the game was up when the older of the two officers picked up the package. She was still in Maryhill Police Station six hours later.

The world stopped that day for the Fairnies. The children were taken into care and their mother was charged with drug-dealing and sentenced to eighteen months. Moira lasted four weeks before she was found hanging in her cell. All this, thanks to Sean Coyle. Gerald Fairnie had sworn he would get him if it was the last thing he ever did.

And now there he was, large as life; the fates

had delivered him, tucked up good and proper. The situation was made even more satisfactory when it became clear that Sean hadn't a clue who Gerry was, before he caved his head in. With a bit more luck Sean wouldn't remember who he was after such a blow.

A decent shave and haircut made Gerry doubly sure no-one in the pub that day would recognise him. There was no way he even remotely resembled the supposed gangland assassin of years gone by. He grinned like a Cheshire cat, maybe things were on the turn. He couldn't have planned it better, and to top it all off he had a meet with Paddy Coyle the next day to sort him out an earn. Gerry had done his bird, kept schtum and now he was going to collect what was due, but not necessarily in cash.

The Hospital

"Dear God, Paddy, look at him," Lizzie sobbed as she almost collapsed at her son's bedside. Sean was deathly white and wired up to God knows how many machines. "Who could have done this to my boy?" she whimpered.

Neither Bridget nor Paddy answered the old woman, but both were thinking similar thoughts. Half of the Glasgow underworld was baying for Sean's blood although there were few who would challenge the Coyles' position.

"Hello, I'm Doctor McLeod. I'm the senior registrar in charge of Mr Coyle's case. Can I ask who his next of kin is?"

"His mother," answered Paddy, "but she's in no fit state to deal with any questions, so talk to me, I'm his oldest brother." There was no sign yet of either Marie or Michael. "First, I want the top man on his case and move him to a private room," demanded Paddy.

"Mr Coyle, as I said, I am the senior registrar. If you were to go private you would simply get the same staff and a whopping great bill. Your second request is not possible either because we cannot move your brother at the moment. He's in a critical condition and requires dedicated nursing and constant observation. That's not possible on a private ward. We are doing our very best to stabilize him. He has sustained serious injuries to his head and a knife wound which has caused severe internal bleeding.

"He will be all right though, doctor?" challenged Paddy.

"I can't tell you that at the moment, Mr Coyle. As I said, your brother is in a critical condition and the next few hours are crucial. It is possible we may have to operate to relieve the pressure on his brain and I need you to sign the permission form."

"You didn't understand me, Doctor, that wasn't a question." Paddy was almost nose to nose with the young man.

"Are you threatening me?" the medic faced up to his aggressor.

"No, laddie, I'm stating a fact. *He'll be all right.*"

Dr McLeod stepped back and looked Paddy square in the eye. "Mr Coyle, I have no intention of standing here being subjected to your ridiculous threats, wasting precious time, when I could be attending to your brother. So, if you'll excuse me. And by the way, the answer to your question is, pray, sir, pray. That's probably your brother's best chance." The medic walked off.

Despite himself Paddy was impressed with the young man's nous. There were few men who would stand up to him, especially under such stressful conditions.

Catching the end of the conversation Bridget rounded on Paddy. "Dear God, man, you've not been threatening the medical staff, have you? Who do you think you are? Your brother's lying in there, probably dying and you're off on some ego trip. Jesus, Paddy, I really don't know you at all nowadays. Go and sit with your mam, she's the only one still impressed with you, and while you are at it, ask yourself what that idiot brother of yours was up to that landed him here. It wasn't for anything done on your instructions, was it?"

Fuck, he couldn't do right for doing wrong with his wife these days. She just refused to see that he only wanted what was best for the family, as he had always done. It wasn't unreasonable to make sure his brother had the best medical attention money could buy. After all, a huge proportion of what Bridget spent, and boy could she spend, was earned by this man. As for why he was in that particular area, God alone knew. Sean was a maverick; he went wherever the wind blew. He could have been on the prowl and upset a boyfriend or husband, or chasing a debt; they would only find out when he came to, not if, and he would come to, of that Paddy was sure.

Michael and Marie arrived. The brother and sister had travelled together, giving them the opportunity to discuss the events of the past few days. Neither were surprised at the situation in the least, and both, given Sean's behaviour over the past few months, were only surprised that it had not happened before.

It was telling their eldest brother about the patient's escapades that was sure to cause ructions. They had wondered whether they should wait a bit, until they saw how Sean's condition was, before upsetting either Lizzie or Paddy further. Either way, the shit would hit the fan and they were in for a rough time.

"I want to know who did this, and now!" Paddy demanded of Michael.

"For Christ's sake, Paddy, Sean spent all his bleeding life upsetting folk. It would take the whole of Strathclyde Constabulary to pull everyone in who had a grudge against him."

"I don't give a fuck! We have to be seen to be tightening up and anyone, and I mean *anyone*, making noises or idle threats gets hammered. Don't you want to get even with whoever did this? 'Cause they were not kiddin' around."

"I think it was an opportunist hit," Marie put her tuppence worth in.

"Don't talk nonsense," snapped Paddy.

"What do you mean nonsense? Think about what we know."

"Well, that'll take a while," her brothers spoke in unison.

"Listen, if you were going out to get someone, you'd be tooled up, yes?"

"Yes, well you wouldn't depend on a beer bottle and a chib, now, would you?"

Paddy was mulling over his sister's theory and actually it made a lot of sense. It had more credibility than one of their rivals arranging a meet and then doing him over, as Marie said, with a random choice of weapons. But still, he had to be seen to be doing something; Paddy had to make someone pay.

Truth

Over the following few days Bridget and Lizzie kept vigil at Sean's bedside. His brothers and sister visited several times to check on his condition, but business was business and Paddy kept up the pretence that they were pursuing the culprit, or culprits.

The barman on duty that day had been pulled in by the brothers, with no success, but he was out of action for a number of weeks until his face less resembled a pumpkin. Most of the customers were easily located, all being creatures of habit, and despite a few slaps, their memories failed them. Even the tempting ransom on offer brought no fresh information. No-one could remember who had been in the pub that day and the description of the gangland assassin varied between a dead ringer for Osama Bin Laden and television presenter Richard Madeley. The family were beginning to believe Marie's theory that Sean had simply been in the wrong place at the wrong time, and the attacker might well have been a random jakey with a sore head after all.

Despite the initial confrontation with Dr McLeod, he and Paddy rubbed along reasonably well. The young doctor kept the family up to date, always addressing them in layman's terms, so that even Lizzie understood what was happening and what they could expect. It had been decided, because of Sean's drug habit and alcohol consumption, that he would be kept in a controlled coma.

Dr McLeod explained that this procedure was to alleviate the withdrawal symptoms and give Sean's internal injuries and the swelling on his brain a chance to heal, without any undue stress.

"Do you think he can hear us?" Lizzie asked her daughter-in-law. "Often I see his eyes flicker as if he knows what we're talking about."

"I'm sure he can, and if not, it certainly won't do him any harm," replied Bridget.

"What's going on with you two? I've never seen either of you in a strop like this." The old girl was upset and hated the fact that there was strife between husband and wife.

"Don't worry, Lizzie. It's something and nothing and we'll sort it out when this is done," Bridget pointed to the bed where Sean lay.

"Bridget, I'm not stupid, and don't treat me like an auld daftie. I can see there's something serious going on, and if you don't fix it now you might be too late. My son loves you, any damn fool can see that, and I know you feel the same. So swallow your pride, girl, and get things back to normal."

"If he loves me that much, what the hell was he shacking up with a twenty-year-old stripper for?"

"Rubbish. I don't believe a word of it. Who the hell told you that nonsense?"

"His sister."

"Marie?"

"Well, to the best of my knowledge she's his only sister."

"And a feckin' shit-stirring one at that."

"Now Lizzie, she doesn't know she told me. It was something she let slip and I put two and two together and got the gold star."

"Paddy wouldn't cheat on you, lass."

"Lizzie, he's taken the odd flyer from time to time since we got together, but they've never bothered me. And I know how much he *did* care for me, but this one was different. It wasn't a one-nighter, and I suspect he only came back for a clean shirt, but all this got in the way."

"I'll feckin' skin him alive, and Marie too, for that matter. She should keep her big gob shut."

"Lizzie, it would have come out sometime. So don't go blaming anyone, this is all down to Paddy being Mr Big and I'm not having it."

"What are you going to do, darling? Whatever it is, I'll stand by you, son or no son."

Bridget knew how much it took for Lizzie to say that, her family came first before everyone.

Confessions

Michael was well pissed off at his twin brother. Despite him being in a coma, it seemed he could cause agg even from a hospital bed. Michael's car had gone missing. Sean had taken the liberty of using it while his was supposedly in the garage, and it had not been seen since. Sean's car, a brand new Jaguar, was in the garage all right, but in bits, never to be re-assembled. A fact he omitted to relay to his brother.

"When he recovers, he's being assigned a feckin' Sinclair C5 and if anything happens to it, he'll take the bus. Three cars in four months, Paddy. Two wrecks and one only God knows where. Have you any idea how much that's cost? I'm telling you, he's a bloody liability and not just with cars."

Paddy's head shot up from the accounts book he was studying. "Are you trying to tell me something, Mick? By the way, this doesn't balance." He pointed to the old-fashioned ledger. "I've checked it and double-checked, but there's still a difference of almost ten big ones. It looks like it's just been written off."

Despite the installation of the most up to date technology, the real book keeping was still done by hand, in code, in old leather-bound ledgers.

"You're not going to like this, and I was going to tell you, but with Sean in hospital and you on your 'jollies', I have to say I pretty much forgot about it."

"Are you telling me that we've been fleeced for ten grand and you forgot about it?" Paddy was incredulous. "Michael, I remember when we were kids and a lad in your class borrowed ten bob off you. You were still going on about it after you'd left school, so don't give me that old fanny that you forgot ten grand was missing. Who are you covering for, or do I have to ask?"

Michael had not expected Paddy to pick up on the discrepancy, but it just went to show that nothing got past the Big Man. "I wasn't covering exactly, and let's face it, Paddy, if I had the inclination to hide money none of you would ever find it."

"Okay, point taken. So what else am I not going to like?"

"I had to pay off Joe Malloy."

"Joe Malloy? Why the fuck would you be paying him off?"

Paddy had known the man in question for twenty-odd years, they went way back to Borstal and never in all that time had either party had a problem with the other.

"Sean had tickets all round town and a few faces were beginning to get jittery, saying we weren't good for the dough, so I paid him. I tried to get hold of you at the time, but you and he had gone walkabout."

"Why would the word go out we had problems, for Christ's sake?"

"The debts were months old and Sean was avoiding everyone. And, of course, you weren't to be seen. You know better than anyone how fast news travels, especially bad news. That's precisely the time we would move in for the kill. So why would the same not happen to the Coyles?"

"Because we *are* the Coyles," Paddy snapped back. "Who's been sniffing around? I think I need to go visit a few 'friends'."

"I agree you need to make your presence felt, but we need to sort our own house first, everyone else will keep."

Paddy reluctantly agreed with Michael; it was time for him to get back out on the streets and be seen, but God help anyone not playing ball. He would extinguish them, with or without Michael's blessing.

"You need to have a word with Marie, she's toiling a bit and I have to say, Sean was giving her a seriously hard time."

"I heard a few rumours from . . . well, from when I

was away," blustered Paddy. "How serious is the drug problem?"

"Bad enough, but his behaviour is so fucking erratic, thank God he's where he is."

"Surely a few weeks will get him clean and then we can send him off for a bit of R & R?"

"Fine. I can live with that, we've got plenty muscle, but who's going to do his collections?"

"Tiny Carter has been working the round with him for the past year and I've just taken on Gerry Fairnie. He got out of stir a couple of weeks ago."

"Christ, I'd forgotten all about him. Didn't his missus top herself or something?"

"Yeah, bad situation. She got done for possession. The kids got taken off them and she, well, she couldn't hack it."

"Are you sure he's up to a job on this scale?"

"We'll soon know. He's not a guy you would argue with and Tiny knows the score. Funny, he seemed quite taken that he was filling in for Sean."

Official

"Sign here, here and here," the woman on duty at the service desk said to Bobby. "That's fine, and now, Mummy, you sign here and here."

When she had completed the remainder of the form, the council official congratulated the young couple, "Ryan McLelland is officially registered as being born in the City of Glasgow," she said as she handed over the certificate. "That will be ten pounds, please."

"If you don't mind, I'd like a copy too." Bobby turned to Erin, knowing that this was his best chance of obtaining the document without an inquisition.

"Sure, no problem. But why?" Erin puzzled.

"I know it sounds crazy, but if anything were to happen to either of us, well . . . I'd just like to have it."

"That's another ten pounds," said the lady behind the desk.

Handing over the money Bobby felt like he'd just bought a couple of bottles of beer. Officially becoming a father had completely underwhelmed him. Ryan was a grand wee chap, and he certainly was the absolute image of Pete, Bobby's dad. But for Bobby that was it. There was no wave of emotion, in fact, no emotion at all. He didn't feel that this lad was part of him, he was just a kid. And as for the mother? Well, she was a good-looking chick, but no way could he settle for only her. Nope, he was desperate to get back to his life in Marbella, and that was just around the corner. They left the Registry Office in silence.

The cousins were waiting outside in a brand new Porsche.

"Jesus, are you crazy?" said an indignant Erin. "You're bound to get caught driving this around town and we'll all end up getting nicked."

"Naw, you're more likely to get caught driving a pissing Ford Mondeo than something like this. I'm telling you, it's all about nerve. No-one would ever suspect a car like this, being driven round town, would be nicked. You just have to front it, man. You're a right fucking wimp for being Paddy Coyle's daughter."

"Shut up! Do you think I'm worried what you pair think? Listen, I'd just be embarrassed to be caught in a stolen car, especially one cheaper than those parked in our drive. My father would kill me for letting the side down, and the reason he never gets a tug is that he doesn't pull juvenile stunts like this." She turned to Bobby, "You can do what you like, but I'm off."

For the second time they parted company outside

the Registry Office. Only this time he had what he wanted.

He jumped into the Porsche.

"Okay, where to now?" asked John.

"This is your Captain speaking; we are flying at a height of . . ."

The cousins were sorry to see Bobby go, but with the promise of an invite to the christening and a holiday in the sun, they celebrated by dumping the Porsche and disappeared out of the multi-storey car park in their most daring steal to date. The Lord Provost of Glasgow would be riding in a black cab for the foreseeable future.

My God, this was luxury, thought John. Maybe he'd take their mammy to the bingo in the limo tonight . . .

Discovery

"Morning, boss," old Tam, the night watchman greeted Paddy. "Don't often see you this early. Been thrown out?" the man chuckled. "Wait here till I get the boys." His piercing whistle brought two sleek, vicious-looking Doberman Pinschers from the depths of the yard, straight to his side.

Although the dogs knew Paddy, they were in attack mode until their master commanded otherwise and Paddy knew better than to move. One word from the old fella and the two dogs frolicked like pups around the men, their duties abandoned.

"Anything interesting, Tam? Has anyone been snooping around?"

"Naw, quiet as a grave. The lads here would put anyone off paying us a visit. Would you take your chances against them?" he laughed.

"No way, worth their weight in Kennomeat they are." Paddy handed the man a score as he made his way into the office, "Here, buy them a juicy bone from their uncle Paddy."

"Sorry, boss. Actually there *was* something," Tam called out. "I was going to leave a note for the dayshift guys. Michael needs to shift his car. The boys will be working that area with the cranes over the next couple of days and it could get damaged."

"Michael's car?" Paddy frowned. "Where is it?"

"Round at number two bay. It's well in, and if these buggers hadn't been chasing a friggin' huge rat I would never have seen it." Tam was far too canny to offer an opinion as to why the car was hidden so well.

"Show me."

And the two men walked together to the far end of the scrapyard.

This was Sean's work, thought Paddy, and he obviously wanted the vehicle out of sight, but why? There were no bumps or scratches which would get Michael's temper up. The car looked intact.

"Thanks, Tam, I'll get Michael to move it as soon as he arrives, but not a word to anyone else, okay?"

It was really too early to phone Michael, but Paddy was sure that there was no spare car key in the office. What the fuck had Sean been playing at? There was obviously something he wanted kept hidden. Contraband, guns or drugs in the vehicle. Why else would it be stashed out of sight?

"Michael, you up?"

"What the fuck is it with you lot? Its five o'clock in the fucking morning. I only got to bed an hour ago. This better be an emergency."

"I found your car."

"It's been missing for nearly a month, a couple more hours wouldn't have mattered."

"It was hidden."

"Not that well if you found it. Look, Paddy, I'm fucking shattered, let's continue this conversation later. I'm glad you found my car, thank you very much." The line went dead.

Paddy hated anyone, including his brothers, getting the better of him. He had a feeling about this situation and wanted the car well out of the way before the yard opened at eight.

The constant ringing permeated his dream. "What the fuck?" Michael gave Margee a sharp prod with his elbow. "Somebody at the door," he muttered.

"What?"

"Somebody's at the door."

"Well, get up and answer it," his sleepy partner grumbled.

"For fuck's sake, give it a rest. I'm coming!" Michael bawled at the visitor.

"Sorry to get you up, but I need your spare keys."

"Spare keys for what?"

"The keys to your car, I told you it's been found. Any chance of a coffee?"

"Fuck off." Michael rummaged through drawers, a fruit bowl and eventually located the keys in the obvious place, on a board marked 'Keys'. "Here, now piss off. I'll be in later," and he slammed the front door closed.

Back at the yard, and accompanied by the dogs bounding back and forth, Paddy made his way to bay two.

He was aware of a loud humming sound, as if an engine had been left running. He sprung the boot open and the reason for the sound became evident. He was faced with his worst nightmare; the interior of the car was a seething, crawling black mass. It was like something from a horror movie, but this was real and Paddy was shocked rigid.

The dogs were yelping and squealing as they ran for their lives from the terrifying black swarm. Hundreds of thousands of insects swamped them as they raced for safety towards their master, who stood open-mouthed at the scene unfolding.

Paddy fell to the ground, desperately trying to cover himself with his coat, as swarm upon swarm of insects smothered him. They were in his hair, up his nose and he lost count of how many he swallowed. He was covered in the living, seething mass, which flew from the boot in seemingly endless waves. But it was the smell that floored him completely. Never in his life had he inhaled anything like this disgusting, malodorous stench of rotting flesh. Gagging and retching, he staggered to his feet. He had to get away, but how? He couldn't see. Eventually, after what seemed to be hours, he struggled into a nearby vehicle which gave him some shelter. What the fuck had created that mass? Paddy had to find out, but he wasn't sure if he'd ever be ready to face what lay in the missing car.

Paddy Coyle had certainly not lived a sheltered life and had been responsible for many atrocities in his day, but the sight of the putrefied body of a young boy, seething with maggots and flies, would haunt him to the day he died. And to think that a brother of his was responsible made him even sicker to his stomach.

It took old Tam the best part of an hour to calm his boys down. The dogs were spooked like he'd never seen them before. They clung to him like a couple of beaten puppies, shaking and trembling. Nothing, it seemed, would induce them to venture anywhere near bay two. This was no good. Tam had to get them over their fear. He wasn't feeling too clever himself. At seventy three he would never have believed he could run that fast. He'd managed to get into the office before the swarm caught him. But what the fuck had caused it?

Paddy had drunk almost half a bottle of Johnnie Walker, but he could still taste those fucking disgusting creatures, covered in rotting flesh. Shuddering at the thought and still gagging, the Big Man knew he had to pull himself together and deal with the problem.

"Tam, get yourself home and take the next couple of nights off, I'll get someone to cover for you." He peeled a few notes from the bundle he always carried.

"Here, have a drink on me and I'll see you later in the week. Any problems, phone me direct."

Making his way back to the car, Paddy was relieved to see that there were only a few insects left in the car, a few die-hards. The smell too, was not so intense, having been exposed to the fresh air, but it was still bad enough. Reluctantly, he closed the vehicle up, preferring to wait for his brother before disposing of the evidence. Loathe to disturb Michael again, Paddy decided to make an early morning visit to the hospital.

Unwanted Visitor

Someone was talking to him in a low guttural tone. Sean thought he knew the voice, but the name was just dancing out of reach. The voice was angry; he didn't want to listen to an angry person. Why would anyone be angry with him? Everyone liked him and Michael. Who was Michael? Was it Michael who was angry with him? No, he didn't think so. Sean was frightened of the voice, but what could a little boy like him do? He wasn't going to listen, no. He would close his eyes and go back to sleep till Mr Angry had gone and his mum came for him.

As he stood over the hospital bed Paddy could hardly look at his brother. The evil bastard was sleeping peacefully with not a care in the world. Well, he hadn't, had he? Sean had nothing on his conscience, nor had he any guilt. Why would he have, when he had everyone else to clean up his shit?

Paddy wanted to wring the bastard's neck. He

wanted to smash his face in. The longer he watched Sean, the more intensely the anger mounted. He was clenching his teeth in fury. To think he had been taken in for years by this devious pig of a man, and that his mother and sister were in such a state over him. Whatever the excuse, and there *would* be an elaborate excuse, because Sean never put his hands up for anything. Whatever the reason for the death of this young kid, Sean had carried out the deed way before his attacker had struck.

There had been police bulletins on the news for the past couple of weeks concerning a young lad who'd gone missing. His young nephew had also spoken about the abduction at some time over the past weeks. The missing boy was his friend and he was devastated. Reports of a dark 4 x 4 vehicle having been seen near where young Billy had been abducted had meant nothing to any of the family, but this could put Michael away for years. They had all been wrapped up in Sean's world, nothing else mattered. The Coyles had been concerned about Sean and nothing else. Never for a moment had they thought that the bedside at which they had all kept vigil held the fiend responsible for such a heinous crime.

God knew what Paddy would do to Sean if he ever recovered; maybe it would be best for them all if he didn't. Better his mother grieve over him now, than find out what a lowlife piece of shite her son had turned out to be. Pondering on his next move, Paddy was interrupted by Dr McLeod and his entourage doing their morning rounds.

"Good morning, Paddy. Early visiting today? I'm going to have to ask you to stand outside for a few moments."

"Doctor, I need to ask you something, man to man."

"Go ahead."

"What are his chances?"

"Honestly, Paddy? I can't tell you. I'm confident he's out of danger, but we'll have no idea what level of brain damage he sustained until we bring him round. If all goes well today then we should begin the process soon, but you have to understand, it may take several attempts."

Brain damage. The fucker had been brain damaged since birth, only none of them had realised it. It was as though the twins were chalk and cheese. Michael was a good man, a good son and a good brother. A brother that Sean didn't deserve, a brother who had covered for his twin, time after time, but in doing so had allowed this twisted evil bastard to wreak havoc without fear of retribution. Well, it stopped now.

Bending over his brother's still form, Paddy kissed him on his right cheek, the kiss of death. One way or another Sean's fate was sealed.

Incommunicado

For a smart guy, Bobby could be a real idiot, thought Erin. How could he put both her, and himself for that matter, in danger of being arrested? He'd never exhibited this type of behaviour in Spain and he would have shied completely away from anyone remotely uncool like the cousins. So what was he playing at here?

My God, if he thought Paddy hated him now, she dreaded to think what her father would be like if the police turned up at the door with her in handcuffs. Christ, there really would be blood spilt.

Erin had called in to see Carol for a coffee and a catch up. The salon wasn't particularly busy that morning and it was obvious Carol was dying to find out what was happening in Chez Coyle.

"His phone seems to be switched off, or maybe it's out of battery." Erin informed her friend. "I haven't seen him since we parted company outside the registry office. Him, or Tweedle Dee and Tweedle Dumb."

"Is this his way of keeping you in check? Tit for tat? You dumped him in town in front of his family, so he's stringing you along?" Carol asked. "After all, he got what he wanted – his name on the birth certificate and a copy of it."

"He can't do anything without my signature since we're not married."

"I wouldn't be so sure. I've told you before, you need to be careful, our Bobby is not all that he seems and I've never trusted him, as you know. Try his phone again."

"It's switched on, but hey! Bloody hell, listen," she handed her phone to Carol. "You know what that means?"

"He's back in Spain," Carol cried out. "The bugger's skipped off and he's back in Spain. I knew it. Damn. I knew he would pull a stunt like this."

"It's gone to voicemail, should I leave a message?" Erin asked her friend, holding her hand over the mouthpiece.

"Why not? He's going to know you called anyway."

"Hi, Bobby it's me. Ring me when you get this." She furiously threw the phone into her bag. "Two can play that game."

"What game would that be?" quizzed Carol.

"If he thinks he can keep me hanging about, well, he's got another think coming. It'll be a cold day in hell before I answer to Bobby Mack or McClelland, whatever he wants to call himself."

"Block his number, then you won't be tempted to

change your mind and he'll know you've done it when all his calls are rejected."

"Good thinking, 'cause he's a plausible devil. He'd probably talk me round." Erin retrieved her phone and tapped away. "There, that puts 'Big Head' out into cyberspace. What do you think he'll do?"

"Well, when he can't get you on your mobile he'll try the house phone."

"Yeah, but no-one at home is going to answer an international call, so that cuts that route off."

"He can't phone me, he wouldn't know the name of the salon, not that I would speak to him anyway."

"Betcha he'll send the cousins to see me. They'll roll up in a Bentley or a Ferrari next week sometime, with some feeble story."

The girls gloated at the prospect.

"Chase them," said Carol.

"No, I'll just set my mum on them," laughed Erin. "She's worse than a Rottweiler when she gets started."

"She's fab, is Bridget, but you're right, I wouldn't want to get on the wrong side of her."

"It's funny how everyone rates Marie and Granny Lizzie as the tough ones, but my mum could sweep the floor with both of them."

"The cousins have no chance, Ferrari or no Ferrari."

They both laughed.

Early Riser

Paddy spotted Michael parking Margee's little red sports car as he pulled into the yard. His brother had been reduced to using his girlfriend's car since his had been hijacked by their brother. God knows how Michael would react to Sean's latest fuckup. Paddy himself was still reeling from this morning's events. Every time the incident crossed his mind he physically shuddered, and his gag reflex was on overdrive. He could still feel the beasts crawling all over his skin, especially his scalp, and he was constantly scratching.

"Okay, what's the emergency? What the hell was so important about finding my car that you dragged me out of bed twice?" Michael sauntered over to Paddy as he got out of his vehicle.

"In the office, I'll fill you in there." The brothers crossed the yard to the portacabin.

The cabin was where all their serious business was carried out. Furnished with a couple of old comfortable leather chesterfields and a huge desk that Paddy had rescued years ago from a skip, the cabin was free from prying eyes and ears.

"You better sit down," Paddy told his younger brother.

"Christ, don't tell me you found the trunk full of bodies?" joked Michael, watching Paddy add a dash of whisky into the two steaming cups of tea.

"Hmmm," was his brother's only response.

"Fuck's sake, Paddy, you're starting to scare me!"

"Scare *you*? I had one of the most sickening experiences of my life this morning and it will probably stay with me forever. I looked in here on my way to work this morning, around five."

"On your way to work?" interrupted Michael.

"I know it was early, don't ask. And I got talking to old Tam."

"And . . .?" Michael knew things between Paddy and Bridget were fragile, but a five a.m. start?

"And in the general conversation he dropped the bombshell that your car was parked way back in bay two. He wanted it shifted before the boys started working there, and I have to tell you it was well hidden. The person who'd parked it up didn't want it seen, and because of that I wanted it out of the way before the dayshift boys arrived. There was no way of telling at that point what the damn thing contained."

"I take it that's what the phone call and visit were all about?"

"Michael, believe me, I wish to fuck I had left the

bloody thing alone. It was like something out of a freaking horror movie. As I walked up the yard I could hear this humming noise, but I had no idea where it was coming from. It sounded like there was a motor running and the closer I got to bay two the louder the sound."

"What was it?"

"Fuck, it makes my skin crawl just thinking about it," Paddy shuddered. "The noise was coming from inside the car. It was a seething mass of insects. Millions, and I mean fucking millions of flies, bluebottles, fuck-knows-what swarming out. Jesus Christ, I have never seen anything like it in my life."

"Fuckin' hell!"

"The dogs were covered in the things. They ran for it, but they were still spooked hours later when old Tam took them home, and you know how vicious those two buggers are. He wasn't too bad, he'd been down this end of the yard and he managed to get inside here. Me? I thought I was finished. What a fucking way to die. I was covered, they were up my nose, in my mouth, and I couldn't breathe. I can still hear the buzzing. I'm sure that some actually got inside my ears, and I was swallowing and choking on them, all covered in rotten flesh."

"Jesus fuck. Where did they come from?"

"Where did they come from? I'll tell you where. From the decomposing body of the kid who went missing a few weeks ago. He's in the fucking boot."

"The boot? For fuck's sake, how did he get in there?" Michael, astounded though he was, didn't for a moment think that Sean had anything to do with the crime.

"Playing hide and seek! How the fuck do you think he got in there, you stupid bastard? Your beloved twin must have dumped him in there."

"Sean? How could it be Sean? He's been unconscious for weeks."

"True, but he wasn't when this poor kid met his maker."

"But you've no proof it was Sean, Paddy."

"Well, you tell me who the fuck else had access to your car? And if Sean had nothing to do with it, why the hell did he hide it? Not really the actions of an innocent man."

"Holy fucking Moses, what the fuck are we going to do?"

"Well, we're not going to broadcast it to the world for a start! We'll come back tonight and sort it."

"What about old Tam?"

"He's kosher. He was down here when I opened the trunk. He didn't see the body, only the swarms. I've given him the night off and told him I'll get cover, but that'll be us, bruv. We'll crush the car and then dispose of it elsewhere. Let's face it, even though it's crushed, the DNA can still be traced."

"Paddy, Sean's a fucker all right, and he pushes his luck to the limit, but murdering kids? No way, I don't believe it."

"Well you'd better, and trust me, this is just the tip of the iceberg."

It was not the time to disclose to Michael Paddy's plans for their brother's future, or lack of one.

Second Childhood

Why had the angry man kissed him on the cheek? He didn't think he liked it. Boys didn't kiss boys and he was sure it meant something, but what? Something not nice, he reckoned. Here was another question he couldn't answer. That seemed to be all he did – try to solve puzzles. All his thoughts and questions seemed to be dancing around in his brain just out of reach and it was making him mad.

He must have dozed off again, there were now two voices, one on either side of him. The angry man was back again and he had someone else with him. The other voice was quieter and sounded sad. Who were they? What did they want with him? Maybe they'd found out he knew who'd stolen the money Paddy had hidden in the graveyard. It was Canon O'Farrell, that's who. He was a bad man, making the boys do bad things, but he said he would tell the polis that the Coyles had stolen goods and Paddy would stay longer in jail. No, it wasn't that, Canon O'Farrell wouldn't snitch on him. And if he did, he'd tell what he made the altar boys do. No, it wasn't about the canon. There was something else bothering him. Bad things, things he knew that Paddy and Michael wouldn't like. There they were again, the names. Who were Paddy and Michael? Were they his brothers? He was sure he'd thought of them before, but he couldn't remember. What were they saying now?

One voice was low and difficult to hear. Something about drugs: that Sean (he was sure that was his name) was selling them. How could he, a little boy, sell drugs?

The other voice, the kind one, kept saying it wasn't true. He liked that voice. He wanted the other one to listen. He wanted the nice voice to keep on telling the other that it wasn't true, but he thought it might be. Maybe he had been selling drugs for the canon. No, he was being daft, how could a little boy sell drugs? His mother would thrash him if she found out.

He needed to go back to sleep.

The Rain in Spain

For the first two or three days back home Bobby spent the majority of his time lazing by the pool, topping up his tan, and his evenings on the pull. Thoughts of his son and Erin were very few and far between.

His mother had wasted no time while he had been gone. There had been a number of changes; the main being that Diane had finally got her wish and emptied the old man out, to Bobby's extreme disapproval.

"Listen, Bobby, he had to go. The staff were beginning to talk. They were well aware he had taken up residence in the pool house." Diane told him. "This is a six-bedroom villa for goodness sake, why on earth would a guest have to sleep rough? No, it was time for him to move on."

"So where is he, and who's looking after him?" Bobby knew the ex-priest had been pushing his luck, but he felt a sense of responsibility towards him. After all, he had been his father's business partner, even if he didn't approve of the merchandise. At the back of his head, buried deep, was the faint hope that if this old bugger had survived then maybe his father had. A long shot, but who would have put money on the priest making it?

"I've set him up in a nice little apartment in the old town, one your father apparently used from time to time," she sneered. "And old bugger-lugs knew all about it. In fact, it was him who told me of its existence. As for who's looking after him, well, I'll let you find out for yourself. Believe me, he's well catered for."

When he met the young boy who answered the door, Bobby understood right away what his mother had implied. She was right, the old coyote seemed to be extremely well looked after.

"So, you're back then?" croaked the old priest. "What reception did you get from the Coyles? I'm sure they were all delighted to see you and welcomed you into the bosom of their family." Bobby thought he could detect a note of amusement.

"Oh, they took to me to their bosoms alright, especially the Big Man. He couldn't have been more pleased to see me, so much so, he moved out for most of the time to give me space," said Bobby sarcastically.

"Well done boy, well done, you've certainly stirred up a hornet's nest. What about the girl? How did she take to you appearing on the scene?"

"Yeah, she was fine. She seemed pleased to see me – a bit lippy, but I soon put her in her place. By the way, how you lot can live in that godforsaken place, I do not know. Even when it's hot it's bloody cold and everybody's miserable."

"There's not a finer city in the world than Glasgow, believe me."

"I'll take your word for it."

"So how did you leave things? What's happening about the child? Any chance you can get her to visit here?" asked O'Farrell.

"Well, I don't think I'm Mr Popularity right now. I skipped off without telling her."

"For God's sake, laddie, why?"

"They were all getting on my nerves and to be honest, I think I would have really blown it if I'd stayed much longer, so I jumped on the next flight and headed for home."

"That wasn't the cleverest of moves, Bobby, you were supposed to keep her sweet and make her do your bidding."

"She will, don't you worry. I know enough about women. When I whistle she'll come running. Anyway, enough about me. How are you?"

"I'm fine, lad, just fine. And I'm well taken care of."

"I knew Mum would turf you out the minute my back was turned, she's a stubborn mare."

"Look, she was right. It was time for me to move on and this place has everything I need, and a bit extra," he chuckled.

"Good, but if you need anything, just give me a bell," Bobby rose, making ready to leave.

"Did anyone mention me, by the way?"

"Not directly, but then, very few folk know we're acquainted. I did hear one or two express their sorrow at your passing, which absolutely creased me up. I couldn't help thinking, if they only knew what the old bugger was up to they'd wet themselves." Both men laughed at the image.

"Keep in touch with the Coyle lassie, son. Don't get her back up. I've an idea how to sort them out, but it means you have to stay in her good books."

"I will, as long as it doesn't entail me going back there in the foreseeable future."

"We'll see, laddie, we'll see." The old priest drifted off to sleep.

Predictable

"You were right, it *was* a Ferrari and Bobby sent them because he thought there was something up with the phones in the UK, would you believe?"

"It didn't strike him that because he was able to contact Dumb and Dumber the phone system might be okay and it was just that you didn't want to talk to him? Arrogant bastard," sneered Carol. "So, what was his excuse for running off without telling you?"

"I'm not sure if I believe him, but apparently his mother collapsed and was carted off to hospital and he had to leave immediately. A bit suspect, don't you think?"

"Very convenient. Ten minutes after he gets your son's birth certificate he has to make a mercy dash. Like you say, very suspicious."

"He's still blocked on my phone. I really don't want to speak to him just now, although I'm going to have to soon."

"Why?"

"Ryan's christening. My mum's on my case to set a date, and now that Uncle Sean's out of ICU we can go ahead and make arrangements."

"What's the story with Sean?" asked Carol. "You know, I've gone in a couple of times, but I've never liked to ask either your mum or your gran. I just know he's semi-conscious, but is he going to be okay?"

Erin knew there was much more to the Uncle Sean story than met the eye. Her dad and Uncle Michael had barely visited him since the first few days when it was touch and go. They were using work as an excuse and the fact that Sean seemed to have regressed back to his childhood also seemed to be influencing why the brothers were giving the hospital a wide berth.

It was spooky, listening to this big scary-looking man babble on like a ten-year-old with occasional flashes of clarity. Erin was really uncomfortable with him. She felt like he was pretending to be a child, but no-one else seemed to notice.

"He's improving and the doctors are confident he'll regain most of his memory, they just don't know when. It means, however, that we can plan ahead now he's out of danger."

"How long will he be kept in hospital?"

"A few more weeks then he's moving back to Gran's to convalesce. You know, I was going to ask him to be godfather to the baby, but obviously I can't now."

"What about Michael?"

"It was to be both of them, but when I broached the subject with my dad, he was dead against it. I thought it might help bring Sean on, but Big Paddy was having none of it."

It was strange to hear Erin call her dad by his first name, but it showed her friend how far removed from their old father and daughter relationship they now were.

"What about godmothers?"

"There's you, of course."

"Me? Don't be daft. You've got loads of relatives and rich folk who would be honoured to be Ryan's godmother."

"I know, but I want you. If ever my boy was to be left on his own, then you'd be the one I'd want to watch over him."

Tears were streaming down Carol's cheeks. There wasn't a day went by that she didn't bless the god that had sent Erin Coyle to her. How her life had changed, and all because of a random act of kindness. She now lived in a beautiful flat in the best part of town, her daughter went to the best kindergarten and she herself had qualified as a stylist with a part-share in a salon. Now her friend had bestowed this blessing on her. To be a child's godparent was a major honour and to be the godparent of a Coyle, well! What could she say?

"Are you sure? What have your mum and dad got to say?"

"It was my mother's suggestion."

"I don't know what to say," snuffled the young mum.

"Just say yes. We thought of asking Diane if she would like to choose someone. She is his grandmother and it might help to keep the peace. Mind you, I don't think Paddy's been told of the plan, so I wouldn't count on it."

"So when is the christening going to be, and where?"

"In about six weeks from now. We need to check with Father Jack. And the 'bun fight' will be in Gleddoch House."

"Gosh, smart or what?"

"Well, he is Paddy's first grandson."

"I wonder who the McClellands will choose? You can bet your boots it'll be someone your folks will hate."

"That'll be the cousins top of the list, then. I can just see them – identical in Burberry and driving a Hummer."

"I can just imagine it, *and* the look on Paddy's face."

Crushed

"I'm on my way. I'll be there in ten to fifteen minutes. Make sure the men are finished and gone for the night." Paddy hung up on his brother.

It was years since he'd operated the crusher. Jesus, he hoped he could remember what to do. There was no chance Michael would be of any use; the closest he'd ever come to crushing anything was a bag of walnuts at Christmas, and even that posed problems.

Paddy couldn't get the poor lad out of his head. By all accounts he was a proper little fucker, but loveable with it. Certainly their Errol was taking it bad. There had been a heart-wrenching appeal by his mother on television only last night. The distraught woman had pleaded for the return of her son, or for any information concerning his whereabouts. The police were still investigating a black 4 x 4 seen in the area at the time of Billy's disappearance and appealed for the driver to come forward so he could be eliminated from their enquiries. It was absolutely imperative that Michael not be associated with the crime. And they would deal with Sean in good time.

The scrapyard looked deserted, but Paddy knew his brother was around somewhere. He parked his car on the other side of the cabin, away from prying eyes, walked back to the gates and secured them from the inside. No chance of some nosey bugger gaining access. He was dreading the job ahead, but he knew it had to be done.

"You're here, let's get on." Paddy knew fine that Michael would be dreading this even more than him, but, like his brother, knew there was no other way. "What the fuck . . .?"

He couldn't believe his eyes. There was Michael with his mother's bottle of holy water, liberally sprinkling it over the vehicle.

"Say what you like, but this young fella didn't deserve to die and certainly not like this. So shut the fuck up and let me finish." Michael took a rosary and a bible and placed them on the passenger side of the car. "Okay, let's finish this."

The sound of the powerful crusher starting up filled the air and several tenement windows flew open to investigate the racket. Every onlooker, without exception, realising the noise was coming from the yard, slammed their windows shut again immediately. The few windows still open were no threat to Paddy and Michael, being the homes of members of the Coyle clan.

"Need a hand there, boss?" called one.

"Naw, you're fine, son. Just a health and safety check," Paddy called back. "Away in and finish your tea, it's nothing we can't handle."

It was impossible to reach the vehicle with the grab crane from its position in bay two and neither brother relished the thought of entering the car, never mind driving it.

"Give me the keys, Paddy. I'll do it."

Without hesitation he relinquished the job to his brother.

"Oh, shit," gagged Michael. He'd never smelled anything like it. He rolled down the window and drove the car to the crusher. Thankfully it was only a few yards away.

It took some time to reduce the immaculate, shiny black car to a heap of scrap metal. Paddy, being unused to the machinations of the crusher, twice got the gears jammed and the screech of metal on metal was deafening.

"Fuck! We're going to get a visit any minute," wailed Michael.

"Just shut the fuck up or you'll be in alongside him," snapped Paddy.

Finally the job was done and they loaded the remains of Michael's pride and joy onto the truck.

The two men drove most of the way in silence until they arrived at an old, disused quarry. With a great deal of heaving and shoving they managed to position the truck and its contents over the quarry's edge. Paddy opened the tailgate and the mangled vehicle dropped into the lake of slurry below, quickly sinking below the surface.

Paddy heaved a great sigh of relief. "I'm sorry, mate. This one got to me. He was only a kid. We'll need to sort the mother out, but not just yet. Let the dust settle bit."

"What are we going to do about Sean, Paddy? Even though I've seen it with my own eyes I still can't believe it."

"You know he was the one punting the gear all this time?"

"I had my suspicions," admitted Michael. "But I didn't really know for sure."

"Oh, it's for sure alright, but let's wait to see how he recovers first. This could be payback for the cunt. He murders a child and ends up one himself. My Erin calls it karma."

Yes, it could well be payback, thought Paddy as the two men made their way back to town.

Awakening

Just as Doctor McLeod had predicted, Sean was back in the land of the living. His physical injuries had healed, but he hadn't got off scot-free. There were serious complications; the patient had recovered consciousness thinking he was a ten-year-old boy.

It was most disconcerting to interact with this bear of a man, jabbering on about skateboards and Rubik's cubes and wanting to go and see the latest *Star Wars* movie when it was released. His condition was such that the physicians could tell the family little more. They were confident that his memory would return, but when, and what percentage would return, was anyone's guess. Doctor McLeod had known only a few cases of this magnitude and in each case the patient had suffered a trauma prior to the incident which had rendered them unconscious.

Had that happened in Sean's case? The two brothers just looked at one another. Fuck, if they only knew.

"Should we tell him, Paddy? It might make a difference."

"Oh, it'll make a difference alright. The daft bastard would be carted off to Carstairs Mental Hospital and the key thrown away."

"I suppose so. It's weird seeing him like this. I wonder if he'll ever get back to normal."

"Normal?" jeered Paddy. "That fucker was never normal. And you want him back to run around stealing from us and disposing of anyone who gets in his way? 'Cause that was what he was up to."

"I suppose so," replied Michael.

"Naw, I'm quite happy with Sean as a ten-year-old, eating fish fingers and playing with Action Man, because when he comes to properly, I'm going to have to do something about him and quite frankly, I don't want to."

"Michael, when can I go home? Sure, I've been picked to be one of the altar boys next week and I don't want to miss my turn."

"Don't start, Paddy. He doesn't know what he's saying. Anyway, it was Father Jack who put that in his head. He was in to see him yesterday and Sean pestered the life out of him. Jack agreed, to keep the peace. Fuck, can you imagine it? The place would be in an uproar. A thirty-odd-year-old dressed as a fucking altar boy?" Michael dissolved into gales of laughter, for the first time in a long time.

"Aye, I could get him to officiate at the bairn's

christening. Can you imagine Lizzie and Bridget's faces? It would be worth it for that alone."

"How are things back home?" Michael asked.

"Well, I'm not leaving at 5 a.m. anymore, if that's any consolation, and thank fuck that Spanish twat has gone. There's been trouble in paradise, from what I can make out, but nobody tells me anything. If it wasn't for the boy, I'd pack up and leave. Michael, I'm a stranger in my own home and believe me, I'm not going to put up with it for much longer."

"Who's the Spanish twat?" asked the occupant of the hospital bed.

"What did you say?" Michael asked Sean.

"I didn't say anything," the man-boy replied. "Honest, I didn't say a word."

"We'd better watch what we say in front of him. You can't tell how much he's taking in or understanding."

"I wouldn't trust the bugger as far as I could throw him before this, so you can guess how far I'd trust him now," answered Paddy.

"Don't you like me anymore?" Sean whinged to his eldest brother.

"No, I fucking don't," snapped Paddy. "I don't like you one bit."

"Why, what have I done to you?" Sean smirked and stuck his tongue out.

"Because you've been a very bad boy and you need punishing."

A howl came from the man. "Go away, you're a bad

man, not me. Go away! Tell him to go away!" Sean pleaded with his twin.

"Oh, I'll go away, you murdering bastard, but woe betide you if I find out you're at it."

By this time Sean was sobbing loudly which brought the two nurses on duty to his aid. "Calm down, Sean, No-one's going to hurt you, calm down."

But Sean was on a roll. He knew somehow that the more mayhem he caused the better it would be for him.

Conference

It was the first time in a long time that they'd all been together as a family, all squeezed round Lizzie's kitchen table. Except for Sean; he was bundled up in the big chair. He'd only recently been discharged from hospital and was finding everything mighty strange. He was also finding it difficult to keep up with the conversation.

"Is it my christening?" he asked Paddy.

"No, it's Ryan's, Erin's baby."

"But Erin's too young to have a baby, she's just the same age as me," persisted Sean.

"For fuck's sake, Ma, get him out of here, he's talking a load of shite." Paddy had no time for illness and found Sean's bizarre behaviour more than he could tolerate.

"Give it a rest, Paddy, he's just confused. Talk nicely to him, he'll settle down and go to sleep in a few minutes."

But Sean was bright and alert and enjoying the attention. He had no idea where he was, or who most of the people were, but certain sounds and smells were jogging his memory. His thoughts were like butterflies just fluttering out of reach.

A loud knock at the door and a strident voice announcing her arrival had Sean clapping his hands in excitement. "It's Theresa, it's Theresa!" he cried. "Have you brought me a present, Theresa?"

There was a stunned silence. How had he known who she was? He hadn't seen their neighbour since before his attack.

"How do you know this lady?" asked his ma. "Tell me again who she is."

Immediately Sean picked up on the vibes; maybe it wasn't good to remember. "I don't know," he said in a quiet voice. "Who did I say she was?"

"It's okay, Sean," his sister cajoled him. "We're just happy you might be starting to remember people."

"Don't you recognise Theresa from next door? You love Theresa, she makes you laugh."

Sean looked at Paddy. "He's not happy, he doesn't like me. I heard him and the other one," he pointed to Michael. "I heard them saying they were going to do bad things to me, they think I've been naughty. Tell them to go away. Mam, tell them to go away."

"What a fucking palaver. I thought we were here to sort out the christening, not to listen to that fucking moron. I'm off. Sort it out yourselves or maybe I *will* do bad things." Paddy stormed out the door.

"See, I told you they want rid of me," whinged Sean.

"Enough," shouted Lizzie. "Or *I'll* be doing bad things. Shut up, Sean, and behave," she spoke as she would to a ten-year-old.

With Sean sulking in the corner and Paddy absent, the subject of the christening was well and truly thrashed out.

The women settled on the godparents, the date, time, and venue. The subject of the McClellands was the most controversial, but in the end it was agreed that they should be included. The Coyles had to be seen to be doing right. So, an invitation would be extended and the opportunity to name a godparent was given, as long as it met with the Coyles' approval.

"I'm quite glad your dad left, we would never have got any agreement out of him, but now, as far as I'm concerned, anything we do was sanctioned by him in his absence. We'll get started on the invitations tomorrow."

"What do you think of Uncle Sean, Mum? Do you think he really has lost his memory or is he kidding us on?" Erin asked her mum as they walked to the car.

"What a strange thing to ask, Erin. Of course he's lost his memory. Your Uncle Sean isn't bright enough to fool all those doctors. Just because he called out 'Theresa' probably means that he gets flashbacks, and I'm sure one day he'll be okay, but we have to be patient."

"What about him being godfather? Do you think he would even know what it was all about? Imagine if he started shouting and swearing in church, Granny would have a coronary."

"She would set about him with that bloody great handbag and do even more brain damage."

"No, I think we'll pass on Uncle Sean this time."

"How many times do you think there's going to be?" laughed Erin.

"We'll have to take a rain check on that one," smiled her mum.

The following morning mother and daughter set off for St. Jude's to speak with Father Jack.

Delighted to have the Coyles back en masse in the parish, Father Jack would have moved heaven and earth to accommodate them. The date and time of the christening was agreed on, and then it was a short walk around the corner to Lizzie's for a quick cuppa.

"My God, what's going on?" Erin clutched at her mother's arm.

Whatever it was, the whole street had turned out.

"Mum, it's coming from Granny's." Erin set off at a run, leaving her mother pushing the stroller.

She crashed in the back door of number 28 just in time to witness her Uncle Sean lift his fist to her gran. The feisty little woman was facing up to her big son fearlessly.

"What's going on?" The girl shouted at the pair.

"Oh, it's nothing, dearie. I fell in the kitchen again and Uncle Sean was just helping me up."

"It doesn't look or sound like you fell. The whole street's turned out."

"I'm telling you I fell. And okay, I probably did make a bit of noise, I got such a fright."

"And what have you got to say for yourself, Uncle Sean?"

"Me? Nothing. It's just as your granny says, she fell in the kitchen."

Just then Bridget arrived with the baby. "What the devil's going on, Ma? You've got the whole bloody street out."

"Christ, can't a body have a tumble without it making the six o'clock news?"

"Put the kettle on, Erin, and see if you can find any cups that didn't throw themselves down the stairs to save your granny."

Sean went into his room and stayed there for the duration of their visit.

"No bull, Lizzie. What happened? Did he hit you?"

"Don't be feckin' ridiculous. To think that one of my boys would raise a hand to their mother!"

"Well, it looked like it when I came in," ventured Erin.

"Well, I'm telling you he did not, and that's all there is to the matter. The boy's had a terrible time and he was a bit anxious, that's all. Now come and have some tea and tell me how you got on with Father Jack."

Both Erin and Bridget noticed how badly Lizzie's hands trembled as the old lady poured out the tea. There was something amiss here and both promised themselves they would keep a watchful eye on the situation.

The forthcoming christening was discussed and dissected by the three women until there was no more to be said.

"I'll ring you later, Gran. And remember, if there are any more anxious episodes, phone my dad."

"There won't be," smiled the old woman, waving them away as they drove down the road.

Christ, if her Paddy knew what had gone on in this house today, he would skin Sean alive.

Lizzie tried hard to convince herself she wasn't scared witless of Sean. He'd always been a handful, but this lad she'd brought home from the hospital was not the lad she'd given birth to. But, he was her son and she'd stand by him, whatever.

Invitation

"Did you know about this?" shouted Diane as she waved a letter in Bobby's face. "Did she not say anything the last time you spoke to her? In fact, when was the last time you spoke to the little tart?"

"Calm down, Ma. No, I know nothing about any christening, and I haven't spoken to her since I came back home. Despite what you think, she certainly isn't a tart. She's the mother of your grandson."

"Crumbs off the table," his mother was ranting. "Crumbs off the bloody table. We can pick a godparent as long as he or she meets with their approval. Who do they think they are? With their approval indeed! I've a good mind to choose your Uncle Walter."

"Who the blazes is my Uncle Walter?"

"Your dad's brother and the real black sheep of the family. Even those two daft buggers you hooked up with will have nothing to do with him. He's an alky and an old pervert. You name it, he's done it. His claim to fame is that he's been barred from nearly every pub in Glasgow."

"You're not saddling my son with a godfather like that."

"I thought you didn't want anything to do with the boy? I thought he was nothing to you?" his mother levelled at him.

"I still wouldn't want to lumber the kid with him," said Bobby. "Don't you want to play the doting grandma? Let's face it, you'll outshine every other woman there." This was exactly the right thing to say to Diane. He knew how vain his mother was, and with very good reason; she was a corker, was his mum.

"What are you going to do? Are we going or not? And if we are, who's going to look after business here?"

"I'll fly over and back on the day. You can stay and have a bit of time with your family and maybe get to know the kid a bit."

"Seems like a plan," answered Diane. "What about the godparent? I honestly don't know who I'd pick. I can't think of anyone in the family who'd want to be associated with the Coyles."

"Okay then, what about someone from here, someone prestigious? Someone who could be an asset to Ryan in the future?"

"I don't follow you." Diane was puzzled by her son's proposal.

"Look, we of all people should appreciate that you

never know what's round the corner, and it would do the boy no harm to be the godson of some rich, influential person who could help out should he ever need it."

"Sure, but I hope to God we've had all the trouble we are going to have. Who do you suggest?"

"What about Dell Knight? He owns half of Marbella and was great pals with Dad."

"Good choice. Only one problem, if he puts one foot on British soil he's going down for a twenty."

"Shit, who else is there? Nick the Greek?

"Same problem, only with a longer stretch."

"What about Mayor Munozo? He's as crooked as the other two, but he and Dad were good buddies."

"Okay, I'll invite him to the club tonight and test the waters."

"That would certainly put Bridget Coyle's nose out of joint."

"What are you up to tonight? It would be good if you were there when the mayor comes by."

"I'm going to visit Frank for a bit and then I'll be in about ten. I've got to say goodbye to my latest conquest. She's a beauty, been on the cover of Vogue, no less. She wants to stay here and have babies."

"For heaven's sake, boy. Haven't you learned to keep it in your pants yet? No more babies, or else."

True to his word, Bobby arrived at the club around ten with his latest squeeze in tow.

"Your mother and I have been reminiscing about your father. He was a great friend of mine, Bobby, and I miss him."

"I know, sir, and I know my father held you in the greatest respect. And because of that, my mother and I have a favour to ask of you."

"Go on, I will do anything in my power for the son of my friend. Are you in trouble?"

"No, sir. It's nothing of that sort. We were hoping you would stand as godfather to my son."

A sigh of relief passed from the mayor's lips, he had been sure he was going to be asked for a favour of a different kind. "Of course, my boy. I would be honoured to stand for the grandson of one of my closest friends."

"Before you agree, I have to say the ceremony is not in Spain, but in Scotland."

"No problem, send me all the details and I will be there. I must tell you again that I am honoured to be chosen."

Bobby signalled to the waiter who had appeared with champagne and glasses and the small party toasted the forthcoming celebrations.

On The Mend

S ean was watching from the living room window; his mother would appear any moment on her way back from early mass. It was the only time he had to himself, between 5.30 and 6.15 each morning, and that was when he went rummaging.

He knew his mother had a stash of money somewhere in the house, but so far he'd been unable to find it.

Unknown to the rest of the family, he had regained most of his memory, but there were still chunks missing. He was fly enough not to let on and he was so good at maintaining his childlike persona that he was sure no-one really suspected him.

He spied his mother walking with Theresa from next door, heads bent against the dreich Scottish weather, whispering to one another. Whispering about him? He was paranoid about who his mother spoke to and what she spoke about. He knew it was mostly about him and his business. She was always spreading lies about him. He would have to put a stop to it. How could his beloved mother have turned against him? So often he had to remind her who was the man of the house and who her loyalties should be with. She shouldn't be telling bloody Theresa any of their business, she wasn't family.

Lizzie was dismayed when she saw her son peering out of the window. "Damn," she muttered under her breath, "I hope he's in a better mood than last night." The old woman rubbed her right arm. It wasn't quite so painful this morning and it would ease once the bruising came out.

Feck it, she thought, if he starts his nonsense this early, I'll lamp him with the poker.

Lizzie was exhausted. She was getting on in years and wasn't up to coping with her son's behaviour. If the truth be told, Sean was breaking his mother's heart. Never in her life had Lizzie dreamt that one of her sons would lay hands on her. They had each, in their own way, provided for her and made sure she had the best that money could buy. Sean had changed. He'd changed long before the attack, but the head injury had made things much worse. She knew he was on the mend and had regained much of his memory. When he got into one of his tempers he would let slip and revert to his old self. But it was the hatred of his brothers that most appalled her and this, she was convinced, was down to the attack so therefore it wasn't his fault.

Because of this, she would protect him and cover for him.

She busied herself around the kitchen, preparing breakfast. She never knew how many would arrive; her kitchen was open to all and sundry. Her three sons and their workforce were welcome any morning. Before he had been hospitalized, Sean had been a regular at the table for breakfast. It was a chance for the brothers to catch up and it was always an enjoyable start to the day. Now, however, Sean would hurriedly consume his meal before anyone else arrived and disappear through to his room. He wouldn't come out until the last plate had been cleared, except for the few occasions when Tiny Carter and the new guy, Gerry Fairnie, came to eat. Gerry went out of his way to draw Sean out and never spoke or referred to him in the way the others did.

Lizzie liked the young man and sympathized with his predicament. His children were in foster homes and he wasn't allowed to see them. And the poor lass he had been married to, taking her own life the way she did. Lizzie had known Gerry's wife since she was a child and a nicer girl you would not meet, but she had been led astray and paid a hellish price.

Gerry seemed well taken with Sean which was most unusual, Sean being a hard man to like. But he and Gerry got on like a house on fire and the old woman encouraged him to visit.

Sean had a bee in his bonnet about Theresa this

morning, wanting to know what she and Lizzie had been whispering about on the way home.

"Don't worry, lad, I didn't let slip that you've taken to throwing your weight about in here and that your poor old ma has bruises the size of dinner plates. Because if I did, big and all as you are, she'd bray you from here to hell and back again. The truth is, lad, I am black affronted at what you've become. You're a woman-beater."

"What are you cawing about, you stupid old bat?" Sean sneered at Lizzie. "When did I ever beat you? If you'd lay off the bottle you'd be steadier on your feet, that's how you get the bruises. Don't blame me or I *will* give you the back of my hand. So shut your blethering and fix me some breakfast."

"You can wait till the others arrive. I'm running behind and I can hardly use this arm, thanks to you. As for me laying off the bottle, I'd have to fight you to get near it."

Sean turned away, the anger blazing across his face. Slyly, he moved the huge griddle his mother used to make her famous tattie scones and positioned the metal handle over the naked gas flame. He left it in position until the handle was almost glowing red. The kitchen was beginning to fill up, Sean sneaked the iron plate back to its original position and waited for the fun to begin.

For the first time in weeks Marie and Errol had joined the throng. Marie got up to help her mother.

She broke several eggs into the frying pan. The bacon was already fried, as was the black pudding, and only the scones were left to be done.

"Don't let her do them, Ma, they'll be burned," called Michael.

"'Well done' is the phrase you're looking for," Marie bit back.

Sean watched the proceedings with bated breath, he didn't care which one of them got burned. He hated them both.

Marie let out an ear-piercing scream as the red-hot metal seared into her hand. The kitchen was in an uproar as Lizzie and Paddy tried their best to tend to Marie's hand. It was already blistering.

"What the fuck happened?" Paddy demanded.

"The handle was scorching hot and I lifted it."

"It must have been over the gas flame," said one of the lads.

"No, it was over there," Marie said pointing to where the griddle had been positioned.

"It's the hospital for you, young lady," stated Michael.

"I can't, I've got an important meeting at eleven this morning."

"I don't care. This needs seen to, and no argument."

"Look, let's go straight to the Nuffield and get her sorted right away."

Marie was sheet white and looked like she was ready to pass out.

Sean didn't open his mouth, he just sat there taking everything in. But Lizzie's weren't the only pair of eyes watching him.

Acceptance

"Good God, Mum, would you look at this?" Erin opened a thick envelope and removed the contents. Inside was a sheet of heavily embossed writing paper: the acceptance from Diane Mack.

"Jesus, I don't think the queen would have more superior notepaper than this," her mother chuckled. "Talk about ostentatious, but more to the point, what does she say?"

"She thanks us for the invitation, she's delighted to attend and requests invites for twenty guests. Christ, the godfather is none other than the mayor of Marbella, Julio Munozo."

"I'm quite disappointed," said Erin. "I was expecting George Clooney or Pierce Brosnan, the way she larges it up."

"The mayor of Marbella will do nicely, thank you. Though it puts our choices a bit in the shade. Should we rethink?" pondered Bridget.

"Don't you dare suggest such a thing! I wouldn't want anyone but Carol to stand for him, and if the mayor of bloody Marbella knew what these lowlifes got up to, he wouldn't be so keen on offering his services."

"Well, this family is not exactly shining white, are we?"

"C'mon, Mum, you can't compare what Pete McClelland and the canon did with my dad's business."

"I should bloody well hope not." Paddy stomped into the room. "And why am I being compared to those illustrious gentlemen?"

"We've just had a reply from the other grandma," said Erin.

"I trust it's a 'thanks but no thanks'?"

"No, she's accepted and would like us to invite a few of her close family." Bridget handed the list over to her husband.

Paddy made only one comment, "No fucking chance." He screwed up the sheet of expensive notepaper and threw it in the wastepaper basket.

"Sorry, Paddy," said Bridget retrieving the crumpled list, "but we've already agreed and I certainly won't be made to look stupid because you decided to storm off from the family meeting."

"So, because I couldn't handle Sean and his shenanigans I've got to extend the hand of friendship to a bunch of mongrels? Who is this Julio Munozo? What does he have to do with anything?"

"He's only the mayor of Marbella," Bridget replied smugly.

"Do what the fuck you like. I'm not sure I'll even be there."

"What?" Mother and daughter exclaimed.

"Just what I said, I'm not sure I'll be there."

"I swear to God, Paddy, if you embarrass us in any way, you'll rue the day. And that's not a threat, it's a promise." It was Bridget's turn to storm out.

"This is all your fault, lady," he turned on his daughter. "Yeah, it's all your fault for bringing that mob back into our lives."

"So you wish Ryan had been aborted, do you? You wish you had no grandson?"

For once her father was stuck for words.

"Of course not," Paddy muttered. "Oh, do what you like. You pair always do anyway."

She would tell Bobby tonight when he phoned that her mother had agreed with his family's requests. He had taken to phoning her most evenings around seven, this didn't interfere with his plans and kept him, or so he thought, in her good books.

The blinkers had certainly fallen from her eyes. Erin had no illusions about Bobby; he was a spoiled, egocentric playboy, who played every woman he came into contact with, including his mother, to get what he wanted. Nevertheless, she was still madly in love with him, but she had no intentions of simply joining the ranks. It would be all or nothing for Erin Coyle. She played the long game . . .

Nosey Neighbours

Pacing back and forth on the pavement in front of the telephone box, Theresa finally plucked up courage and pulled open the heavy door. Money at the ready, she dialled the number written on the scrap of paper.

"Bridget, is that you?" Theresa roared down the mouthpiece. She hated using the phone and avoided them like the plague. Normally she would get Lizzie or her daughter to make any calls she required, but this one she had to make herself.

Lizzie Coyle and she had been friends since they had moved into Lomond Gardens, both young mums, over forty years ago. During all that time the women had seldom had a cross word. They had helped each other through many a crisis and there was little one didn't know about the other's life.

Theresa was convinced without any doubt that her friend was in real trouble. For the past while, in fact, since Sean had been discharged from hospital, things had been going downhill. Lizzie had lost her cheery disposition and never had time for a chat. She was always on the run, fetching and carrying for the invalid. Only Theresa wasn't so sure that Sean was still an invalid. He had come out of his coma with the mentality of a ten-year-old. But it wasn't a ten-year-old yelling and cursing at his mother night after night, wearing her down. This was a man, and a sickening bully of a man at that. His mother seemed terrified of him.

Theresa knew she'd get no thanks from Lizzie for talking about what was going on, but she'd risk her precious friendship before she'd let something happen to her pal. She was frightened enough by what she heard to believe that it was a possibility.

"Yes, Theresa, it's me. What's happened? Has Lizzie had another fall?"

"Well, she says she has, but she's getting mighty clumsy in her old age. I need to talk to you or Paddy. There's something going on, Bridget. She's covered in bruises and the door's been on the chain for the past two weeks. But it's the arguments that go on, hour after hour, that I'm worried about most."

"Who is she having arguments with, Theresa?"

"With Sean, of course. Who else is in the house?"

"Surely she would tell us if he was too much for her?"

169

"Don't talk daft, woman. Lizzie Coyle would no more disrespect her boys than the Pope would change his religion."

"Look, I'll pop round to yours tonight."

"Don't let them see your car. Park it in the next street. Are you bringing Paddy?"

"No," replied the daughter-in-law. "I can always call him if I need to, but it's better I see what's going on first, before him storming in."

"Okay, Bridget. I'm sorry to phone you."

"Not at all, Theresa. You'd never forgive yourself if things got out of hand."

"Thanks, Bridget, I've been worried sick. I'll see you later." And the phone went dead.

God almighty, cursed Bridget. Was there never a moment when this family were normal and lived normal lives like normal people? God forbid if Sean was tormenting Lizzie, his other two brothers and his sister would skin him alive. She thought back to what Erin had said a few weeks ago. Maybe the girl had been right.

Strangely, she wasn't surprised at the accusations, although she should have been. Lizzie's family adored her, and quite rightly so. She was a mother in a million and had worked her fingers to the bone for them all, but Sean had changed, and it wasn't the attack that had changed him.

When she and Paddy were first married the twins were teenagers and full of fun and nonsense, but over the years Sean had distanced himself bit by bit. She knew from what Paddy had told her that the boys had only work in common now.

Michael had more or less settled down with Margee and Bridget was sure a wedding was in the offing. Sean, on the other hand, was a womanizer. He had no regard for the opposite sex and never saw the same female twice.

There had been some trouble involving him just before the attack. She truly hoped Theresa had got the wrong end of the stick, but in her heart she knew the woman had not.

Friends

Lizzie heaved herself out of her chair, cursing whoever was ringing her doorbell. Lord above, she'd only just sat down, having been on the go all morning.

"I'm coming," she called.

To her surprise, there, waiting on the step, was young Gerry Fairnie.

"Hello, son. I'm sorry, you've just missed the boys. They left five minutes ago."

"Hi, Mrs Coyle. It's not them I'm after. I just called round to see how Marie was."

"Och, she's fine, son. It would take more than a bit of a burn to keep our Marie out of action," Lizzie answered the big fella. "Mind you, she got a sore one. Thank God it was her left hand because it'll be a wee while before she can use it properly."

"Strange how it happened. She swore she hadn't left the handle over the gas flame, but what else could have caused it? Well, as long as she's on the mend."

"Fancy a cuppa? I've just made a fresh pot. Sean will be down in a minute."

"Aye, that would be nice. Do you think Sean would fancy a bit of a run out? I've a wee delivery to make across the water."

"Oh, laddie, that would be grand. It would let me get on a bit in the house, it's like a tip." It would also give me a break from that malicious big bugger, Lizzie thought.

"A tip? I don't think so." Gerry laughed, scanning the spotless sitting room. "It's a far cry from a tip, but we'll see if he fancies it or not."

"Who fancies what?" Sean addressed his mother and his new best friend.

"I was just asking your ma if you'd fancy a change of scene, Sean. I have to go over to Helensburgh this afternoon for Paddy and thought you might like to come."

Clapping his hands like an excited child, Sean dashed to the front door, grabbing his coat on the way.

"I think you've got your answer," smiled Lizzie, relieved at the possibility of having the house to herself for a while.

"Now behave for Gerry," she called to her son.

Sean stopped dead on the pavement, refusing to go any further. He stared at the big black shiny car and then about-turned, back into the house.

"No, no. Stay home," he said, throwing himself on the sofa.

"What's wrong, Sean? Don't you like the car? It's brand spanking new. Michael just took delivery yesterday and we're certainly honoured to be allowed to use it."

"Not Michael's old car?"

"No, I don't know what happened to that, mate. It was stolen or something. This one was delivered only yesterday. I daren't get a scratch on it or I'm dead."

Sean became even more agitated. "Who's dead?" He repeated. "Who's dead?" It was if he couldn't quite catch the thought.

"Well, it looks like rain has stopped play," Lizzie sighed.

Gerry wasn't for giving up. "C'mon, Sean, let's christen this beast. There's nothing to be frightened of, and I won't go too fast."

With a tad more coaxing, mother and friend managed to get him into the shiny new car. Gerry took off like a bat out of hell before his passenger could change his mind.

It was a fairly silent journey with Gerry pointing out well known landmarks and territories along the way. They joined the M8 and crossed the River Clyde on the Erskine Bridge.

"Take the A814 out of Dumbarton, along the coast to Helensburgh," said Sean, to Gerry's surprise.

"What did you say?"

Sean, realising his mistake, tried in vain to cover his tracks, "Nothing."

"You didn't say nothing, you told me to take the A814 to Helensburgh."

"Sometimes I get flashes, I don't know where they come from and I can't always remember or repeat what I said."

Gerry knew it! He had sensed from day one that Sean was a devious bastard and had no conscience at all about deceiving his mother and brothers. There was more to this than met the eye, but he had no intention of upsetting the man. He would bide his time and, as his mother used to say, 'have his day'. Gerry was definitely playing the long game and Sean Coyle would pay for what he had done to his family. Oh, he would pay alright.

"Don't worry about it, mate. The more you stress the worse it'll get. Just relax, sit back and enjoy the ride."

He'd have to be more careful. Thank God Gerry was such a gullible fool. If he'd said that in front of either brother, they'd have strung him up. Gerry was a nice enough guy and would certainly come in useful in the future.

The delivery made, they headed back to the city.

"I've got a few deliveries towards the end of the week if you feel like a trip? It's surely better than being stuck at home − I'd go stir crazy. So what do you say, will I pick you up?"

"I'll have to ask my mum, but I'm sure it'll be okay." The young Sean was back, much to Gerry's annoyance. How much of a fool did this eejit take him for?

"Okay, we'll ask Lizzie when I drop you off."

"Maybe Errol could tag along?"

"For Christ's sake, Sean. I'm doing deliveries for Paddy, it's not a fucking Sunday school outing. Forget it, I was only trying to break the monotony, not run the Coyle crèche."

"Sorry, Gerry, sorry. I wasn't thinking."

Gerry noted that not once had Sean queried what the deliveries were all about.

Spying

"I should be back around 9.30 p.m. I'm just popping round to your ma's because she's not been feeling too good." Bridget told Paddy as she was serving his evening meal.

It was about the only time they seemed to talk nowadays. They had become like ships that passed in the night. He usually left the house to do his rounds of the clubs and saunas around ten in the evening and would seldom be home before daybreak. She couldn't complain as that was when their money was made.

"What's wrong with her? Not another fall?"

"Well, I'm not sure, but I hope to get to the bottom of these falls and dizzy spells quite soon," Bridget said cryptically.

"What does that mean?" Paddy challenged his wife.

"I'll tell you tomorrow. Don't worry, she'll be fine. And if not, I'll bring her here for a while."

"What about Sean?"

"What about Sean? He can do for himself if need

be, but forget it for now. I'll try to be home before you go to work."

Erin was tending to the baby as her father put his head round the bedroom door.

"Everything okay? The wee man settled?" he asked his daughter. Despite his feelings toward the McClellands, and Bobby in particular, he was besotted with the baby and would take him out of his pram or crib at any opportunity.

"*Dad!* I've just got him down. God knows how long it'll take me now and I wanted to watch a film starting in half an hour."

"Off you go, I'll watch him."

Erin didn't need asking twice. Off she went, leaving the two men in her life delighted to be in one another's company.

There was a huge pile of acceptances for the christening on the desk and Paddy idly leafed through them. He couldn't believe he was going to play host to his worst enemies. Fair enough, he'd disposed of the head of the clan, but not without good reason. He couldn't bear to think this wee chap had any McClelland blood in him – the thought made Paddy heave. He'd racked his brains to figure a way out of the celebrations, but had come up with nothing – well, nothing that wouldn't stop Bridget leaving him. There had to be a way, though. Otherwise there'd be another murder.

*

178

"You're sure they didn't see you?" Theresa asked Bridget for the fourth time.

"They didn't see me. I came in the back way, through the drying green. Now calm down."

"I'll put the kettle on. It's usually quiet till about eight, but he's been out most of the afternoon with the new fella. You know the one, lost his wife 'n' kids while he was inside."

"Gerry, Gerry Fairnie?" Bridget didn't think for a moment that Gerry would have anything in common with Sean, but there you go, you just never knew.

On the other side of the wall Lizzie was settling down to watch her soaps, hoping against hope that Sean was too tired by his trip, that he would stay in his room and give her peace. Just a couple of hour's peace would be fine.

Night after night he started. He found fault with everything. Arguing and berating her and as often as not giving her a clump or a push. Lizzie knew it was going to have to be dealt with, but pride stopped her. She had always walked with her head held high, proud of her sons. Proud of how they looked after her. How could she tell the family what Sean had become, what he had done to her? Her body was a mass of bruises and she was sure that last thump had left her with broken ribs. She was finding breathing painful and difficult. No way could she go to Dr McPhail; he'd get to the bottom of what was going on in two shakes of a lamb's tail. Nosy old git.

179

It was nearly nine o'clock and, three cups of stewed tea later, not a sound from next door.

"I can't believe it, Bridget. Honest, I can't believe it. These past couple of weeks not a night has gone by without some fracas or another. You know I wouldn't cause trouble. Honest, I can't believe it. I was scared something would happen to her."

"Look, don't worry. Thank goodness he's leaving her alone. Maybe it's the television you've been hearing. Whatever, it's not happening tonight. I'd better be off. Don't worry, Theresa, we should be thankful."

"Hello, son, can I speak to Bridget?" Lizzie had no idea she was just about to start World War III in the Coyle household.

"She's not in, Ma. I thought she was at yours." replied her son.

"No, I haven't seen her since the end of last week."

"I'll get her to call as soon as she gets home." Strange, thought Paddy, she was definitely planning on going to his mother's. Obviously she'd been waylaid. The sound of tyres on gravel announced his wife's arrival.

"Hi, luv," Paddy addressed his wife. "How was the old dear?"

"Fine, absolutely fine. I got completely the wrong end of the stick."

"Oh, you did that, darlin'. My mother is just off the

phone asking for a word with you, and telling me she hasn't seen sight nor sound of you since last week. So whoever you were tending to, it wasn't Lizzie Coyle."

"I can explain, Paddy. It's not what it looks like."

"What *does* it look like, Bridget? And this better be good because it sure as hell doesn't look good from where I'm standing."

"I was and I wasn't at your mother's, if you know what I mean."

"No, I don't know what you mean."

"Well, I was next door with Theresa, but Lizzie doesn't know I was there. I promised to keep the reason to myself."

"Why on earth would you be at Theresa's and not call in on my mother?"

"I can't tell you, but I had my reasons and so did Theresa."

"You're standing there, expecting me to believe that my mother's friend would confide in you before her? I don't believe a word of it," and he marched out of the room.

He returned a short time later with a holdall. Of course he believed Bridget; the one thing he could be sure of, she wasn't a liar, but this could be his way out of attending that fucking farce of a christening.

"Where do you think you're off to?" Bridget shouted, barring Paddy's way to the front door. "If you leave now, Paddy Coyle, don't come back. I have never lied or cheated on you since the day we met, not that I can say the same about you. If you leave this house tonight it will be for the last time."

"Piss off," he snarled at her and slammed the front door behind him.

The Car

Paddy had only stayed away for a couple of nights after the Theresa episode. He had never disbelieved Bridget and knew there would be a good reason for her actions, but right at that moment he had other fish to fry.

The police investigating the vehicle seen at the time of Billy's disappearance had eventually got round to checking the one owned by Michael Coyle. This was serious stuff, and Paddy could see Michael having a hard time if they couldn't produce the car or a report that it had been stolen.

The only way out of this mess was to doctor the vehicle just recently acquired. They would swap VIN numbers, which was a dodgy venture at the best of times. But in a car one connected to the disappearance of a kid, Forensics would go over it with a fine toothcomb.

The answer to their problem came via Gerry and Tiny. A certain Mr George Dodds owed Paddy over five grand, which had been used to finance a bank job that had gone wrong. Unfortunately for Mr Dodds the debt was still in place and he was toiling with the payments. George was probably the best wheel man in the country; he could pick up and disguise a car better than the manufacturers. The plan was to change the VIN number, run the clock forward and hand the car in for examination. It would then disappear from the pound. It was chancy, but they had no alternative and George Dodds would be debt-free.

Over the years Paddy had built up a whole network of bent cops and judges throughout the city. It was time for a few to earn their crust. Facing him was D.I. Higgins, an old acquaintance. Higgins and his wife had enjoyed many a Caribbean cruise, courtesy of the Coyle family, but it was payback time. Like most villains, Paddy hated the police in general, but he hated bent cops even more. To get collared fair and square was one thing, but to get put away by bent filth was intolerable. That's what could happen to Michael if they didn't get this matter sorted. To put Sean in the frame, guilty or not, was never going to happen. Paddy would exact his own revenge at a suitable time.

"So you want me to let some wee tea-leaf have the run of the pound and take his pick? I don't think so, Paddy."

"It's Mr Coyle to you." Paddy walked round from his side of the desk holding a small ball-peen hammer.

"That wasn't a request, Higgins. It was an order. You will allow my man access to the pound and not only that, you will personally make sure everything goes smoothly."

"But Paddy, sorry, Mr Coyle, it's never been done before."

"Well, you're just the man to make it happen," Paddy smacked the hammer against his hand.

Higgins was rigid with terror. He'd taken Coyle's brass for years – to such an extent that he considered it part of his salary. It was reasonable payment for the favours Paddy asked in return, but this, this was way out of his league. He had no idea how to pull it off, but the alternative was staring him straight in the face. If it went awry he'd probably never walk again, courtesy of the ball-peen.

"The car will be available next week. Michael will hand it over, late on Friday. It's unlikely the forensic guys will work on it straight away. Our man will collect it that night. Don't think going off on the sick will save you, Higgins. If you mess up on this you'll be on long term sick. This should cover your expenses." He threw a bulky envelope onto the table.

Higgins left the lounge bar of the Ingram Hotel, where he and Paddy had met, a far less jaunty fellow than when he'd entered the building. He had no idea how he'd pull this off and there was no-one he could run it past. He could hardly ask one of his colleagues for advice on how to stage a break-in to the highly secure police car pound. But he had only a few days to accomplish the task or his time was up.

The car now sported a new VIN number and had allegedly clocked up over twelve thousand miles. It was delivered by Michael to his local police station in London Road, together with all the requisite documentation, and D.I. Higgins was duly notified.

The brand new 4 x 4 arrived at the scrapyard at just after eight that night and was crushed and rendered unidentifiable by nine. How Higgins had accomplished this was of no interest to the Coyle brothers, nor was the fact that Higgins had gone off sick the following morning.

The theft had been relatively simple. The police officer had easily acquired a full set of keys to the pound which he gave to the wheelman whilst ensuring he was at no time out of camera range while the theft was taking place so that he was never under suspicion.

Michael Coyle eventually received compensation from the Greater Glasgow Police Force for the loss of a top of the range Range Rover, stolen from their secure pound and the vehicle was dropped from their enquiries.

Guilty

"It's started again, Bridget. He was at it for hours last night and only stopped when I knocked on the back door."

"Okay, I'll call round later. Are you absolutely sure it's not the television? Because she does have it pretty loud."

"Fuck's sake, Bridget, do you think I don't know the difference between Coronation Street and your mother-in-law being abused? Gimme some credit."

"Sorry. Look, I'll see you tonight and yes, I'll park my car well away."

Bridget wasn't really surprised to hear from Theresa. Things had been far too quiet on the Sean front of late and she had been quite taken aback at her mother-in-law's appearance at the christening.

Oh, she was well turned out as usual, but there was something not right. Lizzie, always the life and soul of any party, was great company and often quite outrageous. She was always game for a laugh, but not so on this occasion. It was as if she'd lost her sparkle, even Paddy had remarked on it. God help them all if what she suspected turned out to be true.

Lizzie was at her wits' end. Sean was becoming more and more volatile by the day and seemed to take vicious pleasure in tormenting her. She knew Theresa was aware of what had been going on over the past few months, but any time her neighbour referred to what she called 'her situation', the old girl vehemently denied anything was wrong and insisted if her friend continued to accuse her family, she would be a friend no longer. Despite this, Lizzie knew that she had to stand up to her son or things could really get out of hand.

Thankfully, the trips out with Gerry had become a regular occurrence and Gerry seemed to calm Sean down, for which Lizzie was immensely grateful. Unfortunately her saviour had been engaged on other duties most of this week which had left Sean cooped up in number 28. By the end of the week he was obviously stir crazy.

Gerry was finding it harder and harder to maintain a pretence with Sean, and to prevent himself doing the man a severe injury, he had stayed away for the best part of the week. He was still reeling from their last journey. Things had nearly come to a head as they were driving down Munro Street, where Gerry had once lived. Sean, babbling on as usual, suddenly went quiet.

"What's up?" Gerry asked his passenger.

"I remember this street. I used to collect down here, but for the life of me I can't remember who from."

Gerry repelled the overwhelming urge to smack the fucker in the face and tell him exactly who he'd collected from and what had happened as a result. It was, of course, his wife. The strain of keeping the information to himself was too much and before he blew his cover, he dumped Sean home as quick as he could, foregoing the customary drink at the Saracen's Head.

"What the fuck's up with you?" growled Sean, used to always getting his own way.

"Nothing, mate, I'm just knackered. I've been doing a few extra shifts at the yard and it's catching up with me."

"That's not my fault. I look forward to having a drink and you said next time I could have a shandy."

"Fuck off, Sean. I do the best I can. No other fucker bothers about you, so stop moaning or this'll be the last trip."

Any normal person would have apologised and been grateful for Gerry's attention and done their best to get back in his good books, but not Sean. As usual, he behaved like the spoiled ten-year-old brat he was pretending to be.

Stomping into the house, Sean announced his return and obvious bad mood. He demanded his mother fix him some grub as he banged and crashed his way through the house, smashing a number of Lizzie's precious possessions: a statue of Our Lady she'd bought on her first pilgrimage to Lourdes, a vial of holy water from Jerusalem, given to her when Marie was ill, worthless, but precious to her.

She placed a plate of eggs and chips before him and poured a mug of tea which he scoffed, all the while insulting and berating her. Lizzie turned the volume on the television up to drown him out, but this simply enraged him more.

On the other side of the wall Theresa's husband, Peter, was demanding that she go and tell those inconsiderate bastards that there was a sick man next door who needed peace and quiet. Just at that moment Bridget arrived. And would you believe it − sod's law − the noise stopped.

"It's fucking ridiculous what we have to put up with," moaned Peter.

"Shut up, you moaning, miserable old git. I'm more concerned with why it's gone quiet. I hope to God he hasn't hurt her."

The words were hardly out of her mouth when the shouting and swearing started with a vengeance.

"Dear God, I can't believe she has to put up with this nonsense." Bridget was appalled.

"That's nothing," verified Peter.

"Okay, I've heard enough," said Bridget as she went next door.

"Will I come with you?" offered Theresa.

"No thanks, I'll deal with this."

Using her spare key, Bridget let herself into number 28 in time to witness her mother-in-law cowering behind a chair and her brother-in-law threatening all manner of atrocities. The room, usually spick and span, was a wreck: smashed crockery, ornaments and food debris everywhere.

"What in the name of God is going on here?" shouted Bridget as she went to help Lizzie.

"He's had a bad day, love. He doesn't mean me any harm," the old woman hobbled to her chair.

"Doesn't mean you harm? Well, fuck me, God help you when he does."

"Let me look at your eye," she motioned to Lizzie. "This needs seeing to, it's deep. Wait till Paddy finds out about this carry-on. You're a dead man, Sean Coyle, and you deserve everything that comes to you."

"No, no, Bridget. He can't help it, it's all down to his injuries. Sean was never like this before the attack. Please don't involve Paddy, or Michael. I can handle him."

"I have to tell him, Lizzie, for Sean's sake as well as yours. This can't go on."

"If you split my family up I'll never speak to you again, Bridget, and that's a promise. I bet it was that nosey bugger next door that got you involved?"

191

"Theresa had nothing to do with this, you're damned lucky to have a neighbour and friend like her. No matter what you say, I'm telling Paddy."

Sean meanwhile was crouched behind the sofa, acting his heart out and playing the ten-year-old up to the hilt.

"Shut it, Sean. It's not washing with me, not one iota. My Erin was right when she said she thought you were taking the mick."

"Please. Please, Bridget, let me deal with it. I promise you, if he dares to lift a finger to me again I'll tell you and Paddy can sort it out. But he's my boy and it's not his fault."

Now it was Sean's turn to beg for leniency. "Please, Bridget, I didn't mean it. It's the voices that make me angry."

"Voices, what voices? Well, buster, listen to this one. If you as much as raise yours to her, I'll have Paddy and Michael here so fast, you won't have time to hear the answer. Understood?"

"Yes," he mumbled and went upstairs to his room.

"Right, lady, this is what's going to happen. That big arsehole is moving back to his own place and we'll hire someone to look after him. You know, Lizzie, he's a lot better than he makes out. But if you don't agree I'm straight back home to get the boys."

"I don't have a choice, do I?" said a relieved Lizzie.

The Rain in Spain

"If she wasn't a Coyle I'd do my best to persuade you to settle down with her."

"You only want to get your hands on the kid. Let's face it, you've no more interest in her than I have," replied Bobby.

"Do you *really* not feel anything for the wee lad? Does he not mean anything to you?" Diane puzzled.

"No, not really. I wouldn't wish any harm to come to him, but then, I wouldn't want anything to happen to any kid."

"Christ, you're not your father's son there then," came the quick retort from Diane.

"No, not in that way, but I have no compunction about using him to get my own back on the Coyles. Paddy Coyle will rue the day he harmed our family." Bobby still could not bring himself to say that his father was dead.

"Don't underestimate them, son. They are a force to be reckoned with and if you harm Erin or his grandson he'll hunt you down like a dog, make no mistake. My advice, although I know there's no chance you'll take it, is to forget vendettas or revenge. In a way your father had it coming. It was inevitable that one day he'd get his comeuppance. Unfortunately he crossed the wrong family.

"You've got a great life, Bobby. You're young, you've got the pick of the totty, the club, friends and money. Why put all that at risk for a man not fit to clean your boots?"

Diane knew she was flogging a dead horse. Bobby might not be like his father in many ways, but in others he was a true McClelland, and she knew in her heart her son would not rest until he had made someone pay. It was up to her, therefore, to keep the lines of communication open. She was not losing touch with her grandson and was determined to have Erin and the boy over for a holiday as soon as possible. But to succeed she would require Bobby's assistance. He would be the bait, but would he play ball? Even though it went against the grain she would enlist the canon's help. That should be no problem; he hated the Coyles almost as much as she did.

The interior of the church was cool and still as ex-Canon O'Farrell finished his devotions. Despite his nefarious deeds and guiltless conscience, he still considered himself to be a good Catholic who attended early morning mass religiously.

"To what do I owe the honour?" the old man mockingly bowed to Diane.

"Cut the bullshit, I've heard it all before."

"Always the charmer, eh, Diane? So how can I help you? I take it this isn't a social call?"

"I need help with Bobby. I need him to play the doting father for the next few weeks until we can get the Coyle girl over here. Once she's here we can see what can be done."

"That's not going to be easy, my dear. Bobby is his own man and will do exactly what he wants without interference from us. We have to get him in her good books, make her think he can't live without her and that he is missing the boy immensely."

"Loathe as I am, I have to agree with you. She needs to think it's Bobby she's coming for, but trust me, she's one smart cookie. She'll not be easy to fool."

"He seems to think she'll come running if he snaps his fingers."

"I'm not so sure. She's certainly besotted with him, any fool can see that. But she's pretty clued up and that baby will come before anything and anyone."

"You need to get him to start calling her again. That seems to have petered out," the ex-priest observed.

"I've tried, but he's not interested and he certainly doesn't want her over here interfering with his social life. We need a plan."

"We do, but in the meantime you call her, befriend her and make excuses as to why Bobby is off the radar.

One way to get her over here is to persuade her he's serious about another girl. I'm sure that would stir things up."

On the drive back through Porta Banus, Diane mulled over the conversation with her husband's ex-partner. She might well hate the sight of him, but he was right, the way to get Erin over to Spain was to make her think she was going to lose Bobby. A few subtle hints would stir things up.

She smiled to herself as she caught sight of her wayward son with a crowd of friends on the deck of their magnificent yacht, preparing to set sail. Why would Bobby give all this up? He was young, free and single and if they could somehow get custody of the boy . . . Well, that would more than pay Mr Paddy Coyle back.

The Beginning of the End

The sound of a plane overhead just served to annoy Paddy even more. "That's probably her off on her jollies," he muttered to himself.

Erin had left that morning to visit the McClellands, the Macks, or whatever they called themselves in Spain. Fucking Spain. Despite all his arguments and cajoling, she was not to be persuaded to leave his beloved grandson at home.

Well, he was done with her. Let her get on with it, see how hard life could be without Daddy at her beck and call. And her bloody mother could do the same. The pair of them were always ganging up on him. Oh, they thought he hadn't sussed them out, how fucking stupid did they think he was? Well it was over; they were both were in for a shock, wife and daughter.

Paddy ranted and raved to himself all the way into town on his way to his mother's, recalling incidents that had happened years ago – situations well settled that should have been long forgotten, but obviously had not been. He was in one of his rare tempers and woe betide anyone crossing him today.

There was something fishy going on. He could feel an undercurrent. His wife and Michael spent more time sorting out Sean than the bloody doctors did and now they had co-opted Big Gerry as a permanent fucking babysitter. It was fucking laughable. Sean was a thirty-odd-year-old man who, it seemed, thought he was ten, and who couldn't blow his nose unattended. And yet, out of the blue, these daft bastards had decided he was capable of looking after himself and ready to stay on his own. What a proper fiasco that had turned out to be. The bloody idiot had set the house on fire. Paddy knew that the insidious bastard had done it on purpose. He just knew it.

It was his poor ma he felt sorry for. It was obviously too much for her, looking after that half-wit. She looked absolutely hellish and here she was, two days after the 'big move', with him back on her doorstep. Paddy knew that Bridget was angling to bring him back to theirs, but no way. He found it nigh on impossible to be in the same room as Sean. And to have the treacherous bastard in his home? No chance, he'd be up for manslaughter within a week.

As he gave his mother a hug, Lizzie let out a low groan of pain.

"Dear God, Ma, what's wrong? I didn't mean to hurt you."

"I know, son, it's nothing. I tripped going out into the yard the other day."

"Must have been a mighty trip, you look like you've done ten rounds with Mike Tyson and that's some cut above your eye." Paddy could see the nervous looks pass between Bridget, Theresa and Michael, as well as Sean's shifty demeanour.

"What's going on here?" demanded Paddy. "What have you two been up to, and what are you looking so guilty about?" he pointed to Sean. "So, c'mon, tell me what's been going on." There was silence from all five. Sean slunk back off to his room.

"It's that daft bugger, isn't it? What's he been up to? Has he been nicking stuff again?"

"He's not done anything, son. It's me, it's old age and I'm not too steady on my feet."

"Rubbish, you're steadier on your feet than any of us. I don't believe a word of it and if we have to stay here until this time tomorrow, I'll get to the bottom of this."

"Paddy, it's your imagination. Mother fell outside and she's a bit bruised and battered."

Bridget was interrupted by the next door neighbour. "It's Sean, Paddy, he's hitting Lizzie," blurted out Theresa. "I don't care if none of you talk to me again. I can't stand back and let my friend get beaten up by that big bully."

Paddy said nothing, but the expression on his face said it all.

Bridget barred his way to Sean's room, "No, Paddy. This is exactly why we didn't tell you. You have to let us deal with it."

Paddy's voice was cold and quiet, "I'll kill him."

But his mother was having none of it. "Paddy, if you harm a hair on his head, I will never, and I mean never, speak to you for the rest of my life. And if you harm your brother it won't be a long one."

"You mean you're going to let him get away with this? Michael, are you telling me you would stand by and let him beat up a seventy-five-year-old woman, your own mother?"

"Of course not, Paddy. I only just found out what's been going on half an hour ago. Bridget's right, this is exactly why they didn't tell us. He needs treatment. He needs help and it's the after-effects of the attack that's made him like this."

"Rubbish, he's been an evil bastard since the day he was born. I told you before what he was like, but you wouldn't have it. Oh no! You said he'd be alright. Well, he's not. So what the fuck do we do?"

"We look after him as we would look after any of the family, until he's better," said his mother.

That'll be shining bright, thought Paddy. That fucker will pay dearly for what he'd put their ma through, that and for the young lad too.

But Paddy wasn't the only one planning Sean's demise.

The Trip

Bobby spied Diane driving along the front. Where in God's name had she been this early in the morning?

The cafés and restaurants were only just opening their shutters and his mother was most definitely not a morning lady. Christ, he hoped she had no suspicions about his plans for the day. She was no fool, his mother. No, she was driving on past, presumably on her way home. He breathed a sigh of relief. It was a beautiful morning, as always in Marbella, just the weather for a day's cruising with friends.

As far as anyone was concerned, especially those in authority, this was simply a pleasure cruise to commemorate his late father's birthday. Being a long term resident and co-owner of the most prestigious club in Marbella, it was highly unlikely that his movements would draw suspicion, but should that happen he was well covered.

The plan was to make a quick trip across the straits

to spend the day in Tangiers, collect his consignment and return home just before nightfall. His previous trips had been uneventful, but until the package was delivered and paid for Bobby would remain on tenterhooks.

His father had made this trip successfully, countless times, for years. Pete had established an exclusive clique including the glitterati of Marbella, the chief of police, the mayor and various other town dignitaries. That elite had given him immunity on the few occasions the trip had been interrupted; the embarrassment of a dignitary on board securing a clean bill of health.

The canon had introduced Bobby to his father's contacts and re-established the excursions. However, it was the beautiful people Bobby cultivated, not the influential friends of his father, which increased the risk level somewhat.

The trip was glorious; the champagne flowed and for some time they were accompanied by a school of dolphins, much to the entertainment of the guests on board. The pod of magnificent creatures performed their acrobatics to the delight of their audience.

His guests were free to explore the old souk whilst Bobby went off to complete his transaction. He had decided that for the time being this would be his last trip. The profits from the deals were fantastic, but not enough for the risk involved, he fancied. It was only his determination to deal with the Coyles that had tempted him.

Drugs had never been his thing and he was loathe to become involved. However, clubs and drugs went hand in hand and he knew that no matter what his opinion was, they would be dealt. Therefore, the scene was better under his control than some other greedy dealers, cutting the coke with who knew what. After this trip he would hand the enterprise over to his two partners. Frank would have to be involved, but he'd make sure the old coyote played his part. The days of him sitting back with his hand out were long gone. If he wanted an 'earn' he'd have to get off his old, wrinkly backside and get his hands dirty.

The ex-man-of-the cloth had been back on his case about Erin and the kid. Bobby knew he was right and in order to put his plan into action they would have to be in Spain. Thankfully, his mother seemed to be on the ball. Having really taken to the boy, and being a grandma, she talked about him constantly and was forever buying gifts for him. A nursery was even starting to take shape in one of the guest rooms.

The trip to Tangiers went off without a hitch and the two pool cleaners, Bobby's partners in his first venture, were now two of the main suppliers in town.

Bobby now had the financial means to carry out his revenge and his first task would be to get his son within his grasp.

Compromise

On the days that Sean went out with Gerry, Paddy would visit his mother. He couldn't trust himself to be around his brother, it was better they were apart. Lizzie was looking much more like her old self and, despite all her threats, she and Theresa were back to normal. The old biddy appreciated that it was concern for her that had made her pal spill the beans.

"I'm no grass, Lizzie, but there was no way I could stand by and let this go on. If it were the other way round what would you have done?"

"Well, if it was your Peter, I'd just have taken the poker to him and sorted him once and for all."

"Aye, but look at the size of Sean. Joking aside, I take it things are okay? He's behaving himself?"

"Good as gold and when he's with Gerry I get a bit of peace, except for nosey neighbours, that is," laughed Lizzie.

This was a joy to her old friend, who'd not heard her laugh for a long, long time.

"Here's your Paddy. I'll get myself off and see you later." Theresa made for the door.

"Hello, son, how are things?" Both Paddy and Theresa knew exactly what things she was talking about.

"Seems to be fine, Theresa, but you keep a watch for me." Peeling a twenty pound note from his wallet, he handed the money to her. "Here, go and buy his nibs a drink to make up for us disturbing him."

"Don't be daft, Paddy, he moans about everything," Theresa offered him the money back.

"Take it, Theresa. I'll be offended if you don't."

"In that case, then," she quickly pocketed the money. "You take care now, son."

"Well, Ma, how is he behaving? No more trouble, I hope?"

"No, son, he's fine, but I think he's regressed a bit. He hardly ever comes out of his room, and that's only when he goes out with Gerry. I swear to God, I thank the day you took him on, Paddy. He's good to Sean. I don't know what I'd do without him."

"Well, as long as it doesn't interfere with Gerry's work, I don't mind."

"Michael's good, but he doesn't spend much time with him and Sean senses that Michael can't wait to get away."

"I'm not surprised. Michael feels the same way as me. It's hard for a man to stand by and see his mother beaten, especially by one of her own. So Michael's doing better than I am."

"How long is Erin away for? I fair miss that wee boy."

"I've no idea, no beggar tells me anything. She could be away for months for all I know, but I do miss the lad, he's a smart wee chav."

"Don't tell me you and Bridget have fallen out again? What the hell's wrong with you both?"

"No, we haven't fallen out, Ma. You need to speak to have an argument and we hardly pass the time of day with one another."

"There's nobody else is there? I won't stand for it, Patrick, and neither will she a second time around."

"No, there's no-one else. There never really has been, but I'm a lodger in my own house. And as for my daughter, well! She flew off to Spain without a by-your-leave. I've not heard a cheep from her. I don't know if she's alive or not. She's probably living it large with the McClellands, her new family."

"Don't be bloody stupid, Paddy. If there was anything amiss we would know, and whether you like it or not, they are Ryan's family too. Hey, I can't get over the mayor of Marbella sitting in this room, drinking tea as nice as you like. It was like having royalty here," his mother grinned. "It certainly gave the Catholic Mothers something to chew on."

Happy Families

"This is your Captain speaking, welcome aboard Flight BA345 to Malaga. We are now cruising at 50,000 feet and the outside temperature is minus 40 degrees. Our estimated time of arrival is 12.08 . . ."

It seemed a lifetime since the passengers in seats 1A, B and C had last heard that announcement and how their lives had changed in the past year. For starters, Erin had no fears that her father would storm the plane and demand she return home. No, that fear was gone; mainly because she and Paddy were, again, not on speaking terms. He was furious that not only was she taking his six-month-old grandchild out of the country, but that she was also entering that den of vipers.

His parting shot that morning as she left for the airport had been, "Don't coming running to me when this all goes tits up. You've made your bed, lady. Shame you've already lain in it."

"Oh, piss off, Dad, and give it a rest. I'm only going

207

for a couple of weeks and it's only fair they should get to know the baby. Whether you like it or not he is as much a McClelland as he is a Coyle."

The door slamming shook the whole house.

As usual her mother didn't say a word, but as Erin knew, she ruled the roost and would calm her dad down before the plane had even left the tarmac.

"God, I can't believe we're on our way back," said her companion nervously. "Are you sure you're doing the right thing?"

"It's a bit late now, we can hardly get off at the next stop," Erin laughed. "Look, if it all goes belly up, we take the next flight home, it's that simple."

Carol wasn't quite so confident about their reception in Spain, but once again she was there to cover Erin's back and give her moral support. Whatever happened, she reasoned, it couldn't top their last visit: murder, kidnapping and fleeing the country. Not exactly a Thomson's week in the sun.

"Hey, listen, I'm not taking shit from either of them, especially the mother. She insists she wants to get to know her grandson, so she better play ball with me. This time I'm calling the shots."

"I'm not so sure. Do you think Bobby will be okay? Remember, he's back on his own turf and you don't have the infamous Paddy Coyle standing right behind you."

"No, but Paddy Coyle is only three hours away and Bobby knows that."

"True, but you better not let the boyo find out that Daddy's in the cream puff with you."

"Don't worry, my dad will be fine. A few days without seeing his precious grandson will soon have him begging for forgiveness. Anyway, Mum won't let it go on, not after the last time."

"What sort of reception can we expect? Do they know we're arriving today?" Carol asked her.

"No, they know I'm coming sometime this week, but not exactly when. It sounds a bit batty, but I wanted to be in control from the start, so we'll get the kids settled and have a bit of us-time before entering the lion's den."

"Don't say things like that," shivered Carol. "I can't stop thinking about the last trip."

"Me too, but remember, neither Bobby nor his mother had anything to do with what went on before."

"I'm not so sure. I wouldn't trust either of them as far as I could throw them."

"That's one of the reasons I've kept it low-key. They'll only know we're here when I choose to tell them. Stop worrying, we'll have a nice couple of days, top up the tan, and then . . ."

Just at that precise moment, a stewardess approached the pair, carrying an ice bucket containing a bottle of champagne.

"Miss Coyle?"

"Yes," answered Erin.

"Compliments of Mr Bobby Mack."

The woman expertly opened the bottle, poured out two glasses and handed them to the surprised passengers.

"They don't know when we're arriving? Don't know what flight we're on?" Carol sneered.

"What can I say?" a dumbstruck Erin replied.

"And you think *you're* in control? It's *you* calling the shots? Oh, it looks like it. And what does the card say?" Carol grabbed the small note before her friend could.

"Can't wait to see you. Meet you at three, everything taken care of. Love, Bobby." Well, so much for the 'us-time'," Carol laughed. "Seriously, you need to be very careful, this guy has a lot of pull here. I just don't trust him at all."

Despite her friend's warning, Erin was secretly delighted. There was no way she was going to fall for him the way she had before, but he was the father of her baby and of course she had 'happily-ever-after dreams', but she wouldn't be taken in a second time – she had her son to consider.

Old Pals

"You're going the wrong way, it's next on the left," Sean corrected Gerry.

"Who's the fucking driver?" Gerry snapped back. "I know exactly where I am."

"Aye, but just five years too late, son. This is now a one way street," the twin laughed.

"Fuck!" Gerry made a hasty u-turn. "I still can't get used to the road changes. Okay, the main roads I understand, but these side roads are just plain stupid."

"Where exactly is it you want to go?" Sean asked. Thankfully it was the thirty-year-old persona who was out and about today. The ten-year-old must have been left on the naughty step, mused Gerry.

To any observer their relationship was bizarre, to say the least. Gerry couldn't, and wouldn't, deal with the ten-year-old Sean, knowing it to be a ruse. There was no doubt that Sean still suffered a great deal of memory loss from the attack, but this childish exaggeration was to keep his brothers off his back. If Paddy Coyle knew for certain that this idiot sitting beside him, cheerfully giving him driving instructions, was almost cured, he would beat the evil shit to a pulp. And although Gerry would welcome the justice meted out by one brother to another, he did not want to be deprived of the satisfaction of paying Sean back personally for the wrongs done to his family.

"I need to drop off keys at the yard and I was sure I could cut across town this way."

"It's second on the left, down to the roundabout and straight across. It'll take about ten minutes. I don't think I've been in the yard since I got out of hospital. It's weird, I've always felt I had some unfinished business there, but for the life of me it's gone."

"Maybe you stashed some cash there, or weapons?"

"Seriously, I can't remember. You never know, being there might trigger something."

I hope it's not my face he remembers, Gerry thought to himself.

The lads in the yard stopped work as Sean got out of Gerry's car.

"Hey, Sean, good to see you, man," called one.

"Coming to do a shift?" from another.

"Michael's in the office, I'll bell him." The gaffer spoke into a radio and informed Michael that he had visitors.

"Thanks, boys, see you soon, hopefully." The twosome made their way to the portacabin where Michael stood waiting.

"Hi, mate," Sean greeted his twin. "Haven't seen much of you lately, things okay?"

Michael shifted about guiltily. He hadn't seen his brother since the showdown at Lizzie's. "You know how it is, mate, busy, busy. And as you know, we're one down." He turned to Sean's companion, "You alright, Gerry?" Michael asked the big man.

"Fine, boss, fine. Just came by to drop off keys for the mini. I didn't get round to stripping it last night."

"Okay, just put them on the board. Where are you off to now?" Michael felt guilty that he spent no time with Sean and that his brother's only companion was one paid to be so. They had been close all their lives until now, but Michael couldn't rationalize the heinous crime this man had committed and his treatment of their mother. This was not the brother he knew and loved. Michael had no desire to spend more time than was absolutely necessary with this stranger. The least violent of the brothers, even Michael couldn't trust himself not to do his twin harm, real harm.

"I've got a couple of collections over Dumbarton way and that's me for the day."

Michael handed Gerry a fifty pound note, "Here, have a drink."

"Thanks, boss."

Sean was livid at Michael's handout to someone he considered to be the hired help, but also at Gerry's subservience to Michael. Not once had Gerry ever referred to him as boss, or in fact treated him with any real respect. So, it was back to the old regime, back to being the gofer. Well, they could go fuck themselves, those days were over. Maybe it was time for him to get his act together.

Sean wandered round the yard, hoping that something, anything, would pop into his head, but nothing came to him. Everything about the place was familiar and he recognised right away that one of the cranes had been moved. The bothy, the ramshackle hut used by the workers, had been painted. In his opinion it was purely paint that held it together, but there were no great revelations. The feeling was still there, niggling at him, but he couldn't solve the mystery.

Control

Erin spotted a driver holding a card bearing her name as they weaved their way from passport control and through immigration. As she and Carol struggled with the cases and children, the driver came forward, took control and soon had them settled in the air-conditioned vehicle. Annoyed though she was at Bobby's interference, she had to admit it was much easier to let someone else take the strain. It was obvious the name Mack opened doors.

"Well, I'm delighted to see you're in control," Carol giggled. "I'm sure he'll have an itinerary for each day, hope it includes some beach or pool time. Mind you, I might get all the free time I want. After all, it's you and Ryan he's interested in, not me and mine, which suits me down to the ground. Just you be careful."

"I've already said, the first wrong move and we are on our way home."

It was a short trip from the airport to their hotel and within the hour the girls were splashing about in the pool. Baby Ryan loved the water and, with the aid of his water wings, was paddling about like a little duck.

A shadow engulfed Erin, and there, standing at the side of the pool, was Bobby. Her heart gave a flutter, but she made sure she gave no outward sign that she was delighted to see him, looking even more handsome.

It was odd, that whilst she and Carol had been witness to the deed, and almost been victims, somehow Erin had detached herself from the scene. It was as if Bobby's father had existed in another dimension.

"Welcome to Spain, ladies."

He oozed charm and Carol could see quite plainly how easy it would be to succumb to him. She was going to have her work cut out, stopping Erin from falling head over heels again.

"My mother is waiting to meet you all, so if you wouldn't mind," he indicated they should vacate the pool. "I hate keeping her waiting."

Carol could see this was going to be an uphill battle. The Macks were used to getting their own way and she didn't hold out much hope of Erin 'being in control' for long, if at all.

"Sorry, Bobby, but we had an early start and I want to put Ryan down soon. Tell Diane we'll catch up tomorrow."

"Why not come for an hour? She's dying to see him and she's gone to a lot of trouble. She's prepared supper. What do you say? Just for a couple of hours?"

One nil to the Macks.

*

Diane's new apartment was stunning and the view even more so. A selection of mouth-watering titbits and chilled drinks were laid out on the wraparound balcony. Even little Amy had been provided for. Erin was no stranger to the good life, but this was something else.

Diane was fussing over Ryan amidst piles of designer baby clothes and toys. Both Erin and Carol had to admit the woman couldn't have made them any more welcome and, true to his word, Bobby delivered the party back to their hotel within the allotted time, with promises to spend the whole of the next day with the new grandma.

The two girls settled the kids down for the night and sat out on the balcony, discussing the day's events.

"I have to say I was worried when the champagne was delivered on the plane. It just proved how much influence they have. Then the chauffeur, marching us through immigration and straight out to the car. Did you see the other passengers looking at us?"

"Hey, don't knock it. Surely you didn't want to stand in that queue?" quipped Erin.

"Of course not, but you didn't want to go visit the mother this evening. You told him you were going to put Ryan down, but we still ended up doing what Bobby wanted."

"I know, you're right, but it seemed pointless to argue and start off on the wrong foot. I learned from

Paddy which battles to fight and which to concede, and you have to agree, if you didn't know the history between us you would think she was delighted to have me in her family."

"That's the bit that worries me," warned Carol.

"So, what's the agenda for tomorrow? Are you going to take Amy to the beach while I go visit Daddy and Grandma?"

"Yes, but I'll have my phone so we can meet up later, or if you're not comfortable, just ring and I'll come straight away."

Strolling along the main drag on a glorious Marbella morning, enthralled with all the activity around the marina, Amy began jumping up and down excitedly. "Look, Mum, it's that man," the little girl pointed to an old man, down by one of the luxury cruisers.

"What man, darling? You don't know anyone here."

"It's the man, the man who bought me and Erin ice-cream the last time we were here. See, he still wears funny shirts."

Carol almost froze with terror, but it wasn't possible, was it? She knew exactly who Amy was referring to, the canon, but whoever it was had disappeared on board one of the cruisers.

"It can't be him, sweetheart. That man had an accident and he's in heaven with Jesus." Not that there was much possibility of that old pervert reaching the pearly gates, thought Carol.

"It was," said the little girl, quite emphatically.

Desperately trying to shake off the horrible feeling, mum and daughter skipped along the front, hand in hand to the beach, but Carol was spooked. What if it was him? She was sure she was being daft, but the last trip had been so traumatic and Amy was so positive.

Feelings

Frank O'Farrell seldom ventured out nowadays. He would frequent the tapas bar down the street from his apartment, but it was so difficult to camouflage his appearance. Although the scarring and discoloration from the salt water on his face had improved slightly over the past year, he still had a malevolent, freaky look about him. His was certainly not the face you'd want to meet on a dark night. It didn't bother him one iota. It did, however, make him memorable. One glance would have a child screaming for its ma, which he found perversely funny. He really was the bogeyman. However, this was business and he had no intention of drawing attention to himself.

It was time to put phase one of their plan into action. The canon had sourced Dave Smith and his wife, Sylvia, through Pete's old mucker, Nick the Greek. The couple had landed in Majorca ten years previously and, with the proceeds of a Post Office raid, had bought a small family hotel in the coastal town of Andratx on the south west coast of Majorca. Unfortunately, business had been poor the last few seasons and the family were really struggling. Things were getting serious. Not only were bookings down, but major repairs were needed. The roof was leaking badly and the wiring was lethal. The family barely existed from hand to mouth. They could see no way out of their situation, but selling up was not an option.

The old Irishman's proposition was the lifeline they needed and without hesitation they had jumped at the chance. They would be well compensated and everything seemed to be legal – not that that would matter, they were beyond desperate.

Frank and Bobby had come to the island to finalize the details and check out the family. Although Bobby had no feelings for the boy, he would make sure he was well taken care of.

"How are you going to persuade your mother to give up her grandson? You've got a hell of a job there, laddie."

"She thinks it's a temporary measure while we go through the legal stuff."

"And when she finds out it's permanent?"

"Well, that's a fair way down the line and let's face it, Coyle is not going to give up easily. Thankfully the Spanish legal system grinds exceedingly slow. Remember, possession is nine tenths of the law here, so, as long we keep hold of the kid, there is nothing they can do."

"Are you sure you can persuade his mother to stay on after her buddy goes back?"

"Don't worry about her, she'll stay here as long as I want her to. And when she sees she has a bit of competition, there's no way she'll go back to Scotland and leave the coast clear for some other bit of totty," Bobby laughed.

"You're right there, but don't make her too jealous and certainly don't make her suspicious."

As they pulled into the private jetty, Frank and Bobby agreed the hotel was the perfect place to hide Ryan. It was out of the way, with no nosey neighbours to question the arrival of a new addition to the family. Sylvia was a homely-looking woman and two of her four children clung to her skirts as she came forward to meet her saviours. She would look after the child as if it were her own, in fact even better, she assured the men.

"When do you expect the job to go down?" Dave enquired.

"Towards the end of next week. As soon as the bait is taken, we'll phone and give you an exact ETA. All the relevant paperwork will be in your name. His birth certificate and passport will be completed. All you'll have to do is register him with your local doctor. Do this tomorrow, as further proof that the child has been with you for some time. Everything will be in the name of Ryan Smith. Any questions?"

"No, I don't think so, it all seems okay. There's

just the matter of payment. You said half the amount up front and the balance on delivery, plus a monthly amount of 1000 euros for his keep?"

"Agreed," Bobby handed over a bulky envelope. "Remember, if you renege on the deal, one of your children will pay the price."

"We won't."

Two hours later the cruiser was back, berthed in Marbella. Bobby went off in search of his mother and Erin, who would, no doubt, be shopping in Bonpoint, the most expensive baby shop in town.

Recollections

"Where the hell have you been?" Lizzie demanded. "And more to the point, what have you been up to?"

"Nothing. I couldn't sleep so I went for a wander. Fuck, this place is going downhill fast, Ma. It's a dump. Is it not about time you were getting out of here? If not for yourself, for Errol? Christ, I wouldn't bring a dog up in this place."

"I'm fine where I am. I've told you before, I'll leave here in a box and then you can all move where the devil you like. As for Errol, he's fine. He wouldn't dare step out of line with his mother and me on his case. He's a good boy and I'll make damn sure he stays that way."

"How about a bit of breakfast, Ma? I'm starving."

"You'll have to wait till I get back from mass. There's tea in the pot. I'll be back in about an hour."

What the hell was he up to, Lizzie pondered as she made her way to church. It was good to see he was becoming a bit more independent, but he still wasn't right, and for all their sakes she didn't want Paddy finding out what progress his brother was making.

Mind you, thought Lizzie, looking around her, Sean wasn't far wrong, this estate really was deteriorating. It seemed to have got worse since that little lad had gone missing. It was as if the community had given up. Hurrying towards St. Jude's, she thanked goodness for her church. No matter what was going on in Lizzie's turbulent life, she left her worries at the door and took great comfort from the hour spent in the presence of Our Lady.

Over the past week, since his meeting with Michael, Sean had taken to night-time forays. Not far to begin with, just a quick recce to see how the land lay. It was pleasing to see that, although he hadn't been around for the past few months, he was still immediately recognised. Respect, that's what it was all about. Neither Paddy nor Michael gave him any. He had always been purely muscle in their eyes,. All the big decisions and whatever earns were doled out to him were made at the behest of the brothers. It was if those two were the twins and he was the odd one out.

He'd had a good thing going with the old priest, that had been the perfect alliance. Who in their right mind would ever have suspected what they had been up to? But, thanks to his brother's interference, a good earner was gone, and now he was reliant on the odd twenty quid his mother or sister dropped him. How embarrassing was that? His fucking driver had more in small change than he had in his pocket. For Christ's sake, Sean had always had money or access to it, now he was nothing more than a pauper.

He needed an earn, but what? And with who? Not once while he had been in hospital, had any of his so-called crew visited. It seemed they had moved on to pastures new. Well, bugger them. They were a useless bunch of fuckers anyway. That left Gerry. Gerry was his mate, his one and only. But although the man acted like his best buddy most of the time, there were occasions when Sean just couldn't work him out. It was if Gerry had some kind of agenda, but Sean couldn't believe for a second that it was against the Coyles. Why would it be? Hadn't they taken the guy off the street and given him back his life, after all that time in stir?

He should be grateful, Sean reasoned. Why wouldn't Gerry want in on a deal? It was Gerry, not his brothers, who had upped him. After all it was Sean's job he was doing and it was Sean who had allowed him to be his mate, so why wouldn't Gerry jump at an extra source of income? It was a no-brainer. Sean just had to come up with a plan. But for now he needed a fix.

Motherly Love

His mother, Erin and the boy were in Bonpoint, the shop in Marbella, exactly as he had guessed. They were in danger of buying the place out.

"How on earth am I going to get all this back on the plane?" Erin protested. "My God, it'll cost a fortune in excess baggage."

"So, what if you stay a bit longer? Then the wee lad will at least get to wear some of the outfits for me."

"I'm not sure about that. Let's see how things go first."

"Of course, I don't want to put pressure on you. It's just the past year has been awful for Bobby and me." Tears glistened in the older woman's eyes. "I really miss his dad and seeing this wee chap has brought a bit of light back into our days. But, as I said, no pressure."

Diane caught sight of Bobby outside and gestured for him to come in and view their purchases.

"How did you know where to find us?" his mother asked.

"Where else would you be? My God, how will she ever get all this back?"

"That's exactly what I just said," Erin laughed, thankful for a chance to change the subject and avoid the fact that it was her dad who was responsible for Bobby's father's death. For most of the time she was happy enough to be in Diane's presence. Bobby's mother was extremely hospitable and generous to a fault, and it was clear she adored her grandson. But, the spectre of Pete was always there. It was bearable when the women were out shopping or had some distraction or other, although there were many uncomfortable silences.

Erin felt she didn't know Diane well enough to stay on further. However, there was no doubt a bit of the green-eyed monster was surfacing. She was not at all pleased that Bobby had gone to work last night. No doubt his pick of the week would have been waiting. Surely he could have spent a bit of time with her on her first night? No, it seemed his plans didn't include her; it was all about his boy.

"Why not stay for dinner?" asked Diane. "It would be our first family gathering."

Not much of a gathering, Erin thought. Four, including the baby. "That's very kind of you, but I've already made arrangements with Carol. I've left her on her own all day so I really should be getting back. And this little lad's ready for his bed."

"I was including Carol and Amy. Bobby could go and collect them. Couldn't you, darling?" she turned to Bobby.

"Of course I could. No problem. Give her a ring, Erin, and I'll nip out to get them."

"Look, I don't want to put you to any bother. It's been a long day and he really is ready for bed."

"Well, we couldn't be in a better place." Summoning a sales assistant, Diane spoke to her in Spanish and minutes later yet another pile of clothes appeared, this time night clothes.

"That's everything taken care of and it won't go to waste. I'm sure at some point he can stay with his granny Diane."

Shit, thought Erin, two nil to the Macks.

How presumptuous was this bloody woman?

Dinner was again served on the balcony. Diane had pre-ordered a magnificent spread in anticipation of the girls accepting her invitation. Once again she demonstrated her determination to have her way, as Erin had expected. Ryan, having been bathed and fed, fell fast asleep in the new travel cot. She half-expected Diane to suggest that he spent the night with her, but fortunately that was a step too far, even for Diane.

"I know she's very pleasant and will do anything to make you comfortable, but I wouldn't trust her as far as I could throw her. It wouldn't surprise me, if she ever got Ryan on her own, that she would disappear with him. There's something not quite kosher about this set up." volunteered Carol.

"Don't be so melodramatic, she's just desperate to see as much of him as possible while she has the chance. Really, I don't mind. I think I'd be more worried if she showed no interest in him."

"I know, but it's the constant references to Pete that disturbs me. It's as if you're somehow divorced from your family. It's weird."

"It's certainly awkward at times," agreed Erin.

"Hey, talking about weird. Amy and I had a really strange episode this morning. We were on our way to the beach, passing by the marina, when Amy suddenly got very excited and pointed to some old geezer."

"And . . .?"

"Well, she insisted it was the man who'd bought you ice-creams last year and she remembered his funny shirt."

"What, the canon? He's long gone. She just saw someone who resembled him."

"That's what I thought, but she was adamant and you know how stubborn she is."

"Maybe the last trip affected her more than we thought." A cold shiver ran down Erin's back, as if someone was walking over her grave. "Jesus, it couldn't be him, could it?"

"No, I don't think it's that. She genuinely thinks she

saw him, but I won't say anything and hopefully she'll forget about him."

"What's happening tomorrow?" Carol asked her friend.

"Most likely the same, I imagine."

"Surely not more shopping?" exclaimed Carol.

"I wouldn't be surprised."

The two girls would have been on the next flight home if they had known about the council of war taking place after they had been delivered back to their hotel.

Bad Habits

Gerry knew immediately that Sean was back on the gear, any fool could tell. He'd spent the last couple of hours babbling incoherently about some fictitious deal and how the two of them could make an absolute packet. He kept nodding off mid-sentence and Gerry knew his passenger was hooked as bad as ever. Thankfully, Sean slept for most of the journey, waking only as they approached the city. Gerry was intrigued as to what scam this idiot thought he was capable of pulling off, not that he was in the slightest bit interested but it would do no harm to listen.

"Take me straight home," mumbled Sean. "I'm not feeling so good."

"I thought we might go for a drink and you can tell me more about your proposal."

"Another time, mate, sorry. I'm feeling terrible."

"Sure you don't want to stop off at the Ship Inn for a quickie? I'd like to hear more."

"No, not tonight, pal. I think I'm coming down with

something," Sean squirmed about in the passenger seat.

Too fucking right you're coming down with something, Gerry thought. You're coming down with a God Almighty crash . . .

Gerry now knew exactly how he would take his revenge on Sean Coyle: via the packages he delivered week in, week out.

Lizzie was taken aback at their early return, but one look at Sean told her why.

"What's he been taking, lad?" Lizzie questioned Gerry.

"Nothing while he's been with me, Mrs Coyle. He seemed a bit off when I picked him up and he's slept for most of the day. I think he's sickening for something."

"No, son, it's not him sickening for something, it's us who'll be sickened. Is this the first time he's been like this with you?"

"Aye, he can be moody from time to time, but I usually win him round."

"I know you do, laddie, and I'm eternally grateful. You've been a good pal to Sean and I won't forget it, but whatever you do, Gerry, don't tell Paddy or Michael. We'll have to deal with this ourselves for the moment."

"I'm not so sure, Mrs Coyle. I'm maybe the wrong person to help you."

"No, lad, you'll do fine. My God, I was sure being off the stuff for so long while he was in hospital would have cured him."

"It did while he was away from it, but once an addict, always an addict. If it's any consolation, I don't think he's been on the stuff for long. He's not had any money for a start."

"Hmm, that's not quite true. There's been money going missing for the past week."

"How are you going to cope with him on your own? And there's Errol to think about."

"Don't you worry about Errol. I'll cope fine with him, but Sean has to stay here so as not to raise suspicions. ."

"What about the doctor from the hospital? McLeod, was it?"

"No, son, this isn't a problem caused by his attack. I can't see him being any use."

"He might be able to refer Sean somewhere and let's face it, there's no chance his brothers will be rushing to visit."

"I suppose it's worth a try, although I don't hold out much hope. Hey, if you don't ask, you don't get," Lizzie attempted to be cheerful.

All the while Sean was drifting in and out of sleep, oblivious to the discussion about his welfare.

It took Lizzie almost half an hour to get through to Doctor McLeod.

"He's what?" exploded the physician. "He's taking

what?" The doctor roared down the phone at her. "Have you any concept of how dangerous this is in his condition? I have to tell you, Mrs Coyle, I didn't invest all that time and effort, not to mention the cost to the NHS, for that buffoon of a son of yours to flush it all down the toilet."

"Oh, doctor, there must be something we can do?"

"Normally I would pack him off to rehab and let the stupid beggar take his chances. Sometimes it works, sometimes not, and at least he wouldn't be costing the NHS a fortune. Unfortunately I can't do that because of the complex medication he's been prescribed, and his recent hospital stay means he is still technically my responsibility. I'll refer him to the psychiatrist at Gartnavel Hospital. It may take a couple of days to arrange, but I'll be back in touch."

"Thank you, doctor, thank you," Lizzie wept down the phone.

"Oh, Gerry, we've only got to cope for maybe forty-eight hours and then he'll be admitted."

"What I suggest is, we carry on as normal, don't arouse his suspicions and then when we get word, I'll take him to Gartnavel without telling him where we're going."

"Thank you, son. Don't you worry about Paddy and Michael. I'll make everything alright with them."

Whilst this conversation was taking place, the man in question had divested his mother of the contents of her purse and slipped out the back way. If he remembered rightly there was a young lad dealing at the end of this road, at the junction of Church Street. He had enough cash to score, but he might not have to pay.

As he neared the corner he didn't recognise the dealer. "Hey, gadge, where's the young lad?" he called to the guy strutting up and down at the junction.

"What young lad? This is my pitch and has been for years." This was a slight exaggeration by Tommy Riley.

"Don't talk fucking rubbish, boy. There was a young lad here the last time I checked on this pitch. Don't fuck with me."

Tommy, recognising at once who the big man was, didn't understand why he would be expecting someone other than him to be on the pitch. He was also sure he'd never punted any gear to Sean Coyle. The only person Sean could be referring to was his brother. Had he been around that day? There was something wrong here.

"Do you mean my young brother, Mr Coyle? He sometimes works for me, maybe that's who you mean?" Tommy watched the man intently.

"Yeah, maybe that's who it was," Sean handed over twenty quid to Tommy. "Come on, I've not got all day."

Tommy's gut told him that this geezer had something to do with Billy's disappearance. After all, his brother had only worked for him the once and this fucker had just admitted to having dealt with him. He was shaken, what was he to do? He couldn't tackle a Coyle, that would be like signing his own death warrant. Fumbling about with the money and bags, just as Billy had done on that fateful day, he dropped his merchandise.

"Are you lot all fucking handless?"

As he bent to retrieve his purchases Sean had a blinding flashback as he came face to face with Tommy. The boy. The car. Fuck, where were they? He had to find them. Leaving a dumbstruck Tommy, Sean went tearing back down the road. Shit, the boy was in the car. Where the fuck was the car? The yard, it was in the yard. He had to get there and fast. Thank God Gerry's car was still parked outside his mother's.

Fuck, he remembered now. He'd thrown the boy into the boot of the car. Jesus, he couldn't still be there, could he? He definitely wouldn't still be alive if he was. Surely someone would have found the car by now. That had been months ago. Why had his brothers never said anything? Of course, they still thought he was a ten-year-old and not able to handle it, he reasoned to himself.

Council of War

"There has to be another way," pleaded Diane. "Surely we can keep him with us? Why does he have to be farmed out to people we don't know, people who might not take care of him. And for how long? I'm not happy about this."

"Look, Ma, if that child is here then the Coyles will be parked on our doorstep until they manage to snatch him back, and believe me, they would. You'd need eyes in the back of your head and be on guard twenty-four seven. All it would take would be one small slip and the game would be up. Trust me, there is no other way."

"He's right, Diane, they would sit and wait, knowing at some point someone would make a mistake, and then they would pounce. The pressure on everyone would be enormous," sighed the priest. "There is definitely no other way."

All three were sitting round the dining table recently vacated by Erin, Carol and Amy.

"This way there may well be speculation, but no proof."

"Who fucking died and made you the boss?" Diane snapped at O'Farrell.

"Quit it, Ma. We have to work together on this." Bobby tried to calm his mother down.

"Well, we know who died, don't we, girl?" interjected the priest.

"I don't see why we can't do it legally. We could prove she's an unfit mother and when the courts award him to us, there's nothing Coyle can do."

"Do you really think that would work, Ma? Paddy Coyle has paid no heed to the law for the past twenty-five years, so why would he obey a Spanish court? He'd snatch him. Get real. The child has to disappear and believe me, that will devastate them all. An eye for an eye, as they say."

Bobby Mack hated the Coyles with a vengeance. Because of them his father was dead and his mother had almost been exiled from her own country, not that that was any great loss to Bobby.

"It's all arranged. She'll be arrested outside the club and surprise, surprise, she'll be carrying a significant quantity of drugs, enough to hold her. Of course, the obligatory phone call will be to Bobby, who will, unfortunately, be uncontactable," said the old man.

"But what reason would we give the authorities for the child not being with us?" asked Diane.

"None. Why would we? As far as we're concerned we haven't seen her since the night before when she left to return to the UK with her friend. I'll make sure she goes to the airport. What happens to her after that is no concern of ours. We know nothing about her landing in jail, or why she was carrying drugs. In fact we'll post a reward for the return of the child. It couldn't be simpler."

"I still don't like it. I want to meet with these people."

"No way, not until it's a done deal. No-one but the canon and I know the child's whereabouts. If you don't know, you can't slip up. You have to get her onside, make sure she stays on for at least another week."

"Okay, but you'll have to pay her much more attention, she's not happy with you just now."

"She'll be a lot less happy by the end of the week," Bobby assured the other two. "I'm pretty sure that if she thinks I'm serious about someone else she'll stay. But, as I said, Ma, you need to cement the relationship. Make her think she's family and we're willing to let bygones be bygones."

"Bobby, I'm not sure if I can. I can't forget what they did to us."

"Hey, Mum, get real. My dad and his lordship here," Bobby pointed to the ex-priest, "weren't exactly innocent. They kidnapped Erin and the little girl, Amy, and God knows what they would have done if Coyle hadn't stopped them. So don't pull that old fanny. You don't know if you can do it? You were in it up to your two carat diamond earrings. You knew exactly what business they were in and turned a blind eye because of the lifestyle it afforded you."

For once Diane was almost speechless. She glared at O'Farrell. "When this is over, you and I will settle things between us. I promise you, you'll not drag my son into anything else. This is all your doing!" She stormed out of the room.

"Well, that went better than I expected," chuckled the old man. "She's a fierce woman, your mother."

Clarity

Sean took Lizzie and Gerry completely by surprise when he burst into the front room.

"Jesus, where the hell did you spring from?" Lizzie almost jumped out of her skin.

"What's the panic?" Gerry said, grabbing hold of him. "Calm down, mate."

"I need to go to the yard," Sean blurted out. "I need to go now."

"It'll be closed, man, it's after five. Surely you can wait till the morning? It can't be that urgent."

"It is that urgent," replied Sean.

"Hey, what's up? What's so life-threatening? You've only been back there once since you came out of hospital and you were fine, so surely it can wait till tomorrow?"

Sean realised that it was unlikely he would persuade Gerry to take him and slunk off to his room.

"Jesus, what was all that about? I didn't even know he had gone out."

"God knows, but something spooked him, that's for sure. Maybe you should phone Michael, he's better at getting things out of him."

"I'm not so sure, Michael's been just as off with him as Paddy lately," said Lizzie.

"Look, I'm no psychiatrist, but I think he's remembered something, something bad, and he doesn't know how to handle it. Seriously, I think you should ring one of the boys. Preferably Michael."

Reluctantly, Lizzie had to agree and she picked up the phone. "Hello, son, how are things? Oh, I'm fine, boy. I just need a bit of advice. Yeah, yeah it's about Sean."

"He's not been up to anything. Well, not that I know of, but something has upset him."

"I don't know, that's why I'm phoning you. He was out for a bit this afternoon, not long, and came back in a state."

"No, he just went for a walk, but when he came back he was shaking and I could hardly make out what he was saying."

"No, I don't think he's back on anything. Will you listen to me?"

"As I said, he came back all excited and upset and demanding that Gerry take him to the yard."

"Yes, Gerry was here, he'd just brought Sean home."

"Tell Sean what?"

"Tell him not to worry about the yard, it's taken care of and everything is fine."

"Are you sure? Do I want to know what you're talking about?"

"I didn't think so. And he's to come to the yard after ten tomorrow. Will Gerry come for him?" she gave her co-conspirator a thumbs up. "I'm sure he will."

"Okay, son, I'll go and tell him now."

"Well, that was very mysterious," said Lizzie as she put the phone down. "At least it should put his mind at rest. I'll go and tell him now."

A light knock on his bedroom door brought a curt response from Sean. "Go away, Ma, I'm not feeling too good."

"Okay, son, do you want me to heat some soup for you?"

"No, just leave me."

"Okay, but I've got a message from Michael."

"Michael!" Sean roared. "Michael! Why the hell were you talking to him?"

"I was worried, son. Something had obviously upset you. Anyway, he says the yard is sorted and you're not to worry about it. Your brothers have taken care of things. Now that should make you feel better."

The relief in Sean's voice was almost palpable. "Thanks, Ma, maybe I'll have some soup after all."

His brothers had taken care of things, thank God. As for meeting Michael the next day, well, that depended on how the rest of this day went. If he had nothing to worry about then so be it, he wouldn't worry. It was time he got back in the saddle.

*

As he listened for the door closing, which would signal Gerry's departure, Sean demolished the bowl of steaming soup and the best part of a loaf of bread. For the first time in a long, long time, he felt he was back to his old self. For his family and acquaintances, this didn't bode well.

Holiday

"My God, another day in that woman's company
will have me chucking myself off the bloody
balcony," Erin laughed to her friend. "All she talks
about is Pete, Bobby and Ryan. The king and the two
princes. Honest, it's 'when Pete was alive this . . .'
or 'when Pete was alive that . . .' I'm surprised she's
not had him sanctified. If she's not blurbing on about
Saint Pete then it's about Professor Robert Mack, the
genius. She would have you believe the only difference
between Bobby and Stephen Hawkins is that one is
better looking than the other. Truthfully, you have to
hear it. She actually predicted yesterday that Ryan had
the makings of a lawyer. Honestly, a bloody lawyer!
She could tell by the size of his feet." By this time the
two girls were rolling about hysterically on the bed.

"You're joking, tell me you're joking," Carol was
gasping for breath.

"Honest, you've got to hear the tripe she spouts. I
thought my mother was bad at times, but Jesus, she's

nothing compared to Diane Mack. She's an authority on everything. And whatever Diane wants, Diane has to have. She's determined to have me stay on for a while, but I'm not sure if I can last the remainder of the holiday, never mind adding to it."

"Why don't you let her have the baby today and you come to the beach with us?" ventured Carol.

"You've had a change of heart, have you not? You were the one who insisted she shouldn't be left with him, in case she absconds."

"I know, but let's face it, there's not much chance of her doing that. She's too well known and loads of people have seen you two together. Go on, give yourself a break. In fact, why don't you go and have lunch with Señor Bobby. You've spent virtually no time together since we got here."

"Oh, Bobby's otherwise engaged. He's been with that Swedish masseuse since before we got here."

"Well, all the more reason to get yourself dressed to kill and make him take you to lunch, to discuss Ryan's welfare."

"Do you think Diane will be okay about this?"

"Are you bloody mental?" replied her friend.

Erin went off to get ready and call Bobby.

"Wow, you're looking hot," Bobby complimented her. "Going anywhere special?"

"That depends," said Erin cryptically. "I was hoping you'd take me to lunch, there are a few things I'd like to get sorted before I go back at the end of the week."

"My mother thinks you're going to stay on for a bit."

"I don't think so, Bobby. Two weeks is long enough and there'll be other times. I was going to suggest she looks after him by herself today so we could have time to sort things out."

"I wish you had run this past me yesterday, I've made other plans. Sorry, I can't change them."

"Can't or won't?" she challenged him.

"Both," Bobby replied.

"Come to the beach with us," Carol coaxed her friend.

"I will, but I have to check with Diane first. I'll text you and let you know what I'm doing."

"Of course I'd love to have him all to myself. You go off and have some fun. I'll arrange dinner for around six, so that gives you the whole day. Why don't you arrange to meet up with Bobby?"

"I did suggest it this morning, but he had other plans."

"Damn! It'll be that blasted Swede. She has him besotted. I'm quite worried, I've never seen him like this. He seems to think that she's 'the one'." Diane tormented Erin.

"I hope they'll be very happy together," was Erin's reply.

"It doesn't bother you that he's chasing her? Don't

tell me it doesn't, it's written all over your face every time he looks at you."

Erin's face was scarlet with embarrassment "Whether it bothers me or not, that ship has sailed and I'm not making a fool of myself again."

"You'll lose him. I know my son, and if you are going to stand a chance with him you have to see off the competition. Surely this little chap deserves a daddy? So, you'll have to fight for him and you're not going to win if you're home in Glasgow. You leaving will give her a clear field. But, as you say, that ship has probably sailed." Diane said, turning the knife.

"See you later," she called as Erin left the apartment. Well, that sure as hell hit home, Diane smiled to herself.

In Motion

When Michael walked into the portacabin he was surprised to see Paddy deep in conversation with Sean's babysitter, as the two referred to him in private.

"Gerry," Michael nodded.

"Michael," Gerry reciprocated.

"Gerry's been putting me right on a few things, Michael. It would seem your twin is on the mend, and certainly not the ten-year-old we've been presented with."

"So, how often have you seen him lately and not just relied on third party reports?" said Michael, nodding in Gerry's direction.

"About as many times as you have, pal. C'mon, let's not get into a pissing contest. He's a cute bugger and he knew he was safe enough while we thought he was about as bright as wee Jimmy Crankie," Paddy accused. "I take it he's regained most of his memory?"

"So I believe. I had a call from Ma this morning, didn't I, Gerry?" answered Michael in an equally accusatory tone. "Why hasn't she let on before now?"

"For God's sake, Michael, she'd never betray him, or either of us for that matter."

"I filled Paddy in on the situation, Michael. Sean's way out of control. Your mother has arranged for him to be admitted to Gartnavel in the next few days, but seriously, there's no saying how much damage he could cause between now and then."

"Where is he?" Michael queried.

"At home, as far as I know," Gerry answered.

Paddy, watching his young brother intently, saw the signs that Michael was about to kick off at Gerry. In Paddy's opinion this would not be one of his brother's best ideas. Gerry could, and would, easily take Michael out. This was so unlike his brother, he was always the reasonable one, the least likely to start a ruck. So what was it about Gerry that annoyed him so much? Jealousy, maybe? The twins had been inseparable all their lives and Michael did not like the fact that Gerry and Sean appeared to be mates, but he had to realise that Paddy was paying for the friendship – it wasn't real.

"Okay, Gerry, We'll sort things out. Thanks for stopping by." Paddy stood up to shake his hand. He wanted Gerry out before things escalated.

"That's not all," Gerry remained in situ, shuffling his feet. "I'm not sure how to say this."

251

"Get on with it, man. You don't need to make a bloody drama out everything."

"What?" Gerry didn't appreciate being spoken to in that manner.

"Michael, for Christ's sake, let him get on with it."

"I know I was hired to take over his job and be mates with Sean, but guys, he's fucking psychotic. And the way he's carrying on, somebody is going to do him over."

"Remember, mate, that's our brother you're talking about."

"Well, maybe *you* should remember him from time to time and we wouldn't be having this conversation." The two men squared up to one another.

"Boys! Boys! Calm down."

"Tell him, Paddy. He's trying to mug me off and I've done my best for Sean. You do know everyone's on the lookout for him and the word on the street is that Tommy Riley is convinced Sean had something to do with young Billy's disappearance, and he's going to report it today?"

Gerry knew he had not imagined the look that passed between the two brothers. So it was true, Sean was responsible in some way for the kid's disappearance.

"He's back on the 'brown' and he has no real cash to speak of, so how's he going to feed his habit?"

"Well, it wouldn't take a Philadelphia lawyer to work that out," quipped Paddy. "He'll go on the rob, mugging old ladies for their pension money or turning over small time bagmen for their merchandise. It's not like he hasn't done it before."

"He's talking about setting up a rival crew, which I get the impression he's done in the past. I'm sorry to have to say this, but, he's a real loose cannon and he doesn't seem to have any respect or loyalty for either of you."

"Okay, Gerry, not a word to a living soul about this."

"Goes without saying, boss. Should I pick him up as usual today?

"Yes, just keep him out of mischief and out of sight, by any means you like." Paddy shoved two small packets across the desk to Gerry, "As I said, whatever it takes. I don't want him roaming the streets trying to score."

Gerry took his leave. The stage was set. He would soon give Sean Coyle exactly what was coming to him.

Paddy sat with his head in his hands, a figure of despair. He turned to his brother. "You know what has to be done. I've dreaded this since way before the attack, but honestly I thought that with him losing his memory and getting hurt, I wouldn't have to take those measures, but there's no other way."

"For fuck's sake, Paddy, he's our brother, my other half. I can't stand by and let you murder him, no matter what he's done. How do you know it's not a set up?"

"Who would be setting anything up? The fucking tooth fairy? Michael, it has to be done. He'll bring us all down, and I'm not talking about a couple of years, but a bloody great lump. And I'm telling you, you wouldn't last five minutes. Christ, I'd be hard pushed myself nowadays. He has to be silenced."

"Surely he could be shipped off somewhere?"

"Where? And who with? Because he'd still need to be watched, and if we let him get taken out by a rival firm, we would have to be seen to exact revenge or go under."

"We can't murder our own brother, Paddy. I won't let you. That's exactly what it is, murder. Cain and Abel style. Think what it'll do to Ma and Marie. We have to find another way."

"The wheels are already in motion, mate. I can't let the filth get to him either. Better you don't know the details. If you don't know, you can't tell. The perpetrator himself doesn't know I've just set him up."

Michael twigged immediately that Gerry would be the one to do the deed.

Decisions

Erin strolled along past the marina on her way to meet Carol and Amy, hoping to catch a glimpse of Bobby and his paramour. No matter how much she protested, her feelings for Bobby had grown considerably, rather than diminished as she professed. Life in Marbella really was fabulous, she thought to herself. The weather and the lifestyle were a far cry from Glasgow. But, she had family back home, and even though she and Paddy were having problems at the moment, she couldn't imagine her life without her family in it.

She scanned the busy marina, but there was no sign of the *Lady Di*, Pete's tribute to his wife. The cruiser was already making its way out to sea.

Erin knew she was being played. Diane couldn't give a damn whether she stayed on or not, Ryan was the attraction. The woman would go to any lengths to spend more time with her grandson.

Should she stay longer? There was no pressing

reason for her to return home. Maybe it would teach Paddy a lesson; he would be missing his grandson terribly. On the other hand, what good would it do to stay another week? If Bobby was as keen on this woman as his mother made out, what could she do in such a short time?

As she wandered aimlessly, daydreaming about a life in the sun, her attention was suddenly grabbed by an odd couple making their way along the walkways towards a large cruiser preparing to leave the berth.

She saw an elderly, dark-skinned man in a garish Hawaiian-style shirt and a young boy in similar garb. The man had obviously spent too long in the sun. There was something familiar about him, he definitely reminded Erin of someone. Of course, this must be the person Amy had seen. She could understand the child's mistake. If she didn't know that the canon was deceased and feeding the fishes somewhere off the coast of Africa, she too could have made the same mistake.

"So you escaped the shopping mall?" Carol was pleased to see her friend. "She'll be like a cat with two tails having Ryan all to herself."

"Yes, pleased is an understatement, but it's been a really strange morning."

"What do you mean?"

"Well, Diane has been trying to get me to stay. She's

implying that if I don't, some chick that Bobby has been seeing will capture him and make an honest man of him."

"It'll take more than a ring to do that," quipped Carol.

"She more or less told me that if I return to Glasgow then I can say goodbye to him as Ryan's daddy, because I'll be leaving the field clear."

"I suppose she's got a point, but do you really think Bobby is the type to settle down? 'Cos I don't."

"Truly? I'm not sure. But I do know a week's not going to make any difference and I don't think I could stand being in the same house with her for any length of time without us butting heads. She's far too domineering for me."

"Hmm, I get you. *I* definitely couldn't, but you're far more tolerant than me."

"That's not all. When I was walking along past the marina, I'm sure I saw Amy's gentleman. I definitely did a double-take. There was an old man and probably his grandson, wearing those wild Hawaiian shirts, strolling along the walkway. I could have sworn it was the canon, but this man was either black or really, really, tanned. But he was too far away and I did only get a glimpse."

"Well, you know everyone is supposed to have a doppelgänger, so who knows? I don't want to think about him. Let's face it, if he was alive and living in

Marbella, do you not think Diane Mack would have done something about him? She hates him with a vengeance and she holds him responsible for the mess Pete got into."

"Diane blames everyone except her husband and son for that, but you're right, he's not top of her Christmas list."

Erin was ready for some serious sunbathing and to put the morning's events to the back of her mind. As she spread her towel on the sand, Carol pointed out a figure wandering up to the beachside bar – it was Diane with baby Ryan.

"Christ, she looks as if she could be his mother, not his grandmother."

"Look how she's dressed," Erin whispered. "Who the hell does she think she is?"

Diane, the baby and the pram were all co-ordinated down to the last detail. They looked like they had stepped off the pages of Hello magazine. Diane's was not a hurriedly thrown together outfit; this had been planned. Fabulous though it was, it was a bit sad, thought Erin. Diane might be able to pass as Ryan's mother from a distance, but she wasn't and never would be. Erin shuddered.

Counterplan

It was downright daft to farm her grandson out to a family who were only interested in money. For all they cared they might as well be contracted to mind a dog, not this precious little boy. Why couldn't she hire professionals to ensure his safety, and do it legally? Despite what Bobby and that interfering old sod believed, Paddy Coyle couldn't simply march in and grab Ryan. No, despite their plans, Diane was not planning to give him up without a fight.

As she pondered her dilemma, who did she spot but that bloody girl, her side-kick and Amy, enjoying an iced tea in one of the many cafes along the front. Diane forced a broad smile onto her face and stopped to greet them.

"Fancy meeting you here," the older woman said, pretending to be pleased.

"Small town," Carol smiled at Diane.

"You better believe it. Marbella is basically a village at heart, and nothing gets past the locals."

"Where are you off to, dressed to the nines? Surely that's a bit over the top to be wearing for a walk along the beach?"

"I'm taking this little one to visit his godfather," smiled Diane. "I don't believe he's seen him since you arrived and, by the way, this is not considered to be 'dressed to the nines', simply daywear for ladies here."

Suitably snubbed and put in their place, Diane marched off towards the town hall. Was that laughter she heard, were they laughing at her? She'd soon wipe the smile off their faces. This visit was not without a purpose.

"Buenos Dias, Señora Mack," the receptionist greeted Diane.

"Buenos Dias, Rosa." Diane was a frequent visitor to the town hall and most of the officials and admin staff knew her.

"El Alcalde is waiting for you, if you'd like to come with me?" The young girl showed Diane and her charge into the ornate offices.

"Ah, Diane. Buenos dias, my dear. And who do we have here?" asked the mayor, tickling Ryan under his chin.

"Hasn't he grown since you last saw him?" Diane and the mayor spent the next ten minutes or so exchanging pleasantries and sipping tea.

"Now, down to business, my dear. I have checked

out the position regarding the legal guardianship of the boy and it would seem that Bobby is named on the UK birth certificate so there is no problem there. However, the matter of his mother being unfit is more delicate and extremely difficult to prove. Spain, like most Catholic countries, believes in the sanctity of motherhood and it is very unusual for the father to be awarded custody. Also, it would be almost impossible to be completed quickly.

"But can it be done, Julio? For the right price?"

"Diane, this is not a case of just throwing money around. I can help in most municipal cases but this is a different ballgame altogether. Adoptions follow very strict procedures. At the very earliest it would take maybe three, possibly four months to complete the paperwork. Then there is a period of time to allow the participants to, as you say, change their minds. So, even with my help and backing we are looking at six months from now."

"That's no good, my friend, we have to work more quickly than that."

"I must say, I was surprised at what has been going on. Señor Coyle and his family seemed to be very close and the child looks well enough. But if, as you say, the girl is drinking and taking drugs, then yes she is not fit. Perhaps you should speak to her parents."

"You don't know that family, Julio. They are without a doubt the most powerful and dangerous family in Scotland and if it was thought for a moment that their name was being dragged in the mud, God knows what would happen."

"You can be assured I will do everything in my power, Diane, but unfortunately it will take time."

"That's the one thing we don't have."

Although disappointed at the outcome of her meeting, Diane was still sure that dumping the boy on an unknown family was not the way forward. It was all the more imperative for Erin to stay on for longer.

Legal or not, Diane had no intention of giving up her grandchild to anyone.

Mystery

Since day one Gerry had kept Paddy up to speed on his brother's condition and behaviour. How much of that information Paddy passed on to the rest of his family, Gerry had no idea. But from Michael's reaction this morning, it was clear he didn't know a great deal. However the news of Sean's involvement in the disappearance of young Billy certainly had not come as a surprise to either man. It was obvious that Sean had some involvement in the mystery, but Gerry was no nearer solving it than the whole of the Greater Glasgow Police Force.

Gerry's main concern was that the Coyles could be planning on fitting him up for the crime. No way would that happen. He'd already played patsy for this family and he wouldn't be doing it a second time. Should there be any likelihood of a fit-up, he'd take every bugger down with him.

He was taking his weekly delivery to Dumbarton, but for the first time ever Gerry examined the package, carefully opened it and extracted a quantity of the contents.

When he arrived at 28 Lomond Crescent, Sean was waiting. "Where the fuck have you been? I was expecting you half an hour ago."

"Jesus, Sean, do you want me to clock in and out, or maybe run to the number 23 timetable? I'm here when I arrive, not a minute sooner or later," joked Gerry. "What's up with you, anyway? Somebody rattle your cage this morning?"

"I'm fine, don't you worry about me," said Sean, whose behaviour belied his words. He was considerably agitated and belligerent.

"Look, if you're in one of your moods you can fuck right off. I'm not pussyfooting about today because you got out of bed on the wrong side. So make up your mind. Are we going to have a pleasant day or am I dropping you here and now?"

Sean glowered and mumbled, "I'll be fine, just a bit of a headache."

"Sure it's a headache, mate? You've not been up to anything you shouldn't?"

"Like what?" challenged Sean.

"Like maybe setting up a new crew and excluding me?"

"New crew, what new crew are you talking about?" Sean seemed totally bewildered. He had obviously forgotten the conversation from the day before. "Are you trying to get me into bother? Why would I be going to put a new crew together? Why would I go against my brothers?"

"Hey, don't shoot the fucking messenger. It was you who was spouting off the other day. You were certainly on some kind of recruiting campaign, so if it's off you better hope your brothers don't get to hear about it."

"Don't know what you're on about." Sean shut his eyes and settled back in the passenger seat.

It was the bang that woke Sean up. "What the fuck? What's up, Gerry?"

"This fucking Herbert shot the lights," Gerry got out, hauled the other driver out of his vehicle and had him by the throat over the bonnet of the car.

"It was my fault, honest it was my fault. Sorry, mate," the other driver pleaded with Gerry, who had now realised the predicament he was in. He had to get off his mark before the boys in blue arrived. He certainly didn't want to hang around with his consignment in the boot.

"Look, mate, I'm in a hurry. Call it bump for bump, but remember, I've got your number, so if you make bother I'll be paying you a visit."

Back in the car Sean was twittering on about Gerry's driving, about him making trouble and generally being a pain in the arse.

"Will you shut the fuck up?" Gerry roared at his passenger. "I've just about had enough of your blabbering. Do you ever ask yourself why it's only me you ever see? None of your old mates come about.

Your brothers can't stand to be in the same room as you. Do you never ask why?"

"Don't talk shit, man. I've got plenty mates and my brothers have business to take care of."

"Yeah, yeah," said Gerry, suddenly realising he knew the street they had turned into. His old address. Memories came flooding back and it was difficult to hold things together.

He turned to Sean and asked, "Do you know my surname, Sean?"

The other man looked blankly at him. "What's this, a fucking quiz? Why the fuck would I be interested in what your name is? You're a lackey, nothing more. Here at my beck and call."

The colour drained from Gerry's face. "Do you know what street we are on, Sean?"

"Oh, fuck, it's *Mastermind* now. No. I don't know what fucking street I'm on. Wait a minute, it's Munro Street. This used to be my stomping ground back in the day."

"I used to live here, with my wife and kids."

"Dump you when you were inside, did she? Get a better offer?"

Gerry had taken as much as he could. This was not the time or place, but he was close, very, very close.

Extension

The last few days of Erin's stay flew past in a whirl. Diane appeared to be devastated that she had been unable to persuade the young mum to stay. She had not however, accounted for her son's charm and charisma. On the day before her departure, Bobby took Erin out to lunch to, as he put it, finalise arrangements.

"I'm really going to miss you both," oozed Bobby, taking hold of Erin's hand. They were in a quiet little restaurant overlooking the harbour in Puerto Banus.

"I don't know why, we've hardly spent more than an hour in each other's company since I arrived," said Erin. "Us being here has certainly not interfered with your social life in the slightest."

"But Erin, what was the point? I've always known you were going back to Glasgow. You were never staying here permanently so I wasn't putting myself through all that again."

"All what again?"

Bobby knew she was hooked; it was time to reel her

in. "All the pain. I was heartbroken, you must have known."

"Pain? What pain? You've certainly not been declaring undying love up until now."

"Well, this situation hasn't exactly been conducive to romance, has it? Every time I came across your father, he smacked me in the mouth. It was a bit hard not to take it personally."

"Maybe so," she smiled, "but you went out of your way to upset him."

"For God's sake, Erin! He murdered my father. What did you want me to do, welcome him with open arms?"

"Pete wasn't exactly an innocent in all this. He and Canon O'Farrell held me and Amy prisoner. God knows what could have happened."

"Look, I didn't bring you here to go over old ground. Let's try to put all that behind us. I know it won't be easy, but we can try for the boy's sake. How about staying another week?"

"No, I don't think so. Maybe it's better we leave now and come back in the spring."

"But that's six months away. If you stay, I'll take time off work and spend it with you and Ryan."

"What about your big blonde piece? Won't she be a bit put out?"

"Probably, but so what? Go on, stay. Just a week and we'll see how things go."

"I'll think about it."

He knew she would stay; she was merely playing hard to get. It was a shame really, thought Bobby. She was a lovely girl and it was sad what the future held in store for her. But, an eye for an eye, and Bobby had sworn he'd take revenge for his family.

The girls checked out of the hotel the following morning and made their way to the airport.

"Are you sure you'll be okay?"

"I'll be fine, no matter what, and I'll be back next weekend. Its Granny Lizzie's birthday and my mum would skin me alive if I missed it."

"Okay, remember to let your folks know what's happening and I'll see you next week. Good luck with Diane."

"I'll need it," smiled Erin. "Say bye-bye, Ryan," and the baby extended a chubby little hand.

The apartment was empty. Bobby had some things to take care of and would be back around lunchtime. Erin had no idea where Diane was.

Pleased to have time with Ryan on her own, Erin donned her bikini and made her way to the pool. There was only one other sun-seeker, a young English girl who, she discovered, stayed on the floor below Diane.

The two chatted for a while until a figure appeared on the balcony, summoning Erin to lunch.

"Nice meeting you," said Erin, taking leave of her new friend.

"You too, see you around," replied Sophie. "I try to get a bit of sun most mornings around this time, so I'll maybe catch you again."

As a rule Ryan was a cheery, good-natured little soul, but that day, whether he was teething or perhaps had had a bit too much sun, he certainly wasn't a happy bunny. He grouched most of the afternoon and Bobby, unused to the disruption, was just as grouchy as his son.

"Heavens, I wonder if there's time to catch a flight home tonight, if this is how it's going to be?" moaned Erin.

"Don't be ridiculous," snapped Bobby. "Can't you give him something to shut him up?"

"He's just a bit off-colour and wants his mummy. I think we'll have to put off going out this evening. I can't leave him like this."

"He'll be fine with my mum. We can't put tonight off, I've arranged something special."

"Let's get something straight right now," Erin stated. "If he's not well, I'm going nowhere. I'm sure your mum would do a great job, but he's my son and that's an end to it."

As she suspected, Bobby went into a monumental sulk. Jesus, she thought, it's like having two kids.

Bobby was annoyed, to say the least. His plan depended on Erin going missing on the first evening of her extended stay. It would be too risky and entail a monumental cover-up if she was to be seen the following day. Whatever it took, he had to get her to the club tonight.

The little boy eventually settled for the evening and with great reluctance Erin agreed that she would accompany Bobby to the club, on the strict proviso that if Ryan woke or was fretting then Diane would ring her at once.

Erin had not been out clubbing for a long, long time and as soon as she heard the music she hit the dance floor.

He's in a funny mood, she thought, watching Bobby at the bar. I wonder what the surprise is. She made her way back to the VIP area where Bobby was waiting with her drink.

"Could you get me some water, please? I don't really want to drink in case I have to go back for Ryan."

"Jesus, Erin, forget him. He'll be fine with my mother. She knows what she's doing."

As usual Bobby was at the centre of a crowd, everyone wanted to be in his circle. Absolutely no-one paid attention to the girl in the blue dress, stunning though she was.

"I think I'm ready to go now," she announced.

"Okay, one more drink, then we'll hit the road."

Having expected an argument, Erin was pleasantly surprised, and one more drink was fine with her – it wouldn't have been if she'd seen what he spiked it with.

Birthday Girl

The Coyles had never been big on birthdays or parties. They somehow brought the worst out in them. But this was different; this was for Lizzie. Lizzie, who had only ever celebrated her special day opening a bottle of sherry with her old pal, Theresa. Lizzie didn't hold with drink at any other time. This was due to the years of poverty she had suffered because of her late husband's love of a refreshment or two. But this was different, there had been invitations sent and acceptances received.

"You know, Theresa, I never thought I'd ever be R.S.V.P.ed, did you?" she asked her friend.

"No, Lizzie, I can't say I ever thought you'd ever be R.S.V.P.ed," answered her friend, the sherry beginning to kick in. "Will I ever be R.S.V.P.ed, do you think?"

"I don't think so, hen. No, I don't think so. But you can share mine."

"Can I, Lizzie? That's awfy good of you. By the way, what is an R.S.V.P.?"

"Fucked-if-I-know, but it sounds good, pal. Here, I don't think we should have any more or we'll be in no fit state to meet them all."

"Hey, Bridget," Lizzie called to her daughter-in-law as she arrived to collect the party girls. "Where's Erin and my bonnie wee great-grandson? Don't tell me she's still in Spanish Spain, living with those bloody heathens?"

"Her flight's been delayed, Lizzie. They'll be here soon." Bridget didn't actually know. She'd been trying relentlessly to contact her daughter for the past four or five days, with no luck. Every call went straight to voicemail. The last communication she'd received from her daughter had been a text saying Carol and Amy were on their way home and she, Erin, had decided to stay on.

Carol had assured her that Erin was definitely coming home for Lizzie's birthday party. It had been the last thing she'd said to Carol, but it was now five o'clock on the day of the party and there was no sign of her. There was only one more flight that day, arriving at seven o'clock. Surely they'd be on that one?

The private room at the hotel was decked out with bunting and balloons. Almost a hundred of Lizzie's family, friends and neighbours were there, scrubbed and dressed in their finest to celebrate her special day. The only ones missing were Sean and the errant Erin and Ryan.

"Where's your charge, Gerry? Why is he not here?" Paddy asked him.

"I went to collect him as arranged, but the doors were locked and the lights out. I presumed he had tagged along with your mother."

"Bugger him," said the Big Man. "If he's sulking at home, we can enjoy the party without worrying about him all night. Forget him, mate, let's go and have a drink."

All Alone

You're only a lackey. The words went round and round in Gerry's head. How dare he? How fucking dare he call him that? That psychotic low-life junkie had the nerve to call him a lackey. Gerry didn't know how he'd managed to stay calm, how he had stopped himself from strangling the breath out of Sean Coyle. Well, he knew one thing: he wouldn't be taking any more of his crap.

The man before him was clad in an Armani suit, a Turnbull and Asser shirt, pure silk tie and custom-made Italian shoes. He certainly had the look of a wealthy man about town. But it was all a sham. The best clobber in the world couldn't disguise a junkie.

"What you doing here so early? I'm not ready to go yet." Sean had questioned Gerry. He was annoyed that Gerry had pitched up half an hour before the arranged time. He'd counted on being alone to sort himself out, but this smartarse had spoiled his plans.

"Wait in the car, Gerry, till I call you."

"You're having a giraffe. Since when did you give the orders? Tell me, why exactly do you want rid of me?" Gerry picked up a bag from the bedside table.

"Is it this you need?" he waved the bag under Sean's nose.

"Give me that back! It's fuck all to do with you what I do." Sean lunged at Gerry who dropped the bag, giving him the opportunity to switch the smack Paddy had provided with pure, uncut and one hundred percent lethal heroin.

Sean was beyond hiding his antics. As he prepared himself his fix, he listened to Gerry jabbering on. Why the fuck could he not just piss off and leave him alone? What was it to do with him, that Gerry's kids had been taken off him? As for knowing his surname, as far as he was concerned, it was cunt. Laughing at his own joke, Sean was almost ready, ecstasy was minutes away.

"You still here? What the fuck are you on about?"

"Answer me a question, Sean, and then I'll leave you in peace."

"Fuck off, muppet."

"Just one question, mate."

"I'm not your mate, I'm your employer," Sean snarled at the man standing over him. "For fuck's sake, if it'll get rid of you, go on."

"You told me when I first took you on the deliveries that you used to collect in Munro Street, but you couldn't remember who from."

"Aye, that's right, I did. I remember now. A wee blonde thing, couple kids, old man inside, bit of a goer, if I remember rightly."

Gerry smacked him straight in the mouth. A bit of a goer, was she? He just couldn't help himself and although Sean was panicking, trying to protect his gear, that sly, cunning look had passed across his face.

"For fuck's sake, don't tell me she was your wife? It was you she was cheating on? To think I had a go on that myself. Christ, man, you're better off without her. She was a proper little slapper."

Gerry could feel the bile rising in his throat. He wanted to hammer this excuse for a man to a pulp. He could barely hold himself in check, but he had to do things the way he had planned. That way there was no comeback, no way the Coyles could set him up.

"Goodbye, Sean, I'll see you in the next world."

What the fuck was he talking about, the mad bastard?

Gerry watched Sean out the corner of his eye and saw him insert the needle, the brown liquid flowing down into the syringe. Within seconds Sean's eyes were popping in terror. He desperately tried to draw the liquid back into the syringe, but it was too late.

In Trouble

Erin felt strange as they wove their way through the packed club. She was having difficulty focusing and she was desperate to reach the exit. If it hadn't been for Bobby supporting her, she wouldn't have made it.

"There's something wrong, Bobby. I feel awful." She couldn't hear herself speak. God, was she losing her voice again?

Outside the club Bobby signalled to the two carabinieri patrolling the area. The officers bundled Erin into a police van and drove off. But the situation didn't go unnoticed. Watching the scene unfold was Sophie, the young girl Erin had met at the swimming pool earlier that day.

"Goodness, what was all that about?" asked one of her friends.

"I'm not sure, but I know she's staying with the Macks, so why on earth would they have her arrested?" Sophie replied.

"That's weird, but hey, it's nothing to do with us and you know what the Spanish cops are like." The girls made their way into the club.

God almighty, where was she? She felt awful: her head was pounding and her thirst was indescribable. She looked around. She was in a small, bare room with bars on the window, containing only a bed frame and a blanket, which, it seemed, she shared with a million cockroaches. In the corner was a filthy, disgusting toilet. The smell was overpowering. The clanging of metal doors and the shouting from other inhabitants confirmed she was in a Spanish jail, but why?

The door opened and a large, butch, female officer handed her a mug of brown liquid and some hard bread.

"Why am I here? What have I done?" Erin pleaded with the woman.

"No English," was the response.

"Get me someone who can speak English."

But the officer merely shrugged and closed the door with a clang.

Although Erin desperately tried to recall what had happened in the club and how she had ended up in prison, all she could remember was telling Bobby she was ready to call it a night and, vaguely, leaving the club feeling sick. Then nothing. She'd felt like this only once before, when the canon had drugged her and Amy to hold them captive. But why would someone want to do that to her now? She was no threat to anyone. They'd got the wrong person. Bobby would come and get her. Shit! What if he'd been arrested too? Maybe that's why she was here – because she had been with him. Damn, she couldn't think straight. Ryan, what about Ryan? Diane would take good care of him, he'd be okay.

Her head was all over the place. Were prisoners allowed to make a phone call? Should she call Bobby or her dad? If Bobby had been arrested then there was no point in calling him but her dad was so far away. She'd call Diane, she would sort things out. But how to get the number? It wasn't likely they'd give her back her mobile phone. What about a lawyer? What was she being charged with?

At that moment the same butch officer came back into her cell and, snapping handcuffs around Erin's wrists, led her out to the reception area. Panic was beginning to rise in Erin's chest. What the hell did they think she had done? The officer pushed her into line with other prisoners who were jostling and shouting at one another. No sign of Bobby, so either he hadn't been arrested or he had been taken to a different station. Two prisoners at the head of the line began scrapping. Spanish discipline was by means of a metal truncheon.

The prisoners were bundled into the back of a meat wagon and driven a short distance to the courthouse.

On arrival they were housed in a single cell: five men and three women crammed in together.

One huge brute of a man relieved himself where he stood, as soon as the cell door closed. The stream of hot, stinking urine splashed everyone, but no-one uttered a word.

The morning dragged on and on. The heat in the small, windowless room grew more and more unbearable. One by one the detainees were ushered into court and dealt with accordingly. Just before noon it was her turn. How the hell did anyone know her name? She had been unconscious when she arrived and no-one had taken any particulars. And as far as she knew she had had no I.D. on her. Before she entered the courtroom, a young man rushed in and introduced himself as the court attorney assigned to her. He spoke virtually no English, but he did however, manage to convey that she had been caught in possession of class A drugs during a routine stop and search. He thought it was unlikely she would be given bail, but he would try.

The situation was becoming more and more incredible each moment that passed. Erin was absolutely terrified and had no idea what was going on. The proceedings were conducted wholly in Spanish with no translator. Why would the police think she would be carrying drugs, and where had Bobby Mack been when this was going on? Erin had been around clubs and drugs most of her life and whilst she had never been involved, she was no mug. She'd been set up and it could only have been the Macks, but why?

Her appearance in court was bewildering; it was over in a flash and she hadn't understood a word of what was going on. It looked like the attorney had been paid to make sure she was remanded in custody.

It was all over in minutes. The judge, speaking in broken English, informed Señorita Coyle she had been charged with possession of class A narcotics, resisting arrest and assault. Due to the severity of the charges she would be remanded in custody and her passport held till her trial.

As she was being led out of the court room she was astonished to see a familiar face, but it couldn't be? There in the public gallery, was the spitting image of Canon O'Farrell, but this man smiling at her was black. How could that be?

Farewell

Gerry waited with Sean until the drugs had taken effect and it was all over. He left him slumped on his bed with the syringe still in his arm. He locked Sean's bedroom door and both back and front doors from the inside and left number 28 through the dead man's bedroom window. Thank God Theresa and most of the neighbours were at the party or he would never have got away unnoticed. She was a nosey old mare, but he was out and away on his toes, unseen.

The party was in full swing when Gerry slipped in. Paddy's acceptance that his brother was just being awkward as usual gave him the alibi he needed. There was no way he could be connected to Sean's demise and, having succeeded in his mission to pay Sean Coyle back for the havoc he'd wrecked on his family, he should have been more than a little pleased with himself, but not so.

Gerry had thought he would feel satisfied at

having achieved his goal and disposed of his nemesis in revenge for what had happened to his wife and children. He had promised himself in prison that he would avenge her death when he'd received the news that his Moira had taken her own life.

Why? He'd asked himself a million times and the answer was always the same: Sean Coyle. The vow that he would personally finish Coyle off had sustained him through his sentence. It had been the sole reason Gerry got out of bed in the morning. Now that he had accomplished his mission there was nothing left for him. If anything, he felt even more desolate than before. Sean's passing didn't bring back his beautiful wife and kids. What motive had he now for facing the day? Having taken a life, even that of a low life bastard like Sean Coyle, filled Gerry with unassailable guilt.

His body was found three days later by his landlady. He was lying peacefully on his bed, clutching photographs of a woman and children that she took to be his wife and family; a little group of happy, smiling people. Funny, she had never taken him to be a druggie, but then, you never know.

Family Problems

The partygoers returned home more than a little merry after a great night. Lizzie had to admit to herself she'd been relieved that Sean had not turned up. Like Paddy, she would have spent all evening on tenterhooks, hoping he would behave and not make a show of himself.

His television was still playing and she knocked gently on his bedroom door, "You alright, son? Can I get you anything, a drink, maybe?" But there was no reply, as was often the case. Lord, he could be a right ignorant devil.

"Please yourself, you missed a grand 'do', but I'll tell you all about it in the morning." And off the birthday girl went to bed.

Party or no party, Lizzie was up at the crack of dawn for her cup of tea, and off to mass. There was no sign of Sean, but his routine was erratic, to say the least. He was either up before her or he would sleep until midday and this morning it was obviously the latter.

Hopefully she would get some news from the doctor later today and they'd get him sorted out. No matter how hard it could be sometimes, he was still her son and she would do everything in her power to help him.

But what about her granddaughter? She was quite cross with Erin. Imagine the little madam choosing the Macks over her real family! Bridget had maintained the facade all night that her plane had been delayed. Rubbish. That wee pal of hers had looked like a constipated hen, jumping every time the door opened. There was something amiss and she intended to find out the reason, as soon as she got home. You'd think the older they got, the less worry her family would be. Not hers.

There was still no sign of Sean when she returned home from mass and to her surprise, she had almost a full house for breakfast. It was mid-morning before she had served and cleared up after her visitors and there was still no sign of Sean.

"You awake, son? Do you want me to do you a bit of breakfast?" No reply.

"The big eejit's in the huff," she muttered to herself. Well, bugger him.

She intended to visit Paddy and Bridget and find out exactly what was going on, so Sean could fend for himself. "There's a plate in the fridge, you just need to heat it up. I'll back around tea-time," she said to the closed bedroom door and off she went.

Bridget was on the phone when she arrived and Paddy had a face like thunder.

"She's an inconsiderate, spoilt monkey," stormed Lizzie's eldest son, "and it's entirely your fault," he pointed at his wife.

"And how exactly do you work that out?" She shouted back at him. "She's never not stayed in touch before, never. There's something up."

"What did Carol have to say?" Lizzie questioned the parents.

"Apparently she saw them off at the airport and was going to spend the week with the Macks. Her last words being that she'd be back for your party. I got a text from her saying the same, but nothing since. I was none too pleased that she didn't get in touch for the rest of the week, but to be honest, I've been so busy I let it go."

"See! That's what I mean. She just comes and goes as she pleases, not a bloody thought for anyone else, and now she's taken up with those Spanish fuckers. We'll be lucky if we see her this side of Christmas."

"Don't be so bloody stupid, and mind your language."

"Go to hell." Paddy stormed off out of the sitting room.

"My God, he's certainly got his dander up," said Lizzie.

"He won't admit it, but he's worried sick. I'm going to find Diane's number and give her a ring."

"Good idea. I've left his lordship still in bed, obviously sulking because nobody came back for him last night."

"Serves him right. If he's going to act like a ten-year-old then he can expected to be treated like one. Anyway, it was better without him. You know, this bloody family gets worse as the years go by."

"I was just thinking that this morning," said Lizzie.

Bridget spoke into the receiver. "Can I speak with Erin please?"

"Well, Señora Diane then," Bridget addressed the person at the other end.

"When will she be home?"

"Can you tell Erin to phone her mother?"

"What do you mean she's not there?"

"What time yesterday? Of course she's there. Look, just get someone to call me. It's Señora Coyle, Erin's mother," Bridget replaced the receiver.

"What was all that about?"

"The housekeeper says Erin's not there, that she went home. She's gone."

"Gone where?"

"Jesus, Lizzie, *I* don't know."

"Don't shout at me, it's not my fault," the old lady was getting quite agitated.

"Sorry, I'm a bit worried. It's not like her and certainly not when she has the wee chap with her. Let's have some tea and we'll phone again later."

The two women went off to the kitchen and spent the next hour going over the previous night's events.

Eventually Lizzie informed Bridget, "It's about time I made tracks. You'll call me when you hear anything?"

"Of course I will. Don't worry, it'll be something straightforward. She probably missed her flight. Whatever the reason, I want her back now. I'm really missing her and Ryan."

"I know, lass, I know. Do you think Paddy would give me a lift home? I'm feeling my age today."

"Of course he will. I'll take you if you want?"

"No dear, I want a word with Paddy and he can't walk away if he's driving."

"I take it he's not going to like what you've got to say?"

"No, possibly not, but it's something he needs to know."

"Bye, Lizzie. I'll ring you later."

"Look, Ma, I'm not coming in if he's in the house," Paddy was adamant.

"Please, son. I have to get him ready to go to hospital. I've had a message from Dr McLeod. Sean can be admitted any time after five. I can't do this on my own and Gerry's not answering my calls."

"He's maybe recovering from last night, he certainly tied one on," laughed Paddy. "I never had him down as a drinker, but by God he certainly kept pace with the best of them."

Lizzie heard Sean's television still blaring away as she opened the front door. Surely he was out of bed by now? She knocked on his bedroom door, calling his name, but there was still no response.

"Paddy, he's not answering and the door is still locked."

"Sean!" shouted Paddy, hammering on the bedroom door. "This is fucking ridiculous. He's like a fucking teenager. Sean, open this bloody door at once or I'll break it down."

Paddy put his shoulder to the door and there was the sound of splintering wood. Mother and son gained entry to the bedroom.

"Oh my God. Oh my God, Paddy. He's been lying here all day and me thinking he was just sulking. God above, maybe we could have saved him."

"There's nothing you could have done, Ma. He's been gone a while." Paddy had spotted the syringe and surmised that Sean had probably died the previous evening: his brother was dressed to go out.

"I'll phone the doctor, we have to report this." Paddy knew that Dr McPhail would do the necessary paperwork for them. No need for post mortems or the like. It was plainly obvious what had taken Sean Coyle. The evidence was there for all to see.

Paddy was bemused; he was sure that the gear he'd given Gerry hadn't been pure enough to kill Sean. In fact, he knew it wasn't, but this was no time for quibbling. He had to get the death certificate signed and the funeral arranged as soon as possible.

"Bridget, get over here as quick as you can. We have a problem. Our Sean's overdosed and my mother's in a right state."

"Never mind Erin for the minute, we'll sort her out after. She'll be fine, she's probably clubbing and partying with that idiot. I just hope they're taking good care of my grandson."

"Look, this is no time to be arguing, just get yourself here. I need to get hold of Michael and Marie before word gets out. You know what this place is like, the jungle drums are beating already."

Dr McPhail arrived before Bridget and was consulting with Paddy as she entered the house. Lizzie was distraught, holding her son close, rocking gently to and fro and keening quietly to him. It was the saddest sound Bridget had ever heard. All of Sean's misdemeanours were now forgotten. He was once again Lizzie's boy, the cheeky imp who, with his twin, had scoured the streets of Glasgow for scrap to help keep the family afloat. Everyone had loved him and his twin brother back in the day. He had just lost his way for a while.

Behind Closed Doors

Shivering in the ninety degree heat, Erin Coyle stood naked in a line of women being checked into the infamous Alhaurin de la Torre in Malaga. She was in some sort of reception area and each woman in the line was being intimately searched. They were being subjected to this humiliation in full view of several prisoners, officers and amidst a barrage of catcalls and jeers from the other prisoners.

Erin was totally freaked out. There was no way this was going to happen to her. As two officers approached her, the Erin Coyle who had entered the facility disappeared. She knew this was make or break time. If she showed any sign of weakness she was dead meat. She knew no Spanish and few of her new chums seemed to have much English, so she had no idea what was being said. Her voice was also failing her, as it did from time to time when she became stressed – and life didn't come much more stressful than this. As the officers approached, Erin stood straight and upright, clenching her legs tightly shut.

The standoff lasted barely minutes. The officers were well used to uncooperative prisoners and they came across this defiance on a daily basis. However, they had not reckoned on Erin Coyle's Celtic nature: a mixture of temper, embarrassment and pain. Erin took a mighty swipe at the officer closest to her and, just like her father's signature punch, she floored the woman.

She was bundled, still naked, into an isolation cell with no amenities except a blanket and a bucket. This was barbaric, but thanks to her behaviour she'd already made a name for herself.

If she was going to survive, she had to get used to living like this. For three days she endured her punishment. With nothing except the thin ragged blanket to cover her, she was stifling hot during the day and freezing at night, with only vermin to keep her company. Possibly due to dehydration or sheer terror she had begun to hallucinate. Twice, she was convinced her Uncle Sean had visited her and he seemed anxious to tell her something. Erin, of course, had no idea that Sean had passed away on the first night he appeared to her.

With no-one to talk to and only the briefest contact with the officers who brought food and water, Erin had plenty of time to think. Her infatuation with Bobby was over. She could only assume that her present dilemma had been engineered in revenge for his father's death.

But to deprive his child of its mother was unforgivable. When she got out of here, and she would, she'd make sure that neither he nor that scheming bitch of a mother of his, would ever set eyes on the child again. She also decided that when she returned home she was moving out. It was time she stood on her own two feet. If she was going to endure this lot, she certainly could manage her own life back home. However dreadful this situation was, not for one moment did she doubt that Paddy would come for her.

In the meantime she had to stand up for herself. She gave thanks for the years of karate training that Paddy had made her attend since she was a nipper. In his eyes being Paddy Coyle's daughter was a dangerous occupation. How right he was, but she was confident she could hold her own against most would-be attackers, as the prison officer she'd smacked would attest to.

On the afternoon of the third day she was brought before the governor. Naked, with only the threadbare blanket protecting her modesty, she was still defiant. The governor was not impressed. She had seen thousands of Erin Coyles over the years and in her opinion this one was nothing new.

"You are a very foolish young woman, Coyle. If you think you can break the system, one which has been in existence for over a hundred years, you will endure a very unpleasant stay with us. You are a remand prisoner and would normally be housed in the low security wing. However, because of your behaviour, and to ensure the safety of my officers, you will be held in the main wing of this facility. But to ensure your safety, you will share a cell with a long term prisoner who speaks English. She is an American who, like you, was caught smuggling drugs."

"I have not been convicted of smuggling."

"No, but you will be," replied the governor.

"I was set up. I'm innocent."

"Of course you are. All the women housed in this correction facility are innocent. But until we can prove one way or another, please listen to what your cellmate, Cindy, says and you will not leave here in a wooden box. Do you understand me?"

"Yes, Ma'am," her bravado was beginning to wane. "I need to find out about my baby and contact my family. They don't know where I am."

"You will be allowed one phone call, but not an international call, so you had better think of some Spanish resident who can assist you. Meanwhile," the governor nodded to the officer present, "take Coyle to her cell. And remember what I said, this prison is a very dangerous place."

As Erin walked back through the compound, she drew the attention of many of the inmates who reacted with jeers, catcalls and ribald comments. Erin, thankfully, could not translate them, but she knew exactly what they meant.

*

Her cellmate was Cindy Fairchild, a petite blonde who hailed from Texas, serving ten years for drug smuggling. Cindy had been a naïve eighteen-year-old who had been groomed by some guy twice her age, and who she still believed would be waiting on the outside for her.

This is who I've to take heed of? Erin thought to herself. She must be as mad as a box of frogs. Shit. I'm doomed if *she's* my best hope.

Although Cindy seemed crazy, she knew everything that was going down on the wing and, small as she was, she could take on all-comers. Everyone on the wing, prisoners and officers alike, liked Cindy. She never complained, never caused trouble, was always ready for a laugh and could procure anything.

Although she didn't know it yet, Erin Coyle had just won first prize in the prison lottery.

Finally allowed to shower and dress, Erin was accompanied to her new cell by the same prison officer she had thumped when she arrived. The woman maintained a stream of vitriolic threats on the journey, but of course Erin had no idea what was being said, which was just as well.

Her introduction to Cindy wasn't much better. The officer pushed Erin into the cell with such force that she fell sprawling into the small room, knocking over all of her cellmate's possessions.

"For God's sake," shouted the little blonde bomber, pushing Erin with equal force so that she fell backwards and knocked over the prison officer.

"Shit, I'll probably go straight back to solitary for this."

"No, you'll be okay," came a genuine Texan drawl. "Wanna start over?" the girl held out her hand to Erin.

"We don't have much choice, do we?"

"Oh, we have a choice okay, but I don't think you're gonna like the alternative. So, we gonna start over again, missy?" Again, she held out her hand.

Unbelievably Erin was laughing at her companion. "For a tiddler you've certainly got gumption."

"Gumption? What the hell language are you speaking, girl? They said you spoke English."

"I do. This is the Scottish version," Erin smiled at her.

Hidden Treasure

His plan couldn't have gone any better. Bobby had spiked Erin's last cocktail with a shot of Rohypnol, the infamous date rape drug. For someone like Bobby, obtaining this drug was as easy as buying sweeties.

As soon as he had seen the drug beginning to take effect, he had led Erin outside where two police officers were already waiting. To any observer it would simply be a case of another drunk being ejected from the club, nothing unusual in that. He had paid off enough people to ensure his plan was carried out to the letter and that she would remain in custody for the foreseeable future. But, just in case there was a hiccup and should something go amiss, it was imperative he hid the boy immediately.

"Bobby! Leave him till the morning, you can't wake him now, it's the middle of the night."

"He's going now, Ma. I'm well aware of your plans. Did you really think Munozo wouldn't tell me what was going on? Especially since I'm the boy's father. So go back to bed and let me deal with this."

"Surely there's some other way, Bobby? We can't let him go to strangers. What if they don't treat him properly? Your father would have a fit if he knew what you were proposing."

"My father would agree entirely with me. I vowed to get even with Coyle and there is no better way than this. The boy won't come to any harm and they're being well paid to look after him."

"You can't guarantee that. He should be with us, we should do it legally."

"Enough! It's all in hand. I promise it's only for a while. As soon as it's possible, I'll bring him home."

"Well, in that case I'm coming with you."

"We've been over this before. The less you know, the better."

"Do you think I'm some kind of mug?" she asked. "Listen, boy, I was pulling scams with your father before you were even thought of, so I'm coming. Get over yourself."

"Well, if you know all the dodges, you'll know I'm right. Remember, Coyle will do anything to find his grandson, and if he thinks you have any knowledge of his whereabouts, he'll get the information out of you one way or another and take great pleasure in doing so. This is for your own good, Ma.

Reluctantly, Diane had to concede to her son's request.

The child and all his possessions were packed and transported to a cruiser with O'Farrell already on board. Ryan did not appreciate being wakened in the middle of the night and certainly not by a strange man. The boy screamed for the whole journey; nothing and nobody would calm him down.

"Shit, if anything was ever going to put me off kids, this one would," Bobby groaned.

"He's certainly got a healthy pair of lungs," remarked the canon.

The foster family were waiting on the jetty for their arrival. With the least amount of ceremony, the child was handed over, along with the balance of the cash and Bobby and his accomplice made their way back to Marbella.

Just as the club was closing, Bobby hooked up with his latest paramour, the Swede, who would swear he'd never left the club that night. Across town, his partner-in-crime poured himself a generous measure of cognac and made a silent toast to Mr Patrick Coyle. Revenge was sweet.

Bobby received news the following afternoon that Erin had been remanded in custody and transferred to the infamous women's prison in Malaga. Thanks to a generous backhander to the sister of one of his staff, he'd already been informed that prisoner Coyle had been causing ructions.

The apple didn't fall far from the tree in her case. Sweet and demure though Erin looked, she had the steel core of the Coyles and she would fight her corner. Even better, he learned there would be no chance of her being released early. Her first three days had been spent in solitary.

Towards the end of Erin's first week in prison, Diane received a call from Bridget, looking for her daughter. Diane had managed to avoid speaking to her for as long as possible, but Bridget eventually caught up with her at the club.

"What the hell is going on, Diane? I've been trying to reach you for days. I need to speak to Erin. We've had a bereavement in the family."

"Oh, I'm sorry, Bridget, but I'm a busy woman. Why would you want to speak to me about Erin? She left last weekend. I did try to persuade her to stay on longer, but she had a family party or something to attend."

"Don't talk rubbish, Diane, of course she's with you. Where else would she be? She didn't return home. She texted me to say she was staying with you and would be back the following week."

"I'm sorry, my dear, I don't know what to say to you. I would have loved to have had her and the wee lad here for longer, but it was a no go. I don't think she and Bobby hit it off too well. Maybe she met someone? You know what young girls are like."

"Not my young girl," snapped Bridget.

"No? Let's face it, she managed to bring home more than a donkey and sombrero as souvenirs from her last trip."

Diane's sarcasm was certainly not lost on Bridget.

"So you're trying to tell me that my daughter and your grandson went to the airport, waved their friends off and vanished?"

"I'm not trying to tell you anything, Bridget. I haven't seen them since they left my home the night before they were due to fly out. I'm sorry I can't help you any further, but if I hear anything I'll be sure to call," and she replaced the receiver.

"That bitch is lying, Paddy. She knows fine where Erin is, but for whatever reason she's not being forthcoming."

"Maybe they've gone off and got married?" Paddy ventured. "You know, I wouldn't put it past her. She's changed."

"No, Paddy she hasn't. It's you who's changed."

"Me! How do you make that out?" He didn't really want to hear the answer.

"Look, this isn't about you, Paddy. There's something wrong here. You know full well she would never be out of touch for this long, especially now she has Ryan."

"I can't do anything until the funeral is over

tomorrow. If we haven't heard anything by then, I'll go and find them. Keep trying her number and I'll get somebody to check the hospitals, just in case."

"Oh, Paddy, surely not? She's had enough trauma in her life already."

"Stop worrying, I'll sort it."

There was a line of black limos along the street and round the corner to where Tommy Riley plied his trade. For any other funeral Tommy would have stopped trading out of respect, but not this time, not for that wanker. The shitebag had beaten him to the chase. Before he could report his suspicions, the fucker had gone and overdosed. They were all trying to keep it quiet, but if Theresa knew, the world knew. She didn't mean to open her gob, she just couldn't help it. It didn't explain why Sean's big mate, the quiet one, had climbed out of the ground floor window the night Sean died, but that information would keep for now.

St. Jude's was packed to the rafters and all of Glasgow's top families were out in force. All contrite and professing their sorrow at the family's loss. These were the same faces who, only a short while ago, had been ready to string him up for a measly ten grand.

Much to Paddy's disgust, Sean was given a funeral fit for one of Glasgow's finest, but for his mother's sake he went along with it. If it had been up to him the fucker would have been dumped in the Clyde for fish food.

He and Bridget had to endure hours of the wake, and play the game for Lizzie, Marie and Michael, when all they really wanted to do was go and find their daughter.

"I'm coming with you, Paddy, so don't argue. She's my daughter too," insisted Bridget.

For once Paddy put up no argument. Arrangements with his old pilot pal, Ritchie, had been finalised the day before and by five a.m. the day after the funeral, the Coyles were in the air.

Before most people had finished their breakfast, the pair had arrived in Marbella and begun their search.

The Long Wait

The days dragged interminably. Prisoners were on lock-up for twenty-two out of twenty-four hours, which created a virtual pressure cooker of emotions, and fights were constant.

On her first day in the wing Erin had been accosted by the wing's top dog and her posse. She'd been cornered in the rec room where the gang of women set about her for no other reason than the fact she was foreign. But Erin was no soft mark; years of self-defence classes meant she was well equipped for such a situation. She had fought back as if her life depended on it, which it may well have done. She took out three of them, including the ringleader, before the fight was stopped by one of the screws who had been watching from the sidelines. Apart from a few other minor incidents, Erin was more than able to defend herself.

Her biggest frustration was not being able to contact anyone on the outside. She was desperate to get in touch with her family. Her mother would be beside herself with worry that she hadn't called or texted since the message saying she'd be back at the end of the week. Paddy, despite his gruff exterior, would be just as bad, especially since Ryan was involved too. There had to be a way to get in touch with them, but how? Despite several requests, the governor would not permit international calls. Erin would have to make contact through a third party here in Spain and, other than the Macks, there was no else she could turn to – or was there? Of course. Her son's godfather, the mayor. Why had she not thought of him before now?

Her request to phone Mayor Munozo was denied by the governor as being inappropriate, despite the fact that he was alleged to be the godfather of the prisoner's son. Erin assumed that the mayor was in the pocket of the Macks and would not help.

"Is there no-one at all you can think of?" asked her cellmate.

"Well, a couple of guys who live here helped my dad out last year."

"Surely they're worth a try. Would they know who you are?"

"Oh, they'd know who I was alright. I know it sounds a bit far-fetched, but I was kidnapped here and held hostage by the family who have Ryan."

"Jesus, girl, life sure as hell ain't boring around you. You were kidnapped and now you've been set up as a drugs mule? Shit, don't offer to meet up with me on the outside. We'd probably be sold to the white slave trade."

"That's nothing. I also lost my voice for nearly ten years."

"What?" laughed the American. "You just mislaid it for a while, or you really lost the ability to speak?"

"I lost the ability to speak. Don't you notice my voice comes and goes when I get stressed?"

"Lady, everyone in here is stressed to the max, so a little ole frog in your throat ain't gonna alert the National Guard, honey. How did it happen?"

"A bunch of gunmen shot up my First Communion party and I was so traumatised I was struck dumb."

"Jesus! How did you fix it?"

"I'm not sure if I want to tell you," laughed Erin. "It sounds ridiculous when I say it out loud."

"Go on, tell me." Cindy was enthralled and it certainly made her own story seem tame.

"Well, the father of my baby's father was about to shoot my father and I managed to warn him and save his life."

"Get out!" said the American. "Hey, I'm supposed to be the one protecting you, not that that's an issue. You can certainly stand up for yourself. I have to say, I was worried when I heard Roseanne and her bitches were planning a reception committee, but you were like something out of a Bruce Lee film. I'm sure you dislocated her jaw."

"Yeah, I probably did. Look, this is all very well, but it's not helping me get in touch with my folks."

"No problem. For a small fee most of the screws will help out. There's Marta, for instance," Cindy pointed to an officer standing by the snooker table. "She'll do most things for the right price."

"I've got no money, but I'm sure these guys would see her okay, they'd know my dad would be good for it."

The prison officer leaned against the door jamb, listening to what the girls had to say. "And who exactly is it you want me to get a message to?"

"Two of my father's associates. One is called Charley Taylor, he owns a bar somewhere in the old town."

Marta's eyebrows shot up when Taylor was mentioned. "So, Scotty, you know people in high places, do you?"

"The other one I only know by his nickname, Nick the Greek." The officer's eyebrows almost shot to the back of her head.

"You want me to go and meet with this man? I don't think so."

"Why not?" asked Cindy.

"He is probably the most feared man on the Costas. I can't help you, sorry," She made to walk away.

"Hang on, Marta. If he's so feared, would you not worry that if he discovered you wouldn't help me, he'd be very angry with you?"

"I don't think you have a choice, Marta. You have to get a message to him." Cindy smirked at her cellmate.

"Come back before the end of your shift and I'll write him a note. I'll make sure you are well compensated."

"I don't want anything."

There was no such thing as a private conversation in the prison and by now most of the wing was in the know. The bitches who had threatened and bullied Erin during her short stay were now desperate to get into her good books.

As expected, Marta collected Erin's letter and reluctantly agreed to deliver it. Her first thought was to contact Charlie Taylor and endeavour to get him to pass the note on. She was anxious not to have to deliver it in person.

"I'm sorry, but Mr Taylor is out of town," the barman informed her. "He won't be back until early next week, is there something I can do?"

"No, I don't think so, I have something I must deliver to one of his associates," the officer didn't dare use the name she'd been given.

"Well, Charlie won't be around, so if it's urgent you can leave it here. Most of his mates come in at some point during the day. Who is it addressed to?"

She showed the young man the envelope and he smiled. "I understand why you don't want to deliver this yourself, but sorry, I can't help you." He looked at his watch, "You'll catch him in the Double Deuce. He usually stops off there on his way home, but you'll have to be quick."

Marta dashed back out into the street. She wanted this errand over and done with. Preoccupied, she didn't see the car speeding down the road. The envelope fluttered away on impact.

The Visit

"Hold on, I'm coming." Diane Mack pulled on a silk dressing gown.

Who the hell was banging on the apartment door this early, before her housekeeper was on duty? Diane peered through the spy-hole and her heart almost leapt into her mouth. Christ, they were here already. She opened the door to Paddy and Bridget Coyle.

Paddy grabbed her roughly and snarled right in her face. "Okay, missus, start talking." He pushed her backwards into the huge open lounge. "And don't give me any bullshit, I'm sure you'll remember what I told you the last time we had a situation. Well, the same applies. Where are my daughter and grandson?"

"I told her," she pointed at Bridget "I don't know."

"Shame I don't believe you," growled Paddy.

"I've not seen or heard from Erin since the night before she was leaving."

"That's not what we've been told," Paddy bluffed.

"Whoever you've been talking to knows more than me, then. I tried my best to persuade her to stay, but she was adamant she was going home."

"Something changed her mind."

"I'm sorry to say it wasn't me. What does her friend have to say about it? She's bound to know where she went. I can tell you, you're barking up the wrong tree here," Diane shouted at them.

"That's not what Carol says, and I got a text from Erin saying she was staying with you," Bridget had been quiet until now.

"You're forgetting something crucial in all this, coming in here throwing your weight about. That little boy is as much my flesh and blood as he is yours and there is no way I'd ever let anything happen to him."

She was convincing, no doubt about it, but Bridget no more believed her than she believed in Santa Claus.

"Where's the master of the house? What's he got to say for himself about his child and its mother going missing?"

"I don't think Bobby knows anything about this. He's been away on business and I'm sure, like me, he thinks she's at home with you."

It was Bridget's turn to act. She grabbed Diane by the hair and hauled the woman round to face her.

"Think what you would do to anyone who harmed Bobby. Well, I'll do the same to anyone who harms mine. If you know anything, tell me now, because you won't get a second chance with me." She twisted her hair even tighter, "Understand?" and she delivered the famous Glasgow Kiss.

Diane's face exploded. Her perfectly reconstructed nose was smashed and bruising began to appear around her eyes immediately.

"That's just for starters. I'm much worse than *him*," Bridget looked at Paddy who was almost as surprised as Diane.

"You better put something on that," sneered Paddy.

The couple left the apartment with the promise they would be back soon and if Diane had any sense she would get her son to contact them.

On the flight over, Paddy had managed to get hold of Sam, the feisty holiday rep who had played a vital part in their last encounter with the Mack family. He had arranged to meet her later that morning.

Next stop was his old mate, Nick the Greek. If anyone could find out what had happened to Erin, it was him. Despite his name Nick was a true Cockney, having been born within the sound of the Bow Bells. No-one knew exactly where his nickname originated from and Nick certainly had no intention of enlightening any inquisitors.

"Hello, me old cocker," he shook Paddy's hand and kissed Bridget on each cheek, welcoming the couple. "Good to see you both. What brings you back to this neck of the woods?"

Within ten minutes, Paddy had apprised Nick of the circumstances.

"So you have no clue as to where she went after leaving the airport and you are sure she did return to town? I'm sorry to ask, but well, you know kids," the man gestured his helplessness.

"She definitely left the airport, but we have no proof that she actually went back to the Macks' apartment," ventured Bridget.

"We have to find out what Bobby is up to. Have either of you spoken to him recently?"

"No, I can't get hold of him. He's gone to ground," replied the Big Man.

"We need to get to him. He's the key to finding Erin and the boy. Leave this to me. I'll put the word out. We should know something soon. Don't worry, we'll get to the bottom of this." Standing up, the 'Don' bid them goodbye for the moment.

"What next, Paddy?" asked Bridget.

"We need to speak with Sam, she knows her way round this town like no-one else."

There, waiting in the reception of their hotel, was the girl in question.

"Hello, Paddy, Mrs Coyle."

"Hello, Sam, you okay? We're hoping you can do a little job for us. We have another problem with the same family as before."

"Jesus, I didn't think they'd be stupid enough to take you lot on again," the girl smiled.

"Well, they have. And this time it's not just Erin, but our grandson also."

"Your grandson? That's a turn up for the book. I'm presuming that Señor Bobby is the daddy?"

"Got it in one, but Erin and her baby have gone missing and we," he indicated Bridget, "are convinced the Macks are behind it."

"Wouldn't surprise me. I've known Bobby Mack for years and he's always had a high opinion of himself. Basically he's a nice guy, but lately he's turned into a proper little prick. He swans about town like he's really something. Gets right on my tits. Oh, sorry, Mrs Coyle."

"That's okay. I've heard much worse living with this lot, and it's Bridget, by the way."

"Okay, Bridget, how can I help?"

"First of all, we'd like you to scout about the Macks' apartment, see if you can find out anything. We've nothing to go on except gut instinct. Check out the club, no-one will suspect you, you're well known enough and it goes without saying we'll make it worth your while."

"Hey, I don't need payment for this. I'll get started right away, there could be folk round the pool about this time," she looked at her watch – a smart Rolex, courtesy of her last pay cheque from the Coyles.

"I'll stay in touch. Bye. And nice to meet you, Mrs Coyle, sorry, Bridget." The girl zoomed off on her trusty little scooter.

"Let's go visit Ryan's godfather," suggested Bridget. "You never know."

Somewhat reluctantly, Paddy accompanied his wife to meet with the illustrious Julio Munozo, their grandson's godfather and mayor of Marbella.

The two were ushered into a magnificent room where, rising from behind his desk, Mayor Munozo greeted them effusively.

"Señor Paddy and Señora Bridget, to what do I owe the pleasure of this visit?" Since he'd heard Diane's recent request, the shrewd politician had been half-expecting such an encounter.

For the second time that morning Paddy explained their concerns and the circumstances surrounding their visit.

"You can appreciate my position in this matter, Paddy. I cannot betray confidences, but I will tell you there have been enquiries regarding the boy. I was concerned and surprised. He was not a child I would ever have thought to be neglected or abused in any way."

"Are you telling me my grandson has been taken into care?" Paddy asked, forgetting for a moment who he was dealing with.

"No, no, of course not and anyway, these matters take time. Now I've said more than I should."

"Thanks, Julio. I appreciate your help."

"Well, I do have his welfare at heart. After all, he is my godson. Unfortunately, I must take my leave now. I have someone waiting for me, but if I can be of any further assistance, please let me know. And a word of warning. Bobby Mack was always a good boy, but since his father's death, well, he is not the same man."

The Gatherers

There was only one girl lying by the pool when Sam tipped up to the apartment block. The same old ruse, 'Parcel for Mack, but no reply', always gained access to a gated block.

"Hello there, I wonder if you could help me." Sam asked, catching the girl's attention. "I'm looking for a friend of mine. She's supposed to be staying here, but there's no-one home. I don't want to hang around if she's already left, she may have gone back home. She's Scottish, a tall, dark-haired girl and her name is Erin. She also has a baby boy."

Sam couldn't gauge the girl's reaction from behind her huge sunglasses.

Sophie had a 'don't get involved policy' about life in general. As far as she was concerned there had to be a damned good reason for the young guy on the floor above to have this Erin arrested. Whatever it was, it was none of her business. She had seemed a nice enough girl and the baby was divine, but whatever was going down was nothing to do with her. Life had been tough enough the past year, why invite any more trouble?

"No, I don't think so. There were a couple of girls visiting a few weeks ago and I think one of them had a baby, but I didn't really pay much attention."

"Okay, thanks. I really need to find her. You see, her mother's dying and she's an only child." Sam was laying it on thick. Like the Coyles, she too acted on her gut instinct and she was sure this girl knew more than she was telling.

"Can you imagine what it would be like, out partying and your mother on her death bed?"

Sam saw the girl wince. "Actually, I do. My mum died last year and I wasn't with her." Tears ran down the girl's cheeks. "I may have seen your friend. She lay out here one afternoon with the baby and then later that night she got chucked out of the Marbella Princess. Bobby, the guy from upstairs, was with her. It looked like he got her arrested. That's all I know and I don't want any trouble with them. Your friend was absolutely out of her face and I don't think it was just alcohol."

Bingo, thought Sam. "Can you remember when this happened?"

"Yeah, we were all out to celebrate my birthday. It was the 17th."

Bingo again. Sam thanked the girl, assured her she

wouldn't get any hassle from the Macks, and took her leave.

So, Erin and the baby *had* been in the apartment after leaving the airport. And Erin had been out clubbing with Bobby later, despite his mother insisting she last saw her on the evening of the 16th.

"Hello, Sam here. I struck gold on the first call. I spoke to a young girl by the pool at the Mack's complex and lo and behold, she'd met Erin and the baby on the afternoon of the 17th, the day she was supposed to have flown home. And she also saw her later that night, being ejected from the Marbella Princess. According to her it looked like she'd been arrested. Anyway, she was driven off in a police van."

"Was she on her own?"

"Yes and no. This Sophie and her friends couldn't understand why Bobby Mack was having her arrested, but she said the girl was absolutely wasted and could hardly stand."

"Erin doesn't drink or do drugs."

"Maybe not normally, but this is Marbella and she was on holiday. Maybe someone spiked her drink? It happens all the time here."

"Anything else?"

"No, but I'm going to track down the security guys on duty that night, if I can. See if they remember anything."

"I wouldn't think they'd spill the beans."

"Not normally, but I can try."

"True. See what you come up with and thanks, Sam. Keep in touch."

Paddy turned to his wife. "Sam caught up with a young girl who saw Erin being bundled into a police van and driven off, in full view of Bobby Mack."

"We need to check which station she was booked into and who the officers were who arrested her."

It took just over an hour for Nick to ascertain which police station Erin had been taken to and the names of the two arresting officers who were conveniently on annual leave. They could wait.

"It turned out she was arrested outside the Marbella Princess and charged with possession of a shitload of cocaine, resisting arrest and assault. She was remanded in custody in Alhaurin de la Torre in Malaga and we need to get her out of there. It's a desperate place. It looks like she's been well fitted up, I'm sorry to say. Unfortunately she was up in front of one of the most feared judges and she presented no defence. Some clerk from the Justice Department was instructed to plead guilty on her behalf."

"Why? There was no problem at the christening, they got their own way. The father's name is on the birth certificate and, despite my objections, Mack could have access to the child at any time."

"Revenge," said Nick. "You killed his father."

"To save my own skin. He most definitely would have killed me, Erin and the girl."

"No matter. He's out for revenge. The boy idolised his father."

"But what does he hope to gain? It's just plain stupid."

"You're here. You have interrupted your business. Your daughter is in the worst and most dangerous prison in Spain, and you have no idea where your grandson is. I'd say he's doing a pretty good job so far."

"Suppose so," muttered Paddy.

"First things first, we have to get you a visiting order. Hopefully for today, but if not, then tomorrow. You have to make sure she is coping." Nick picked up the phone and spoke for some time in Spanish. "That's it all arranged. A car will pick you up outside in ten minutes and take you to see your daughter."

"Thanks, mate. You have no idea how much this means to me, and I'll forever be in your debt," said the Big Man, tears glistening in his eyes as he hugged his friend. Of the two parents, Bridget was by far the most composed.

Fear

"Bobby, it's me. I've just had a visit from the Coyles. Husband and wife."

"What do they know?" Bobby asked his mother.

"They're pretty damned sure she didn't go back to Glasgow and I got a broken nose for suggesting she might have other interests here."

"You've got a broken nose?" Her son screeched down the phone. "They actually laid hands on you? I'll fucking kill him, Mum, fucking kill him! He's not on his own turf now."

"Hey, I've had worse off your dad for the tatties being burned. Don't you worry about me. I'm as tough as old boots. This was just a little taster to flush you out. Paddy Coyle knows you would keep me safe by not telling me anything. You were right on that score, by the way. But that means he's going to come after you with a vengeance."

"We always knew that was going to happen, but he

won't harm me because I've got the boy. He'll turn up at the club tonight, nothing surer, but we'll be ready."

"Okay, keep me informed. I'm going to be out of action for a few days until I get this nose sorted, then I'll be brand new." Desperate though she was, she refrained from asking after her grandchild although it killed her not to.

Meanwhile, the Coyles had just entered the high security compound where their innocent daughter was incarcerated. Both parents were dreading the meeting. Bridget knew she had to keep Paddy under control for Erin's sake, but she herself was in bits at the thought of what the girl might have suffered; she'd heard enough stories.

To their astonishment, Erin seemed no different to the girl who had left home a few weeks previously.

"How are you, sweetheart?" Her mother asked, almost knocking the breath from her in a suffocating bear hug.

"You coping, darling? No-one being . . .?" Paddy didn't know how to ask.

"If you're asking if I'm some bull-dyke's bitch, then the answer's no."

Her father, labelled the hardest man in Glasgow, blushed from his neck up. He hated women, especially his women, to talk that way.

"I'm fine, honest. I had a bit of bother at the start, but trust me, all those years of karate finally paid off."

"You mean you've been fighting?" Her mother quizzed.

"How do you think someone like me would survive, Ma, if I didn't stand up for myself? Anyway, forget all that. How's Ryan. Is he okay?"

Mother and father exchanged glances. "We don't know, darling. We don't know where he is."

"What do you mean, you don't know where he is? He's with Diane, that's who I left him with. Bobby insisted we went out to the club. I didn't want to go, but he promised he had a surprise for me."

"He had that right enough," muttered her father.

"Paddy," Bridget warned.

"I left my baby with his grandma, what's wrong with that?"

"Nothing, if she wasn't related to the fucking Borgias."

"For the love of God, will you two stop? What do you remember, Erin?"

"Not much. We had a couple of drinks and I told him I was ready to go. He suggested we have one for the road and I remember virtually nothing after that. I woke up in a police cell feeling like I'd been hit by a herd of rhinos."

"Do you know what you were charged with?"

"Possession of class A drugs was what I was told. The amount they allege I had was ridiculous. The bag I was carrying would hardly take a lipstick and my phone. As for resisting arrest and assault, I was unconscious, drugged and set up. But why would they do this to me? They had to know you'd find out and would come for us."

"Well, that's what your dad and I are here to sort out."

For the first time in weeks, Erin knew things would be alright; her dad was on the case.

But it wasn't that easy. They were in another country and one where Paddy hadn't spent a fortune greasing the wheels of the law.

Guilty?

First thing on the agenda, they had to get a brief sorted. They wanted the best available and one who could speak English.

"Your daughter is in a precarious position, Mr and Mrs Coyle. There is no precedent under Spanish law which allows for a guilty plea to be changed at this time, or for an internee to be released on bail, having been refused so previously. However, we can put forward the case that Erin did not know that she was actually pleading guilty and that it was not her intention to do so. As her representative, I have requested copies of all the documentation relating to the case and details of the evidence against her. So far they have been unable to produce any. It would seem that all the evidence concerning this case has disappeared. If this is confirmed, I would propose she be released immediately, as there would be no case to answer."

"Thank God," said Bridget who seemed to having been holding her breath throughout Señorita Cortez' summing up of the situation. "Thank God. How soon do you think she could be released?"

"I have no idea. It could be as little as one month and as long as twelve. It is up to the judiciary, and drugs are a taboo subject here in Spain," replied Señorita Cortez.

"Have you no influence with them?"

"No, Señor Coyle, unlike the UK courts, the Spanish, they cannot be bought."

"Shame," muttered Paddy. "What about the mayor, could he help us?"

"Perhaps, it can do no harm to ask, but whether he would want to interfere is debatable."

For the second time that day Paddy and Bridget were ensconced in the mayor's magnificent quarters.

"Thank you for seeing us again so soon, but we think you may be the only person who can help us, Julio."

"You certainly work fast, Paddy, and of course, I will be of any assistance I can be."

Once again, Paddy apprised the mayor of the circumstances surrounding Erin's case.

"If you could find a way to bring her case forward, it would help matters immensely. Her lawyer is confident that because of the language problems and Erin's lack of understanding, it might sway the judge."

"But if the evidence is missing, there is no case to answer," put forward Julio.

Paddy and Bridget exchanged glances; he had repeated almost word for word what the lawyer had said only an hour or so ago.

"I will do the best I can for you. I will speak with the legal department in the morning and be in touch."

"Hello, Michael. It's me, your ma." Lizzie shouted down the phone.

"I know who it is, you old bat, and if you shout any louder, you won't need a phone. Just stick your head out the window."

"Don't be so bloody cheeky, this is serious. I'm worried about Gerry. Do you know where he stays?"

"Why are you worried about Gerry, Ma? He's a big lad, he can take care of himself. He lives near the yard, I think, in Seymour Street. But I've no idea what number."

"I've not seen him since the party. He didn't come to the funeral and I miss him. He's a good lad and he was a good friend to your brother."

Michael hadn't the heart to tell Lizzie that Gerry had been paid to be Sean's companion. No point in upsetting his mum now, it would do no good.

"I can't understand why he didn't come to the funeral."

"Maybe he just couldn't hack it. Lots of guys are like that, Mum. Anyway, I'll get one of the lads on it this afternoon. Now you get through next door and have a brew with Theresa."

"Oh, I'm not talking to that big-mouthed erse! I told her something in confidence and she told the whole feckin' street."

"You didn't by any chance tell her over the phone?" Michael asked.

"I did, as a matter of fact, and it was confidential."

"Well, there's your answer. It wouldn't be Theresa that let the cat out of the bag, but you bawling your head off and all the neighbours party to what your confidential bit of news was. I'm not saying Theresa's innocent, can't say she hates a wee gossip, but you're the real culprit, Ma. Go on, knock on her door and make your peace. I'll check on Gerry and get back to you."

Waiting Game

"You still haven't seen him?" O'Farrell asked incredulously. "What the hell is he playing at? I thought you'd be number one on his to-do list."

Bobby had called over to check on the old man and keep him up to speed on what was happening, or not, as the case was.

"Nope, I've not seen hide nor hair of either of them. They turned up at the apartment the day they arrived, but that was the only contact. You know Bridget attacked my mother and broke her nose?"

"Good Lord, I never had her down as the violent type, she was always the peacemaker. Just shows you, a mother will always protect her cubs. Let's face it, your mother would tear anyone limb from limb if they harmed you."

"I know, but I don't understand why he's not been near."

"He's playing mind games with you, son, and it's

working. You're on edge, looking behind you, round corners, because you know he's coming, but you don't know when."

"I'm ready, make no mistake. My theory is that he's waiting for Erin's release, he's not going to jeopardise that in any way. As soon as he secures her freedom, he'll come looking for the kid."

"I agree, and you'd better be ready because he'll come at you all guns blazing."

"More than likely, but he has to keep me alive if he has any chance of ever seeing his grandchild again. There is no-one else except you who has that information and the last person they'd ever go looking for is you."

"Bobby, don't underestimate Coyle. Look at how he got the mayor on his side. You know, it wouldn't surprise me if he's already located the child."

"No chance. I've been in daily contact with them and everything is kosher."

"Just be careful, lad. Paddy Coyle is not to be trifled with."

It was almost a week since Paddy and Bridget had arrived in Marbella and during that time they had left no stone unturned. They now had evidence that their daughter had intended staying with the Macks.

Thanks to Sam, Bridget had arranged to have coffee with Sophie, the girl Erin had spent the afternoon with and who had witnessed the incident outside the nightclub.

"She definitely still had the hots for Bobby, no doubt about it." Sophie told Bridget. "The only reason she was staying on was because there was some other woman in the picture. She wasn't really fussy if the other grandma spent time with her baby or not, it was definitely all about Bobby. I can't stand him myself, big-headed smartarse."

The girl had obviously had a bad experience there, thought Bridget.

"Then later, when we saw him hustle her out of the club, I was gobsmacked. I was standing in the queue with a group of friends, watching what was going on. I didn't realise it was her to begin with. The two cops had her in the back of the van and away in minutes. Thinking back, it was definitely planned and Erin was so out of her face she was helpless."

"Do you think she could have been drugged?" Bridget asked the young girl.

"I suppose so. She was certainly in a state."

"Thanks, Sophie, you've been a great help."

Sam had also tracked down the three doormen on duty that night and, as suspected, for a tidy sum they had agreed to look the other way when Bobby had some low-life junkie ejected and arrested.

Thanks to the mayor's influence, Erin's court hearing had been brought forward and she would be appearing the following morning.

"Please don't think this is a foregone conclusion," Rosa Cortez told her while preparing Erin for her hearing the next day. "Because there is still no trace of the evidence, it should mean that there is no case to answer. However, the judge could grant an extension because it is alleged a large quantity of drugs were involved. But I am confident we can present a good enough case for you to be released."

Bridget had visited Erin every day and was amazed at the girl's fortitude. Although desperate for news of her son, she never complained. She was, however, as vengeful towards both Bobby and his mother as they were to her father.

"As soon as I get out of here I'm going straight for them," Erin told her mother.

"We'll do exactly as your dad advises, dear. He knows what he's doing and we know they're both rattled that he hasn't come after them yet. Sophie heard them going at it hammer and tongs yesterday, so don't you worry, your dad has everything in hand."

"What's Sam doing? She was very secretive when she came to see me yesterday."

"She's a clever girl, that one. She only got herself a job at the Marbella Princess as a promoter, so she can keep an eye on who comes and goes. She's already sussed out all the different entrances to the building."

"I like her."

"Me too."

"I'm dreading tomorrow. What if I don't get released? I could be here for God knows how long. It's a minimum of ten years for a drugs courier. And the Macks would get custody of Ryan here in Spain."

"Don't think like that. You have to be positive, this time tomorrow it could all be over."

"Or just beginning," sobbed Erin.

One in One Out

Without a doubt it had been the longest night of her life. Erin Coyle was almost at breaking point. She'd been assured by her parents, her brief, her cellmate and most of the internees that she had nothing to worry about. The outcome of her hearing was a no-brainer since there was no evidence, it had all miraculously disappeared. But no matter what anyone said to reassure her, she couldn't get it out of her head that until she walked free from the courthouse, there was always the chance something would go wrong.

"I have no idea how I would have survived in here without you," Erin thanked Cindy.

"Just fine, girl, you're made of strong stuff. And don't you worry, this time tomorrow you'll be nursing that little baby and on your way home."

"I've got to find him first. Jesus, Cindy, he could be anywhere, and there's no way Bobby will just surrender him. No way. Not after all the trouble he went to get me off the scene.

"Whatever you think of the grandma, she won't let any harm come to him. Hey, this is probably all for her benefit, to keep him to herself. I'll bet you if you find her, you'll find the boy."

"Maybe, but for the minute he's nowhere to be found. There are dozens of people on the case, out looking for him, but no clues have turned up so far."

"Okay, but once you're out you'll find him. A mother's instinct always works. Try and get some sleep. It's a big day tomorrow."

Erin paced the cell until daybreak.

There were shouts of 'Good luck', 'Adios', and inmates banging on their cell doors as Erin walked across the landing towards freedom, praying as fervently as she had ever prayed in her life.

Bobby answered the call on the third ring.

"She got off and the three of them headed straight to Nick the Greek's place," said the voice on the line.

"Okay, thanks. I'll be in touch," Bobby replaced the receiver and dialled his mother.

"She got out, Mum. Did you do as I asked?"

"Yes. I've packed a case, but where are we going and for how long?"

"Not far, and just for a few days. I'll be there in the next half hour or so."

"I'll be waiting downstairs."

337

"Hello, Señor Coyle. They have just left the apartment block, mother and son, in a white BMW. They are heading out of town on the road to Ronda."

"That's fine, José. Don't let them see you. We'll set off now. Don't lose them."

Paddy's instinct had proved right. He'd had José, one of Nick's men, posted outside Diane Mack's apartment since five a.m. He was sure that they would go underground and that's exactly what seemed to be going down.

"Let's go," Paddy motioned to his wife and daughter. "José has just reported that they're on the way to Ronda. We'll catch up within ten minutes."

"Paddy, that's a hell of a road when it's dry, but in this weather it will be treacherous." It was one of the very few stormy days that occurred in that part of the country and the rain was relentless. "Do you want a driver to go with you?"

"Thanks, but I don't know how this is going to turn out, so better if it's just us. We'll be fine."

"Seriously, Paddy, be careful. It's a bad road and this storm doesn't look like it's going to let up," said Nick.

The Coyles caught up with the BMW and José had peeled off before the road started to climb. This road was infamous for its zigzag course up and over the mountain, with magnificent views and terrifying, sheer drops into the sea below. There was no sightseeing today; the road was treacherous and took all of Paddy's concentration.

"Do you think they are going to collect Ryan?" Erin asked her mother.

"I've no idea, sweetheart, though nobody but a mad person would be on this road unless they were desperate. So they certainly must have a good reason to be out in this storm. Jesus! Paddy, be careful," Bridget squealed as the car swung dangerously across the grass verge and she caught sight of the drop below. She was praying with all her might that they wouldn't meet their maker on this death-defying road.

In the car up ahead, Diane was equally terrified. "Bobby! Take your time. You know how bad this bloody road is. Slow down or it won't be Coyle who finishes us off, but your bloody driving. Slow down," she repeated as the car skidded round a corner.

"What's the plan then, and why have I got to leave town in weather like this?" Although she wouldn't admit it, she was more than a little frightened of the husband and wife team, and now the daughter was on the loose, only God knew what would happen.

"Coyle knows you had no information that could help him, but my guess is he'll take you hostage to trade for the kid. But he can't if he can't find you."

"Bobby, have you honestly thought this through? You know it's not like the movies. The people you're dealing with don't take prisoners. I know you thought your dad was a real tough guy and a successful businessman. But the reality of the situation was that he was a low-life shit who, alongside O'Farrell, preyed on the weak and innocent. He doesn't deserve your loyalty, Bobby, or your blood. Whether you like it or not, Coyle killed Pete in self-defence and to save his daughter who was completely innocent in all this. Keep your eyes on the road!"

Bobby ignored his mother's plea. "I've booked you into a small hotel up in the mountains for a few days. That's all it should take. You'll be quite comfortable. Trust me, I know what I'm doing." The same couldn't be said of his driving

"Christ, Bobby!" shouted Diane as once more, the car veered across the treacherous road, right into the path of an oncoming truck.

The sports car crumpled on impact.

The car behind flew round the corner, screeching to a halt just millimetres from the wreckage.

As the shocked truck driver alighted from his cab the car exploded, putting paid to any hope of survivors. Erin fell to her knees in hysterics at the side of the road. Despite everything Bobby had put her through, he was definitely the love of her life. And now the father of her child was dead.

It took hours to clear the road and recover the bodies, but the Coyles had to continue their journey. Ryan might be somewhere on this mountain and they had to find him.

There were few homes on the road and the Coyles stopped at each one. All were inhabited by peasant farmers who spoke no English and there was no sign of the boy. The last stop on the treacherous road was the Hotel Parador. The owner, Gwen, was a Welsh girl from the valleys and had only recently taken over the business. She was eager to help the desperate souls.

"I have only seven guests booked in tonight – three couples, and a single lady still to check in. A Mrs Glasgow.

"That's her, Dad. That's her," wailed Erin.

"Of course it is. They would book under an alias to avoid us tracing them," said Paddy. "I think you'll have a vacant room this evening, Gwen."

"So it would seem."

"Maybe we should book in, see if anyone turns up?" Paddy proposed. He turned to the hotelier, "I don't suppose you have a double as well as a single available?"

"Yes, no problem, but do you really think someone will turn up with the child?"

"What other reason could she have for booking a hotel room less than twenty kilometres from her home and under an assumed name?"

"They may have had to arrange to collect the boy away from town because they are so well known in Marbella. It's the only reason I can think of for the two of them to be on this road. If Erin had been kept on remand, they wouldn't have had to shift him, but with you around," he addressed his daughter, "it might have been too risky."

"Does this not seem surreal to you both? Ten hours ago I was incarcerated in the toughest women's prison in Spain. Since then I've been in court, acquitted of being a drugs mule, the father of my child and his mother have been cremated before our very eyes trying to escape from us, and now we're holed up in a three star B&B hoping to kidnap my son back."

"Well, when you put it like that," her parents chuckled.

"It's not funny! How can you laugh at a time like this?"

"Hey, don't get uppity with me. I didn't crash his bloody car. And whether you believe it or not, they did you the biggest favour of your life." Paddy snapped.

"WHAT?"

"Did you really believe I could get your son back without blood being spilled? And it might well have been ours, Erin. I'm afraid of very few men and Bobby McClelland certainly wasn't one of them, but don't you think he would have come mob-handed to see us off? That's why I didn't go straight for him when we arrived here. He knew that I was coming, he just didn't know when. I'm not sorry in the least. The stupid, reckless idiot did us a huge favour. We don't have to fight him, and your son, when we find him, is heir to everything."

"How can you even think like that?" his daughter was shattered at his remarks.

"I can think this way because if it hadn't been them, it would have been us. My greatest revenge would be to take everything from them and, thanks to my grandson, that's exactly what has occurred. Karma, Erin, karma. What goes around comes around."

Great Expectations

Two months had passed since the accident and there was still no sign of Ryan. As Lizzie had predicted, Bridget and Erin had stayed on in Marbella to take care of the McClelland empire, but more importantly, to conduct the operation to find the missing child. Despite a significant manhunt mounted by the Spanish authorities, and an equally exhaustive search by Nick the Greek and most of the Costa del Crime, not one clue to Ryan's whereabouts had surfaced, except for one possibility.

A few weeks after the funerals, Erin and Bridget had moved into Diane's apartment.

"I couldn't ever live here permanently," Erin confided in her mother.

"Nor me. I keep hearing her clip clop across the marble floor and I get a waft of her scent every so often."

"She's probably furious that we're in residence. Thank God the grieving rellies are gone. I don't think

I could have been civil to them one second longer."

"Jesus, for a family on the bones of their arse, they had some treasured heirlooms, wouldn't you say?" Bridget smiled. "How the devil are they going to get all that back on the plane?"

"Who knows? They must have diddled us out of the best part of half a million, and that's not counting her clothes. What about all Diane's cocktail dresses. C'mon, can you imagine Diane's sisters, down at the Gala Bingo, dressed in all her clobber?"

"I'd pay to see that. Listen, I'm not worried how much they claimed, they are welcome to it."

Diane's sisters and their offspring had insisted on staying on to the bitter end, on the pretext that they couldn't bear to leave their family's remains all alone on foreign soil, and they were going nowhere until they found their nephew. This was all done at the expense of the McClelland estate. Lazy days spent by the pool and evenings in the Karaoke Bar ended when John and James reverted to type and borrowed a Lamborghini from one of the apartment residents. Marbella wasn't Glasgow and two half-wits riding about in such a car drew attention. One night in a Spanish jail was enough for them. They were back in Glasgow with their spoils the following day; straight up to the pawn shop to cash in their bounty.

On the day Bridget and Erin moved into the apartment

they received a telephone call – short, but certainly not sweet.

A raspy, quiet voice told Erin "You can tell the Big Man he'll never see his grandson again."

"Who is this? What do you know about my son?" Frantically she tried to reconnect the call but the line was dead.

Erin was amazed at her mother's ability in dealing with the McClelland's business; Bridget had once again come into her own. Paddy and the family had forgotten her years of experience in her father's extensive loan outfit. She knew instinctively how to uncover hidden sources of income.

She also recognised the cause for most of the problems between her and her husband. She was bored. Since Erin had grown up there had been nothing in her life to challenge or stimulate her.

So, she worked steadily through the task in hand, unravelling the complex transactions Pete McClelland had been involved in and stunned at the amount of money salted away in a myriad of different accounts. One was even labelled 'Divorce'. She deduced from the documents and a number of compromising photographs of Diane with a series of young men, that he had intended to divorce his wife and ensure she had access to only a limited proportion of his wealth. Ironically, there was a similar file with details of

Pete's goings-on and the relevant evidence gathered by Diane – happy families indeed.

Niggling at the back of her mind was the thought that this fate could be hers and Paddy's if she wasn't careful. Not the stupid photographs and private investigator's reports, but that she and her husband had drifted apart. Things needed to be sorted and soon, but first things first, they had to find Ryan.

Her grandson was now a very wealthy young man. Please let him be alive to enjoy it, his granny prayed.

Every morning Erin left the apartment and handed out leaflets regarding the kidnap to anyone who would take one. She then visited the various banks to check accounts that Bridget had uncovered. She and Bridget had come up with the idea that they should keep Bobby's bank accounts live, despite objections from the bank. The mother and grandmother were convinced that whoever had Ryan was being paid and there was a chance this would eventually show up in the accounts. So far they had traced one recurring payment. The second would appear today and hopefully this would flush someone out.

Ryan had settled in with his new family after only a few days and life for the Smiths blossomed, although their change in circumstances had not gone unnoticed. The change in their fortunes had been the source of much conjecture by the villagers. Their settling of all outstanding accounts with the local tradesmen was the cause of much delight and also suspicion.

"He must have won *El Gordo*," gossiped the fisherman.

"Well, he must have won it twice," joked the baker.

"And a new baby too," from the baker's wife.

"They have brought in tradesmen from Palma to refurbish the hotel," commented another.

"I hope they get paid up front," replied his mate.

"No-one from here would work for them unless they paid beforehand."

"I didn't even know the woman was pregnant and suddenly she produces a six-month-old baby. What do you make of that?"

"Maybe *he* gave birth to the child and that's where all the money came from," laughed a member of the group.

"Everything will be explained eventually, it always is."

The group dispersed, most pondering the Englishman's new wealth.

Too many crooks around here, thought the fisherman as he got ready to make his weekly trip across to Marbella.

Money is the Root . . .

The two fishermen from Andratx had finished their business and were having a drink before heading home. As they waited for the barman to bring their drinks, a young woman approached their table. Neither of the men spoke more than a smattering of English, but they understood there was some problem connected with the child on the poster. The skipper nodded to her, folded the flyer and stuck it in his shirt pocket, merely to be polite.

"David, that was the bank on the phone," shouted Sylvia. "Something about a deposit, can you phone them back?"

David was on the roof, assisting the tilers with the last of the repairs. In the past weeks the hotel had been fully refurbished and was now ready for guests. The wiring and the plumbing were state of the art and every room had been brought up to standard. All their money was gone, but they still had a thousand euros a month to tide them over until the first guests arrived.

"I'll call them when this is finished."

The afternoon flew past as the men endeavoured to get the job done and David forgot all about the call until later that evening. "What was the call from the bank about?"

"I don't know, they wanted to speak with you, did you not call them?"

"No, I didn't finish until late in the afternoon. I'll call them tomorrow. The boy's money should be in the account by now."

"We have stopped the payment as you requested, Miss Coyle. It is payable to a Mr D. Smith in Andratx. This is the second payment. It was set up on the 20th September for an indefinite period."

"D. Smith? Do you have any further information on this individual?"

"Sorry, the account is not held at one of our branches so we have nothing more."

"Thank you. I want to close the account now and ensure no other payments are made to D. Smith."

The payments had been organised the day after she was arrested and this would have been, as the bank official said, the second instalment. Erin was sure she was on to something. She debated with herself as to whether she should contact the police or go straight to Nick the Greek. Correctly surmising that her father's friend would act more quickly than the police, she made her way to his office.

*

"But there should have been a thousand euros paid into my account yesterday."

"So what is the balance?"

"Shit," he muttered. What the hell had gone wrong? "It's a transfer that comes from the Bank of Andalucía in Marbella."

"There's nothing you can *do*?" He slammed the phone down on the cradle.

David stormed into the kitchen where his wife was feeding the baby. "Well, you can stop that right away," he grabbed the spoon from her hand. "He gets nothing till we get what's due."

"What's up? What's the matter? And don't be stupid, we can't just stop feeding the child."

"Oh yes we can. He gets not one morsel of food until this is sorted."

The first contact number he had went to voicemail immediately.

The second went to voicemail after a few rings, asking the caller to leave a message and someone would get back to them.

"The money hasn't gone in to my account and the child will not be fed until we get paid," he screamed. "Phone me back the moment you get this message," and again he smashed the phone down.

"You're kidding?" asked his wife. "Surely you're not going to deprive this child of food? It will be a misunderstanding, something between the banks."

"Well the choice is yours, your children get fed or

this one, you decide, but with no money, there is no food." And again he stormed out. David was a nice man and a good father, but his one big failing was his temper and when he was roused Sylvia and the kids shipped out until he was calm again.

Ryan was hot, feverish and dehydrated; other than a few sips of water he'd had nothing to eat for nearly ten hours. Even the crying had stopped.

"I don't care what you say, he has to have something. What will happen when this gets sorted and you've starved the poor mite to death? A fine pickle we'll all be in then."

David was beyond reasoning with. The money was three days overdue and he was desperate. Why was no-one returning his calls?

Since Bobby's death Canon O'Farrell had felt truly alone for the first time in his life. He was well aware that many would say he deserved it; he, himself, was sure he did, but that didn't ease the deep sadness he felt at losing Bobby.

He had stopped answering the phone and hardly ventured out, there didn't seem to be much point these days. As he rose from his armchair, he was alerted by the new message alert on his mobile. He supposed he'd better answer. He picked the phone up to see over twenty voicemails from an unknown number. He listened to the messages becoming increasingly more and more threatening and knew he had to do something. He couldn't leave Bobby's child to die at the hands of strangers. In fact, he would go and remove the boy and rear him himself.

As she prepared her husband's shirt for the laundry, the fisherman's wife came across the flyer he'd taken from the girl earlier in the day. Like her husband, she could speak little or no English, but it didn't take much to decipher what the message was. A reward of five hundred thousand euros for a baby, just like one the English woman had brought into the shop only a few days ago. That would explain why no-one had known she was pregnant.

She picked up the phone "Hola . . ."

"Hello, David," the priest spoke.

"What the hell is going on? The money didn't come through."

"I'm sorry, but Bobby met with an accident. I should have made arrangements to have the transfer done, but I quite simply forgot. I take it the child is okay? You weren't stupid enough to carry out your threats?"

"No, of course not," the hotelier was beginning to panic. The child had barely made a sound this morning.

"I'll transfer the money tomorrow and I'll come and see him in a few days."

Thank God, he had breathing space. They had to

make the boy well again. His wife was right. He was stupid.

Please God, make this right.

"Erin, we've had a call from someone in Andratx who thinks she knows where Ryan is." Bridget spoke quickly. "We have to get there now, before someone alerts them."

Erin was with Nick the Greek when she received Bridget's call. On hearing the new information he immediately said, "We'll take the chopper; we can be there in about an hour. We should meet the caller first to get our facts right. No point in going in all guns blazing if it's the house next door, or the wrong child."

Meanwhile Bridget was on the phone to her husband. "Please, Paddy, come over. Things are moving and I would feel much better if you were here, or at least on your way."

Ryan was clammy and feverish. His breathing was shallow and he was floppy and lifeless.

"You stupid, stupid man. God knows what they'll do to you if he dies, and I'm damned sure he's not far off it."

"The young bloke is dead, some accident or another. It's only the old one left and he's no problem. We've got until the end of the week to get the boy sorted."

The sound of a helicopter passing overhead drowned out the rest of the conversation.

Payback

While Bridget and Erin were away from home, Paddy had taken to dropping into his mother's most days around tea-time. He hated being in the house on his own and he visited on the pretext of checking in on the old biddy. She had taken Sean's passing hard and seemed to be half the woman she had been. Nothing Paddy could say would lift her sadness.

Over the past day or two he had been aware of young Tommy Reilly hanging about Lomond Gardens. He was a fair distance away from his usual pitch and there was an air of insolence about the way he had swaggered away from Paddy without acknowledging his presence.

"Here, boy, I want a word with you," Paddy called to him.

"You want a word with me? Well, I have nothing to say to you, Mr Coyle," the young lad brazenly called back.

"What did you say, you young cunt? Get over here this minute."

"Or what? You'll do me in? Fuck off." Tommy knew he must have a death wish, but so what? The Coyles could go fuck themselves. All of them.

As Paddy walked towards the young lad, he noticed a deep gash all along the side of his car.

"How did that happen, Tommy?" He pointed to the damage.

"No idea. Maybe somebody doesn't like what you Coyles get away with?"

"Listen, boy, there's only so much disrespect I'll take and you're getting close to the edge."

"Just like my little brother? Was he close to the edge with your little brother? I know he murdered Billy and I also know the big guy who worked for you did the twin in. I saw him leaving through his bedroom window."

"You know nothing and saw nothing, if you know what's good for you. Don't play the smartarse with me. I feel sorry for your ma. It's a terrible thing to lose a son and if you behave and keep your mouth shut, I'll help make things better. Not because my brother had anything to do with it, but to help the family out."

"Fuck off! We don't need your help," the young dealer spat back.

"Tommy, I could put you out of business with one call, so behave yourself. Take what I'm offering and help your mother out."

"Like I said, fuck off. Do your worst. You can't hurt us anymore." Tommy Reilly walked away from Paddy with his head held high.

There would be trouble there. He was worth watching, Paddy thought to himself.

Recovery

The entire village was agog at the sight of the helicopter landing on the beach and a couple running from it, across the sand, to meet with the skipper's wife. What could she have to do with people who rode about in helicopters? Curiosity was buzzing like electricity in the air as the strangers made their way towards the hotel, the one owned by the Englishman.

"Where's the child?" demanded Nick.

"What child? Our children are all down at the beach, looking at your machine." Smith was brazen. If he had known who he was talking to it might have been another story.

Nick pulled out his gun and addressed Sylvia. "Get the child or he's a dead man."

"Don't harm him," Sylvia pleaded. "I'll take you to him." She led them to the boat house where Erin saw her son for the first time in months. It looked like they were too late as the young mother collapsed, grief-stricken.

Nick picked up the child from the makeshift cot. "He still has a pulse, Erin." He shook Erin's shoulder roughly. "Come on. No time for tears, we need to go."

Erin stood up, wiping her tears away, and followed Nick, who was already racing towards the chopper. The nearest hospital was just ten minutes away. Perhaps there was a chance?

Seeing her son wired up to so many machines, battling to stay alive, was almost more than Erin could bear. Paddy, Bridget and she took turns keeping vigil at his side, day after day, with no change in his condition. On the fifth day the little boy opened his eyes and gave a lusty yell. He was back. He still had a long way to go, but he was back.

The nurse who had been caring for Ryan came in to check on her charge. "It was the priest who saved him," she told Erin.

"Priest? What priest? And when? We've never left this room unattended."

"He comes in from time to time, usually when you are asleep. He even administered the Last Rites."

"What does this priest look like?" Paddy asked.

"He's very old, black and has a strange accent," she replied. "It was definitely him who saved your baby. As soon as he left last night, Ryan's breathing improved. You should remember him in your prayers."

It was fortunate the nurse couldn't see Paddy Coyle's expression, it was murderous.

By the end of the week the little boy was off the ventilator and breathing on his own.

"At no time is he to be left unattended," Erin insisted. "I'll get Nick to station one of his men outside."

"Don't you think Nick has done enough? We can't keep depending on him to come to our rescue," answered Paddy. There was that green-eyed monster again.

"He won't mind, I'll ring him and get it arranged." Erin was quite confident that Nick would help her out.

"Paddy, its Nick. Meet me outside my office at ten tomorrow morning. I have some cargo you might be interested in."

Christ, this was it, payback time. What the hell was he going to have to do for all the favours this man had bestowed on his family? There was no such thing as a free lunch. Whatever Nick wanted him to do, he would, without question; he was honour-bound.

The next morning he made his excuses to Bridget and set off for the meeting.

"What is this cargo?" Paddy asked.

"You'll see for yourself in a minute," the crime boss replied enigmatically.

Paddy kept quiet until the car pulled up alongside the berth. The two men got out and walked towards the loading bay. Paddy spied a container positioned away from the main stack.

"This is it," said Nick, signalling to one of the stevedores to open the metal box.

At first glance Paddy thought the container was empty, but he could make something out, way at the back. The heat was overpowering and sweat was dripping into his eyes within seconds. He hoped this wasn't some set up, but in the dark he could just make out the figure of a man, bound to a chair; his hands, feet and mouth taped.

"Do you know who this piece of trash is, Paddy?" With a vicious kick, Nick overturned the chair and sent it sprawling into a pool of urine and faeces.

"No, but I can guess."

"This is the piece of garbage who let your grandson almost starve to death. All because he hadn't been paid a measly thousand euros. It costs exactly the same amount to send this container to the Far East and takes almost the same length of time as the boy has spent in hospital. What do you say? Punishment enough?"

"An eye for an eye," replied Paddy as he swung the heavy metal door shut and sealed it. No-one could hear the muffled cries.

Ryan was to be discharged from hospital the following day. The doctors had just finished their rounds, during which time the guard had nipped out to have a quick break. O'Farrell knew the hospital routine like the back of his hand; this was his only chance. He slipped into the room, pulled the blinds down; this usually indicated the doctors had not finished their examinations. He gathered the child, wrapped him in a hospital blanket, hid him under his voluminous cleric's coat and headed for the lift.

"C'mon. C'mon," he urged the lift to descend. He had only a couple of minutes to get away.

The lift reached the ground floor. The doors opened slowly and he came face to face with Bridget Coyle. He pushed past her, Ryan well hidden beneath his coat. She stood stock still. Who was he? She knew him. Then she heard a baby cry.

"Stop! Stop that man," she yelled at the top of her voice, taking off after him. Fortunately the guard was on his way back when he heard the commotion. What the hell was going on? An old priest was tearing towards him, holding a baby, and chased by the woman whose grandchild he was supposed to be guarding.

He dived on the old man and grabbed the child, who had tumbled from the cleric's grasp. O'Farrell managed to twist free in the melee and disappeared into a crowd alighting from a newly-arrived lift. He walked as fast as he could, head down, making no eye contact in order to avoid attention. He shook off his coat and discarded it in the nearest bin, revealing one of his wild Hawaiian shirts.

He couldn't keep up this pace, he'd have a heart attack. He needed a safe hiding place until the situation calmed down. Turning into Accident & Emergency he spied a nurse walking towards him. Quick as a flash the old man clutched his chest and stumbled to the floor.

The nurse sprang into action and pressed the nearest panic button and within seconds the ex-priest was surrounded by the crash team. Fortuitously they blocked the entrance to the department, thus thwarting his pursuers who sped on in search of the elusive priest.

It was late afternoon before Canon O'Farrell ventured forth into the bright Marbella sunshine. That had been a close shave, but at least he knew his heart was in full working order, he smiled wryly.

Unexpected

"Are you sure you don't mind? It's just that I feel I owe so much to the man. Nothing seems enough to thank him. And we're on our way home tomorrow."

"Of course I don't mind watching my grandson, but are you sure you want to go to dinner with Nick on your own? He's a bit old for you and certainly in a different league. You know his reputation."

"He's thirty-five, Mum, not bloody Methuselah. And I'm only having dinner, not eloping."

"What did your dad say when you told him?"

"I haven't said anything to him, it's none of his business. Look, I'll be back around eleven."

Bridget watched from the balcony as the tall, stunning girl climbed into the convertible and kissed the driver on the cheek. She knew immediately they were a couple, there was no denying it. How the hell was she going to break this to Paddy?

"Have you spoken to your parents?" Nick asked his dinner date.

"Not yet, I just couldn't find the right time. Heaven knows if there will ever be a right time. They're just coming to terms with all that's happened over the past while and I want to make sure we're solid before I go springing this on them. Mind you, I think my mother sus-pects something. She questioned me before I left. She thinks you're too old for me and listen to this – way out of my league."

"She's right, Erin. I am older and I've certainly lived a colourful life. There's always the possibility that I could be extradited back to Britain. It's only natural if you're having second thoughts."

"Second thoughts? Are you trying to put me off? 'Cause you're not succeeding. Let's face it, my family are not exactly goat herders and there's also the two months I spent in jail. That wasn't a Swiss finishing school. I know what I want, and it's you. If they don't approve then that's their loss, but I don't want to fall out with them if I can help it."

"Neither do I, but it's not going to be plain sailing."

Over the past months, since Paddy had asked for his help, Nick had grown more and more fond of the stoic, brave, beautiful young woman who had fought tooth and nail to find her son. Never giving up and seldom complaining, she was definitely his kind of woman. But there were a few major obstacles in their way.

It was unlikely Paddy and Bridget would give their blessing willingly and he could under-stand why: his reputation for starters. Nick was, without a doubt, a top face, both in London and here on the Costas. At the ripe old age of thirty-five he had been married twice already. One ex-wife had met a violent and untimely death at the hands of one of Nick's enemies. The other had turned Queen's evidence, hence the reason for Nick's exile.

They had agreed that Erin would return home for a short while, during which time he would look after her business interests. The Marbella Princess had been leased out to a busi-ness associate of Nick's. This would give Erin and Ryan a good income, no matter how things between them turned out.

The evening went by in a flash. How was she going to say goodbye to him, even for a short while? Only a few months ago she would have sworn that Bobby Mack was her soul-mate and she had been desolate when he was killed. But her feelings for Nick were com-pletely different, totally incomparable. This man kept her safe, would do anything to make her happy and go to any length to please her. He had rescued her son and saved his life. They were made for one another. And the sex was incredible.

By the time Erin arrived home Bridget had completed their packing. Her father was lazing on the balcony with a nightcap. "Nice time?" he asked.

"Mm, yes, we went to a quiet little place down by the marina."

Not quite ready to hear about his daughter enjoying time with Nick the Greek, Paddy changed the subject. "Have you decided what you're going to do when you get back home? Your mother says you're thinking of getting your own place."

"Would you mind?"

"Of course not. You're a big girl now. We'll get on to it as soon as we get back."

"I thought you would have a fit," Erin breathed a sigh of relief.

"Not at all. Now off to bed, we've got an early start."

Erin tossed and turned most of the night. Why the devil was she going all the way back to Scotland, only to return in a few weeks? What was the point? She wasn't going to feel any different. A quick call the next morning confirmed her change of plans.

"Who the hell's here at this time of the morning?" Bridget muttered to herself as she an-swered the intercom.

"It's Nick."

"Nick?"

"Yes. Erin phoned me."

"Why?"

"You better ask her. Can I come up?"

Bridget pressed the buzzer and seconds later their visitor arrived.

"Paddy." Nick nodded to the Big Man. "Bridget." He turned to Erin, "Have you told them?"

"Not yet. Here, take my cases to the car while I explain."

Without a word Nick did as she asked.

"What's going on?" asked a perplexed Paddy.

"It's quite simple, Dad. I asked you last night if you would mind if I moved out."

"Yes."

"Well, I just did."

"Just did what?"

"Moved out. Well, actually, I'm about to move in."

"Where? I don't understand. And what's he doing here? Christ, you haven't asked him to drive us to the airport, Erin? That's taking the piss, girl."

"He's not driving you anywhere, but Ryan and I are going with him. I'm not coming home, Dad. I'm staying here."

"Jesus, not this bloody scenario again, Erin. It's becoming a bit played out, girl."

"Paddy, she's staying here with me." Nick walked back into the room and interrupted the conversation.

"What? Why on earth would she be staying with you? She can't stay out here on her own."

"She won't be on her own, Paddy, she'll be with me."

"With you? What the hell would she be doing out here with you?"

"Do you want me to spell it out?"

"Christ, you're old enough to be her father. No way. She's coming home with us and there's no more to be said."

368

"Dad, I'm staying."

"What have you got to say about this?" Paddy spun round to face Bridget. "No doubt you knew all about it."

"No-one knew anything. We didn't know ourselves until just a few weeks ago," answered Erin. "You knew the night you met Mum that you were going to be together, so why can't it be the same for me?"

"It's just different. Have you any idea what kind of life you'll have with him? He's wanted in God knows how many countries."

"Only two," Nick answered. "And we've already discussed this."

"If you stay here I'll wash my hands of you," shouted her father. "How's he going to feel bringing up another man's child?"

"If it wasn't for him we wouldn't be bringing him up, but burying him," replied Erin. "Please, Dad, give us your blessing. I promise you it's the real thing."

"Give it a few weeks and she'll be back home."

"I can't take that chance, Bridget. I know more than most what she'll have to put up with and I want more for my daughter."

"I give you my word, Paddy. I'll take good care of her," Nick vowed.

"You can't do that. You can't stand there and promise me you'll take care of her because you don't know what's ahead of you."

"Neither do you, Dad. Nor did Diane and Bobby, so I'm willing to take the chance."

The argument raged back and forth for the next half hour or so, neither party convincing the other.

Reluctantly, Bridget persuaded Paddy they should leave for the airport.

"I'm telling you, I'm finished with her." Paddy ranted all the way to the airport.

Checking in was a nightmare and the belligerent passenger cussed his way across the con-course and headed straight for the bar

"For the love of God, Paddy, shut up! There's nothing we can do for the moment."

"There is no 'for the moment'. As far as I'm concerned she's on her own, and don't think for one moment that's a happy-ever-after scenario. That bastard will dump her as soon as he's had his fill."

"Just like you're doing with me?" said Bridget sadly.

"Me dump you?" Paddy asked incredulously. "Whatever made you think that?"

"We haven't exactly been love's young dream lately," his wife replied.

"No, but everybody has ups and down and although your bloody menopausal behaviour has been hard to take, there is no way I would leave you or call it a day on our marriage."

"What about Erin and Ryan? I couldn't live with you if you cut them off."

"You know bloody well I'm not going to do that. But I'll miss that wee boy and I don't want him brought up by the bugger we've just left him with."

"You'll have to learn to trust Erin, she's a smart girl. After all, look who her father is."

Paddy smiled back at her, his temper cooling down.

"Do you ever regret she was the only one?"

"Of course I do, but it wasn't to be, was it?" Paddy drained his glass and made to stand up.

"Hang on a minute, Paddy." Bridget ordered another drink for her husband. "Here, I think you're going to need this." She handed him a large scotch.

"For fuck's sake, Bridget! Can you not leave it till we get home? I don't know if I can take any more shit,"

"Okay, but I did think you'd want to know right now that you're not going to have time to miss Ryan."

"Eh?"

"You're not going to have time to miss him."

"You've not bought a pissing dog, have you? I've no time for bloody walkies. You can take it back as soon as we get home."

"Not a dog, Paddy, a baby."

"A baby? I'm too old for bloody adoption or fostering. Sorry, but it's a no go."

"No, Paddy. Listen, will you? You're right about my hormones, but I'm only thirty-nine. I'm far too young for the menopause, but not too old to be pregnant."

The busy airport almost came to a halt at the roar let out by the big Scotsman.

For a sneak preview of the sequel to
The Betrayal

THE RECKONING

Read on . . .

New Beginnings

"You're what? At your age?" Lizzie Coyle leapt off her chair. The chair she'd barely moved from since the day she'd buried her son, Sean. Hugging Paddy and her daughter-in-law, she could hardly believe their news. "Bridget, pregnant, would you believe it?"

"Yes, I can hardly believe it myself," smiled Bridget. "I take it you're happy at the news?"

"Happy, I'm feckin' delirious," shouted the old lady gleefully. "Well, you certainly must have settled your differences," she chuckled. "Good God, pregnant after all this time. It's a miracle that's what it is, a bloody miracle."

"It certainly is Lizzie, and after all we've been through in the last year it's about time we had something to celebrate."

"What's Erin got to say about this? Where is she, by the way?" Lizzie realised her granddaughter and great grandson were missing.

"She's still in Spain," Paddy informed his mother.

"Still in Spain? Whatever for?"

"It's a long story, Ma. We'll tell you later."

"No, you won't tell me later, you'll tell me now. Is she and the wee lad okay? I take it they're safe or you wouldn't be standing here."

"They're fine, Ma. She's met someone."

"Holy Mother of God! She's been on the pull while her bairn was kidnapped? Well, that takes the bloody biscuit," exploded Paddy's mother. "We're all worried sick about her and she's getting her end away."

"That's not how it was," Bridget jumped to her daughter's defence.

"No?" queried Paddy.

"Look, everything's fine. Don't let's spoil this news by arguing over Erin's decision. She's a grown woman and quite capable of making her own choices. What does a mother-to-be have to do to get a cup of tea in this house?"

Still grumbling Lizzie went off to make tea for her visitors.

"Hey, Ma, what's happened here?" Paddy called through to his mother, having noticed the kitchen window boarded up.

"Bloody kids, that's what. It's the second time in a

2

week it's happened. If I catch the little feckers I'll tan their arses, so I will."

"The second time?" Paddy repeated. "It would have to be kids, there's not a soul brave enough around here to take me on."

"A gang of youngsters have taken to hanging about outside. Drinking and carrying on and when I chase them I just get a load of abuse."

"What does our Errol have to say about it?"

"Nothing, he's very quiet, in fact I think he's a bit scared."

"Rubbish, there's not an ounce of fear in that lad. There's more to this than meets the eye."

"I'm not so sure, you know he's never been right since his wee pal was murdered." Lizzie had never been told about Sean's involvement in the boy's disappearance and Paddy aimed to make sure she never did.

"Bridget, I've got some business to see to so you stay with Ma for a bit and I'll catch you back home."

As Paddy left his mother's house he was aware of half a dozen youths loitering on the corner.

"Fuck off you lot and don't let me see you hanging around here again. Now move." He made to walk toward the group.

They dispersed in different directions, shouting abuse and laughing, all except one. The boy Riley swaggered towards Paddy. "Is there a problem, Mr. Coyle?" The cocky young lad called out.

"You'll have a problem, ya cheeky young cunt, if I catch you hanging around here."

"It's a free country, Mr Coyle."

"Not where my family are concerned it's not. Now fuck off before I get serious."

Paddy Coyle couldn't believe he was engaged in an argument with a two-bit street dealer. "Now, I won't tell you again, piss off."

With the same insolent air, Tommy Riley swaggered off down the road towards his pitch.

Given the circumstances Paddy was prepared to overlook the incident, but brother or no brother, this would be Tommy Riley's last chance.

Errol saw and heard the altercation between his uncle and his best mate's brother from his bedroom window. He knew, as well as the protagonists, that his family had had something to do with Billy's murder and he couldn't cope with how that made him feel. He was sure it was his uncle Sean who had been responsible, but Paddy and Michael had covered for him, so they were just as bad. He watched as his uncle drove off and for the first time ever, he'd not pestered him about the new car. The least he had to do with his uncle the better. What he didn't know, he couldn't tell.

Paddy arrived at the scrapyard and was warmly greeted by his younger brother, Michael. Lizzie hadn't waited a minute to impart the wonderful news. That Paddy might have preferred to tell his brother himself hadn't entered the old girl's head.

4

"So you're not firing blanks after all?" Michael jested with him.

"Seems not, but don't expect a brood over the next few years. One more is enough at my age."

"For God's sake, Paddy, you know what they say, life begins at . . ." he was interrupted by the sound of shots being fired.

"What the fuck's going on out there?" roared Paddy, fumbling with the catch of the gun cupboard.

As quick as they could, he and Michael tooled up and cautiously opened the door of the cabin.

A blacked-out 4 x 4 was reversing out of the gates. Random shots were being fired from the back passenger window and a large object, wrapped in an old tarpaulin, was thrown out of the vehicle as it sped off in the direction of the city.

"Jesus Christ, what was that all about?" shouted Paddy as he vaulted the steps into the yard, towards the object.

Tentatively, the Big Man pulled back the covering to reveal the battered, indistinguishable body of a woman. She had been beaten so badly it was impossible to identify her and, just to finish off the job, they had poured acid over her face.

"Dear God, Paddy what the hell's going on? And who is she?" Michael backed away from the corpse.

"I've no idea," Paddy replied, inwardly giving thanks that this bloody mess wasn't any of their women.

Bridget and his mother were safe indoors, Erin was in Spain and he had just spoken to Marie, not five minutes since. Margee, Michael's fiancé, was visiting her folks so who was she? Why had she been dumped in their yard and by whom?

"My God, what a way to go," Michael murmured. "We have to call the police. There are too many witnesses around."

"Not yet," Paddy said, playing for time, but the sound of sirens in the distance put paid to his plea.